Dear Readers

They say M[...]
tery day, there's nothing better than four sizzling Bouquet romances to warm you from head to toe.

Legendary, award-winning author Leigh Greenwood sets the pace this month with **Love on the Run,** as a woman desperate to clear her name discovers that the P.I. hired to help her may be a danger himself—to her heart. In **Little White Lies,** from favorite Harlequin and Loveswept author Judy Gill, a contented bachelor who needs a fiancée for a month only learns that his "intended" is the one woman he could love forever.

When two stubborn people collide, it's a sure thing that sparks will fly. In Harlequin author Valerie Kirkwood's **Looking for Perfection,** a small Kentucky town is the setting for a story about two single parents who find love in a surprising place. Finally, Silhouette author Mary Schramski takes us on a search for **The Last True Cowboy,** the story of a hard-living rodeo rider—and the woman who's stolen his renegade heart.

So curl up with your favorite quilt, a cup of tea, four breathtaking, brand-new Bouquet romances and dream of spring!

Kate Duffy
Editorial Director

TWO HEARTS DANCING

"Are you all right?"

Zoe flattened her hands against his solid chest. "I am now that you're here."

Mitch curled his fingers around hers. The way he was holding her, the way her hips fitted to his, made him want to move. Dance. Slow dance. And there was only one song to slow dance to. The melody started in his head, then traveled to his feet, impelling them to weave a circle. Hips swaying, he pressed his forehead to hers.

Zoe smiled. Then, closing her eyes, she sent her inner gaze to his thighs, which pulsed against hers to the beat of a song she couldn't hear. "What are we dancing to?"

He raised her right hand in his left, meshing their fingers. "Guess."

Pressing her temple to his cheek, Zoe inhaled deeply of a scent that was both warm and dangerous. " 'La Bamba.' "

"I knew I couldn't fool you."

"No, but you nearly frightened me to death, leaving me alone."

He leaned back, pressing Zoe into the hard plane he'd made of his body. "So you screamed at a cobweb." He thrust his hands along either side of her head, combing her hair back from her face.

Her heart thumping, Zoe closed her eyes as she clasped his wrists. "I guess I was really safe all the time."

"I wouldn't say that . . . exactly." Pulling her hard against him, Mitch brought a hot, hard kiss down on her mouth. . . .

LOOKING FOR PERFECTION

VALERIE KIRKWOOD

Zebra Books
Kensington Publishing Corp.
http:www.zebrabooks.com

ZEBRA BOOKS are published by

Kensington Publishing Corp.
850 Third Avenue
New York, NY 10022

First Printing: March, 2000
10 9 8 7 6 5 4 3 2 1

Printed in the United States of America

For Liz Bevarly, who sparkles on and off the page. Your Destination was South when mine was north, and by the grace of God, and perhaps Bob the Comet, we became friends. Thanks for never Mutinying like Moriah, and for helping me to sing my Torch Song and find Perfection. Here's to the next ten years of friendship.

Acknowledgments

Thanks to Eric Blow of the Jefferson County, Kentucky, Department of Animal Control for patiently answering my questions and sharing some "howlingly" hilarious stories. My favorite is the one about the mailman who repeatedly maced the ferocious guard dog always on duty outside an elderly couple's house. The dog turned out to be a concrete lawn ornament. Thanks, also, to Daniel Logan of the governor's office, and to Marie, a state employee, for information about casinos and gaming laws. To Christine Gee of the Missouri Department of Friendship, a salute for many years of outstanding, on call service to this very grateful citizen. To Judy Fields, who so generously shares her special brand of insanity, and to Jo Wright, my dear friend who introduced us—thanks, I think. Lastly, and once again, humble gratitude to my "team"— Jude, Lucy, John Evangelist, and newest member Francis de Sales.

ONE

"Mo-o-om! I'm completely out of clean panties."

Winding a section of her chestnut hair around a large-barreled curling iron, Zoe Laurence slanted her gaze at Bink's pink-robed, ponytailed, panicked reflection in the bathroom mirror. "Thrilled as I am, isn't fifteen minutes before your bus arrives a little late to be telling me Bianca's Secret? Imagine the possibilities if only you'd told me yesterday."

Folding her arms, Bink rolled her very large, very brown, eleven-year-old eyes. "Mom, what day was yesterday?"

Holding the curling iron in her left hand, Zoe brushed a light apricot blush over her cheekbones with her right. "Is this an open calendar test?" Seeing Bink suck in her dimples, she said, "Okay, just give me a second." She traded her blush brush for a mascara wand. "If yesterday was a recyclables day, but also a no-parking-on-the-west-side-of-the-street day, then it must have been . . . Wednesday!"

"Wrong." Stepping up behind her mother, Bink tightened the belt at the back of the navy blue, pin-striped vest Zoe wore over a cream-colored blouse. "You forgot that it was also an it's-okay-to-play-the-stereo day, because Mrs. McIntyre takes Regina Elizabeth to the sitter and doesn't pick her up until after eight."

"That's right. We had The Backstreet Boys to dinner

last night, at no little risk to this building's foundation, not to mention my digestion." Shifting her gaze to the elder of her two children, Zoe winked. "Which means that throughout greater Chicagoland, yesterday was Tuesday."

"And what does *that* mean?"

Zoe paused, thinking that she was looking at a four-foot, eight inch tall version of Violet Pringle, her boss at the bank. "And what do banks do, Zoe?" the small loans VP had said just yesterday. "That's right. They lend money. They lend money so they can make money, and Zoe, you're not helping the bank to make money." Maybe not, Zoe had wanted to reply, but she liked to think that she'd saved more than a few families from drowning in debt as hers nearly had, no thanks to Jack.

Zoe shook off painful memories. "Obviously, it means that tomorrow's Thursday."

"Mother, really."

"Mother, *really,*" Zoe echoed, "has to hurry." Setting down the curling iron and tossing her mascara into her cosmetics drawer, she hastily fluffed her layered hair into fashionable disarray. "If I don't make the Loop by eight," she added, spritzing her "do" in deference to the odds of a squall veering in off Lake Michigan, "I'll have to park in Des Moines."

"My teacher says you could cut down on carbon emissions and help save the planet if you took the bus."

"Tell her to make that three buses, or an el and two buses. Of course, I could always carpool with total strangers whose bumper stickers say I BRAKE FOR NO ONE and BACK OFF OR I'LL SHOOT." Cocking a hip, Zoe looked at Bink. "You can also tell her that I'm thinking of getting an SUV, and would love to know how she likes the one *she* drives to school every day." Legs bare except for one knee-high nylon stocking, Zoe scurried past Bink, up the hall and into her bedroom.

"Mother?" Bink followed, her Pooh Bear slippers scuffling along the wood floor. "Do you want to know why I'm out of clean panties, or not?"

After yanking the slacks that matched her vest from a hanger, Zoe pulled them on and said, "Only if you will make a habit of telling me you're out of skivvies in time for me to do something about it. Like last night." After zipping up her slacks, Zoe looked around the floor. "Have you seen my shoes?"

Bink peeked in the closet. "They're not in here," she said. "And anyway, you couldn't have done anything about my *panties* last night."

Getting down on her knees and searching under the bed, Zoe blew away a ball of dust. "You'd be surprised what I can do when I put my mind to it."

"Mom, I don't need a role model," Bink said to her mother's posterior, "I need clean panties. And the reason you couldn't have washed clothes yesterday is because it was Tuesday."

Backing away from the bed, Zoe dragged out a pair of navy blue pumps, three knee-high stockings, a Luke Skywalker action figure, and a linty dog chew. "Bianca, I don't have time to run in circles. Didn't I already say that yesterday was—?" Gazing openmouthed at Bink, she slowly wagged her head. "I didn't say that it was a the-laundry-room-is-off-limits-to-the-seventh-floor day, did I?"

Bink plunked herself down on the bed. "I thought about doing a load of wash after school on Monday, but I know you don't like me going down to the basement alone. After that, I just forgot."

Piling everything atop the bed except one of the stockings, Zoe hoisted herself up beside Bink. "Why didn't you ask Poppy to go with you?" she said, planting the heel of her bare foot on the edge of the mattress.

"He was downstairs having coffee with Mrs. Cooper-schmidt." Sliding the multicolored, polka-dotted scrunchband from her hair, Bink rewrapped her pony-tail. "At least that's what he said he was doing with her. I knew what he was really doing, of course."

In the midst of rolling the stocking over her instep, Zoe froze. She had a pretty good idea herself of what her father had recently been doing with the thirty-something divorcée in 602, whose cleavage she'd pri-vately dubbed Silicon Valley. And sipping cafe lattes wasn't it. "And what would that be?" she asked, stretch-ing the stocking's elasticized band before settling it around her calf. The knot in her stomach was tension enough.

Scampering over the bed and behind her mother, Bink adjusted Zoe's collar over her vest. "Reassuring himself that he's still virile."

Zoe whipped around, fixing Bink with a pop-eyed stare. "What do you mean, *virile?*"

Reaching across the bed and taking Zoe's gold hoop earrings from the nightstand, Bink handed them to her. "Mom, I know it's hard for you to think of your own father as a normal man with normal male needs, but—"

"Ow!"

"You okay, Mom?"

"Fine, fine," Zoe chirped, then added under her breath, "I probably won't need more than a few stitches." She rubbed the earlobe she'd stabbed with an earring post when her heart had lurched to a stop. Then, slipping the hoops into her pants pocket, to be inserted when sensation returned to her fingertips, she rose. "Just out of curiosity, Bink, wh-wh-what do you know about normal male needs?"

Tucking her legs beneath her, Bink leaned back on her hands. "Poppy just needs to feel needed, Mom. Mrs. Cooperschmidt lets him carry her groceries and fix her garbage disposal. Things like that."

"Oh . . . like that." Zoe's eyes fluttered shut as, sighing, she gave thanks for not having to talk to Bink about things no parent should have to talk about before a second cup of coffee. After glancing at her watch, she hurriedly stepped into her shoes, grabbed her navy blazer and purse from the chair beside the dresser, then dashed for the door—only to grab onto the jamb, forcing herself to a halt. She sent Bink a quizzical look.

"Do you mean to tell me that your grandfather fixed that woman's disposal when I can't even get him to walk the dog?"

"If you want a man to do something for you, you have to ask the right way. You just don't ask right, Mom." Bink scooted off the bed. "You're supposed to say, 'Daddy dear, would you please take Bruno for a walk?' Not 'Bruno's crossing his hind legs again, Dad.' When you do that, you make Poppy feel guilty."

"For all he contributes around here, he should!" Zoe sprinted for the bathroom, shrugging on her jacket as Bink followed. Selecting a tube of lipstick from her cosmetic bag, she glazed her mouth with a warm, earthy shade that soon came under the cloud which was gathering in her gaze. She pitched the tube into her bag and turned to Bink. "Where did you learn that?"

"What?" Bink replied, delving into Zoe's cosmetic bag and retrieving the lipstick.

"You know very well what. That business about how to get a man to do what you want."

"From Tina," Bink said, studying the peachy brown streak she'd glided over the back of her hand. "She's been reading her mom's copy of *Men Are Weird: Deal with It.*"

Tsking, Zoe snatched the lipstick from Bink and dropped it in her bag. "Don't young girls read *Little House on the Prairie* anymore?"

"Times have changed since you were a kid, Mom." Bink grinned. "Deal with it."

In her daughter, Zoe saw Jack, and recalled how hard she'd had to work to resist the irresistible—to say no to another of his can't fail, get rich quick schemes, only to find that before long she was agreeing to his withdrawing from their dwindling house down payment fund. She wouldn't make the same mistake with the children, she'd vowed after she and Jack divorced three years ago. She'd hold to a firm line with them. *For* them.

"Yeah, well they haven't changed that much, at least not in the Laurence household," she replied. Jamming her cosmetic bag and hairbrush into her purse, she again looked at her watch, then at Bink. "Why aren't you dressed?"

"I have no panties, remember?"

Hiking her purse over her shoulder, Zoe huffed. "Rinse out a pair in the sink, then blow-dry them."

"In five minutes? I'll get diaper rash."

"Then you'll have to go without." Zoe cupped Bink's chin. "Nobody will know but you and your jeans," she said, then headed out the door.

Bink shadowed her mother into the hall. "What if there's a terrible bus accident on the way to school, and I'm rushed into surgery?"

Looking back, Zoe shrugged. "Better no underwear than dirty underwear, I always say."

Bink's forehead puckered in exasperation. "This may be funny to you, Mother, but I'm the one who has to go to school practically naked." Turning on her heel, she stomped toward her room. "I'm going to call Tina and ask if she can run up with a pair of hers."

"Bianca Laurence, don't you dare mention your unmentionables to Tina. She'll tell her mother, and by tonight the whole building will be talking about how I can't keep my children in clean underwear."

Drawing up and facing her mother at the opposite

end of the hall, Bink propped her hands on a waist that hadn't yet narrowed. "Well, it's true, isn't it?"

Her shoulders sagging, Zoe bit the inside of her lip. "All right, forget that the child welfare authorities will come and take you and Toby away from me, and then put you in separate foster homes so that you won't see each other again until *Unsolved Mysteries* reunites you thirty-seven years from now." She drew a breath. "Haven't I told you it's not sanitary to borrow so much as someone else's comb?"

"Tina isn't someone else. She's my best friend." Looking up at her bangs, Bink plucked apart strands of her honey brown hair. "Besides, it's not like she has an STD or something."

Zoe's mouth fell open. "I was twenty, and married a year, before I ever heard that term. I thought it was a kind of motor oil." Walking up to Bink, she gently ran the backs of her fingers down the girl's cheek. "Who did you hear it from, baby. Tina?"

"I'm not a baby, Mom," Bink replied, her skin nevertheless feeling newborn soft to Zoe's touch. "And I heard it from Mr. Scanlon, the guidance counselor, last term. Don't you remember? You were the only fifth grade parent who insisted on checking out his home before giving *your* child permission to take his human development class."

They could call it "human development" all they wanted, Zoe thought, not for the first time. As far as she was concerned, it was still Hormones 101. And in the fifth grade, yet. Smart and precocious as Bink was, she was a child, not a temporarily short adult. She still slept with her baby blanket, for the love of Mike. And contrary to what Mr. Scanlon thought about the habit, Zoe didn't think her daughter needed a twelve-step program to break it.

"All right. So I didn't find *Penthouse* stuffed in the cabinet below his bathroom sink." Smiling softly, Zoe swept Bink's thick, straight bangs to one side. "I know you're no longer a baby, but I can't help feeling that girls your age should still be skipping rope and playing board games and—"

"Wearing panties?"

Turning Bink by the shoulders, Zoe headed her toward her room. "Put on a leotard," she called, backing away. "And make it quick!"

Outside her room, Bink paused in the doorway. "Mom?"

"This had better be important, Bianca," Zoe said, pivoting, "because I don't dare show up late for work two days in a row. Even though The First National We-Can't-Wait-to-Get-Our-Hands-on-Your-Assets Bank thinks small loans officers should be seen and not paid much, this job's all that stands between us and a steady diet of Hamburger Helper."

Bink laid her cheek against the jamb. "I know you're in a hurry, Mom," she said softly. "But I was just wondering . . . Do you think we'll ever have a house of our own?"

Bink's question was so unexpected that Zoe clutched her throat. Long ago, she and Jack used to lie awake nights in this cookie-cutter apartment in a glass and concrete urban high-rise, imagining their small town, Victorian dream house with its spacious rooms and wide front lawn, and a swing set in the backyard for the children. They'd even picked out the small town— Perfection, Kentucky—a Norman Rockwell hamlet on the Ohio River in the western part of the state. They'd chanced upon it during a car trip they'd taken as newlyweds.

At some point along the road to Perfection, Jack had taken a detour—to Las Vegas, with a bimbo.

Since then, Zoe had worked so intently toward putting her financial house in order that she'd never once considered buying a real house. Or that her former dream of owning a home was living on in her daughter.

"I thought you were happy here, sweetheart," she

said. "It never occurred to me you'd want to leave your school, your friends. Or even this apartment. You've lived in it all your life."

Shaking her head, Bink pushed off the jamb. "You know what I think, Mom? I think *you're* the one who's afraid to take chances." She disappeared inside her room, shutting the door behind her.

Zoe stared at the movie poster taped to the door, then cupped her hands around her mouth. *"Titanic* isn't helping your case any!" Suddenly remembering the time she was running out of, she turned back up the hall.

"Aaaaah!"

"Is that any way to greet your father in the morning?"

Breathing deeply, Zoe held her hand over her thumping heart. "Dad, I wish you wouldn't sneak up on me like that."

Curling two weights, each marked 10, Harvey Beck grunted. "How would you *like* me to sneak up on you?"

Zoe tucked a strand of hair behind her ear. "Is that supposed to be funny?"

"I could always make your mother laugh."

"Yeah, well, Mother thought *Gilligian's Island* was hilarious." Barely raising her eyes, she fixed a pinched gaze on him. At five feet eight, she was just a few inches shorter than her father. "Did you want something?"

"Toby's ride's down at the curb. Thought you might want to say good-bye to the boy."

Zoe gasped. "Oh my gosh. Toby." She ran up the narrow hall, calling back to Harvey, "Did you do as I asked, and nuke a couple of pancakes for him?"

"No, I thought I'd let him work up an appetite for the gruel that kindergarten feeds him at lunchtime," he replied, alternating curls. "Of course I fed him. Even though you didn't ask right."

Pressing her palms to the walls on either side of her, Zoe drew up. Over her shoulder and beneath raised eyebrows, she gaped at her father, suddenly noticing that he was really quite attractive for sixty-six. Virile, even. The implications, like a possible sibling thirty-four years her junior, were terrifying. "You know, I don't remember you lifting weights before that Cooperschmidt woman moved in. And don't tell me you're getting in shape just to carry her groceries."

"It's the end of May." Still pumping, Harvey flashed Zoe a naughty grin. "Any day now, she could ask me to handle her melons."

Zoe slid her jaw to one side. "If you'll excuse me, I have to find the other little boy who lives in this apartment." Turning, she wheeled into the kitchen. "Toby?"

No chipmunk cheeks; no gap-toothed grin; no cowlick. No Toby.

No Bruno, either.

"Toby!" Zoe ran through the living room to the front door, arriving in time to catch her six-year-old son heading out with Bruno the Hyper, whose toy Boston terrier eyes bulged as he repeatedly somersaulted at the end of his lead. She took the lead from Toby's hand. "Sweetie, how many times must I tell you that Bruno cannot go to school with you?"

"But he wants to run around on the playground, Mom," Toby insisted, wiping beneath his nose with a pudgy index finger. "He's tired of being all cooped up in this place. He told me so."

"He *told*—? Toby, honey, you know that's just make-believe, don't you?"

Minus his weights, Harvey peered over his daughter's shoulder. "The boy's right, Zoe."

She slanted her gaze at him. "Bruno talks?"

"If he did, he could tell you plenty." Harvey dampered his voice to a loud whisper. "Not that you'd listen."

Zoe snorted. "Meaning?"

"Meaning that you can't even hear your own son

telling you that a dog and his boy need a great big yard to play go fetch and . . . whatever else they play."

Zoe squinted one eye. "A dog and his boy? Dad, you've been watching *Rocky and Bullwinkle* reruns again, haven't you?"

"A man can learn a lot of history from Mr. Peabody and Sherman."

"Uh-huh. Not to mention getting an eyeful of that slinky Cleopatra in the opening sequence."

Harvey flexed his brows. "Natasha's not bad, either."

With Bruno's lead trailing from her fingers, Zoe rubbed her temples. "I can't deal with your erotic fantasies right now, Dad. Come to think of it, I'm not sure I can deal with them later. At the moment, I need you to—" Recalling Bink's advice, Zoe moistened her lips. "Daddy," she began, buttoning the top button on his powder blue cardigan, "would you please take Toby downstairs for his ride?"

Harvey smiled broadly. "Why, I'd be delighted, daughter. Toby, kiss your mother good-bye." When Toby had done so, Harvey took his grandson by the hand and led him out the door.

Zoe stood stunned by the magic she'd worked. Confident in her newly discovered powers, she stepped into the hall and tapped her father on the shoulder. "While you're at it," she said, holding Bruno's lead out to him, "walk the dog."

Turning and lowering his gaze to the lead, Harvey scowled. "Can't," he said, unbuttoning the top button on his sweater. "Mrs. Cooperschmidt's waiting for me to hang some pictures for her. Come on, Toby."

Watching her father and son walk off, their joined hands swinging, Zoe realized that, as a magician, she wasn't ready for the big time. She returned to the apartment, Bruno springing at her side. *"You're* a male," she said, her head bobbing as she affixed her gaze to his. "What'd I do wrong?"

"You didn't *thank* Poppy, Mom." Fully dressed and

munching on a blueberry bagel, Bink bounced toward Zoe. "You just asked for more." Standing on tiptoe, she kissed Zoe on the cheek. "Have a super day," she said, then breezed out the door.

Dazed, Zoe watched Bink disappear. A moment later, she looked down at the still boinging Bruno. "Are you sure you don't want to tell me what's wrong with me? Everybody else has. Speak now or forever hold your—"

Bruno yapped three times. Then landing on all fours, he scooted his butt across the carpet.

"I hope you're saying that you really, really have to go, and not that I should quit dragging my behind about buying a house." Confirming that her keys were in her purse, Zoe shut the door and started Bruno toward the elevator. "Don't you know that moving is one of the ten most stressful things a person can do? A dog, too, I'm sure. And you and I certainly don't need any more stress in our lives."

When the elevator doors opened, Bruno yanked her inside. She hit the L button. "Besides, this location is convenient to church and shopping, and a fire hydrant. Unfortunately, it's also convenient to Mrs. Cooperschmidt, but I'm sure Dad's just going through a phase."

The elevator doors whooshed apart. Bruno pulled Zoe into the lobby and toward Mr. Farnsworth, the building's manager, whose eyeteeth she'd always thought were suspiciously pointy.

"Ah, Mrs. Laurence. A word, if you will."

"Sure." She craned her neck at Farnsworth as Bruno hauled her past the lugubrious manager and toward the entrance door. "Does mañana work for you?"

"*Mrs.* Laurence."

"Works for me."

"Halt!"

Zoe applied what she considered brute strength to Bruno's lead, only to skid along behind him on the smooth soles of her shoes until a column, around which she hooked her arm, brought them both to an abrupt stop.

"About-face!"

Letting go of the column, Zoe slowly turned around. Bruno did not. "He's not much on drills," Zoe said as Farnsworth marched toward her. "But if you're into really cool dog tags—"

"And do they give his weight?"

"His weigh—?" Seeing Farnsworth flash his pointy and perhaps too aptly named canines, Zoe stepped in front of Bruno. "Exactly what *are* you into, Mr. Farnsworth?"

"The rules, Mrs. Laurence. Surely you're aware that we don't allow dogs weighing more than fifteen pounds in this building."

Bruno, whimpering, yanked Zoe toward the door. "I know how this looks," she said, yanking back, "but I can assure you that Bruno's in spec. His fifteen pounds just happen to be all muscle. Now if you'll excuse me, I don't want to be late for work."

With the sleeve of his jacket, Farnsworth polished his brass name badge. "This will only take a moment—"

"Which I . . . haven't . . . got." Her teeth gritted against Bruno's strength, Zoe reached for the door handle.

Farnsworth reached for Bruno, scooping him up and unhooking his collar from his lead. Holding the terrier belly out, he crossed the lobby to his office.

"Just a doggone minute!" After taking a moment to recover the breath Farnsworth had snatched along with her Boston terrier, Zoe charged after him. "What do you think you're doing?"

"Check your lease, Mrs. Laurence," Farnsworth replied, pausing in his doorway. "I have the right to conduct random weighing."

Zoe gaped at the man and then at Bruno, who, to

her surprise, really was crossing his hind legs. "You could at least let me walk him first. Fair is fair."

"If you find a clause in your lease that requires me to be fair, do be sure to let me know." With Bruno as figurehead, Farnsworth sailed to the credenza behind his desk. Then, tucking the little black-and-white dog under one arm, he removed a bathroom scale from a drawer at the bottom of the credenza.

With a derisive laugh, Zoe waved at the scale. "You'll never get him to stand still on that thing."

"We have ways," Farnsworth replied. Taking an imitation bacon dog treat from his pocket, he placed it on the floor in front of the scale, then set Bruno atop the latter. Standing bowlegged, Bruno chewed the treat while Farnsworth read the scale's dial. "Aha! Just as I thought." He gazed up at Zoe, his eyes beady and his expression smug. "You'll want to see this for yourself, Mrs. Laurence."

Kneeling beside Bruno, Zoe whispered in his small, pert ear. "Haven't I told you never to take candy from vampires?" Bruno looked at her without apology, then returned to the leathery chew. Scratching him between his ears, Zoe hunched over the dial. "Fifteen pounds, twelve ounces." She looked at Farnsworth. "So?"

"*So?*" Rising, Farnsworth pointed an accusing finger at her. "You're in violation of your lease, Mrs. Laurence."

Zoe shot up, her eyes bulging like Bruno's. "Are you saying that after fourteen years you'd throw us out on the street because of a measly twelve extra ounces of pooch paunch?"

"Rules are rules, Mrs. Laurence. If I overlook one tenant's infraction of the rules, I'll have an insurrection on my hands."

Hearing Bruno's yap, Zoe looked down. "If I were you, Mr. Farnsworth, I'd be more concerned about what's on my shoes."

Wrinkling his nose, Farnsworth sent his gaze to his wingtips, formerly black, now black and brown. "Egad!"

Zoe had steadfastly denied merit to Toby's claim that Bruno could smile, but as she gazed down at the pug-faced canine, she could have sworn he was grinning from one pointy ear to the other. Picking him up, she hugged him to her. "Good boy. We have ways, too, don't we?" Latching his lead onto his collar, she carried him to the door.

"Mrs. Laurence, your lease is up at the end of the month," Farnsworth called. "If that animal is still overweight, you'll have to get rid of him or vacate your apartment."

Hearing Farnsworth's ultimatum, Zoe halted. Suddenly, she'd had it with being told when she could wash her family's clothes, and with fearing she might run into the Freddy Kreuger look-alike from the fifth floor whenever she did. With being told when she could play her stereo, and at how many decibels. And now, with being told that she had to put a perfectly healthy dog on a diet. She'd had it with Mrs. Cooperschmidt and her melons making a fool of her father, too, and most of all, with trying to raise happy, healthy children in a steel-girdered box.

Cuddling Bruno, she faced Farnsworth. "I wouldn't want to keep you in suspense," she said. "Start looking for a new tenant for 703, Mr. Farnsworth, because you've just threatened my family with eviction for the last time. I'm going to buy a house, and from then on the bank can do the threatening!"

Head high, Zoe marched out the door, slamming it behind her. Instantly, her knees buckled. She'd realized that while she'd freed her family from the Happydale Correctional Facility, she'd also torn the roof from over their heads. No doubt, they'd be thrilled that she'd decided at long last to buy a roof of their own. But, in less than a week's time, how was she going to find one that she could afford that came with walls?

Locating the right house in the right neighborhood at the right price took time. Where would they live in the interim? Hotels were expensive, and short-term leases nonexistent except in buildings where everyone was named Smith and wore wigs and dark glasses.

Zoe looked at Bruno, their noses nearly touching. "How do you feel about sleeping in a homeless shelter?"

His pink tongue shot out from between his jowls, licking a corner of her mouth.

Tucking his head beneath her chin, Zoe squeezed back tears. "Thanks, but I'll check back with you after a week of Dinty Moore stew." Setting him down, Zoe offered no resistance as he dragged her to the door. Once outside under a warm sun, she inhaled deeply, hoping to take courage from the scent of nature renewing itself. Instead, she got a noseful of the diesel smoke a city bus standing at the curb had just belched. That was one more thing she'd had it with, she decided as she coughed the stench from her lungs—city noises and smells, and trees that looked like part of the stunted aftermath of a nuclear blast.

But a house in the suburbs? All that commuting? All that schlepping kids! She'd have to buy a minivan. And a sprinkling system, or the neighbors would complain about her crabgrass. Besides, the burbs were no longer the refuge from crime and congestion they'd once been.

"You know, Bruno, there's only one more week of school, and The Kill-'Em-With-Debt-First-National Bank has branches in Kentucky," she said, gazing down at him as he sniffed out his favorite hydrant. "If we're going to do one of the ten most stressful things anyone can do, we might as well go for Perfection. Whaddaya think?"

Standing on the tarmac of the small regional airport in Winsome County, Kentucky, Mitch Ballard watched the approach of a corporate jet, its sleek body gleaming beneath a midafternoon sun. As always, he gave silent thanks for its safe arrival, even as the very sight of it cut his pride. When a man's main mode of transportation was a temperamental beater that frequently forced him—as it had today—to borrow an iridescent black pickup tattooed with orange flames, he couldn't help comparing himself to the Atlanta-based CEO who commanded a fleet of classy jets. Especially when the CEO was his ex-wife's new husband.

"You've got to give Ellie this much, Mitch. She's come a far cry from Perfection."

Mitch slid his gaze leftward, to the owner of the pickup he'd driven—with embarrassment, and over the limit—up Liberty Avenue and out of town. Catching the glint in her sharp blue eyes, he aimed a sideways smile at her. "Spoken like a true mom. Thanks, Lou."

"You can just put an ice bag on that swellin' up head of yours," LouAnn Ballard replied, brushing back the strand of silvery hair that had escaped the thick braid cascading over her shoulder. "I wasn't referrin' only to the pa-a-arful charms I passed on to you and your brothers."

Shoving his hands in the pockets of his jeans, Mitch cleared a chuckle from his throat. "Spoken like a true mom, and a modest one, despite her powerful charms."

"Well, it 'tain't always easy keepin' a proper perspective—that's a fact." Lou Ballard's gaze narrowed on the plane as it screeched on touchdown. "Course, some people will never have a lick of perspicaciousness, no matter how hard they try. Like that fool Ellie, leavin' Perfection for airplanes you can't hardly stand up in and fancy foreign cars that are worthless for haulin' stuff home from the flea market, and diamond rings that just get in the way when you're plantin' beds.

You know, all them glittery things as you could never give a woman, son."

Inhaling deeply, Mitch took his hands from his pockets. Wrapping his arm around his mother's shoulders, he bent close to her ear. "Where'd you learn to sweet talk like that, Lou? *Crossfire?*"

Lou scowled up at him. "Wouldn't hurt you none to take more of an interest in politics, Mitchell Ballard. Or even run for somethin'. You have a real way with people when you want to."

Grinning, Mitch pinched Lou's cheek. "Another charm I undoubtedly inherited from you."

Lou shoved Mitch's hand away. "At least I'm not thin-skinned, like some folks I know. So what if you couldn't give Ellie all she hankered for? If she'd been the right woman, she wouldn'ta cared. Why, I never once thought to quit your daddy—God rest him—even though he was just a—"

"Poor country lawyer who got paid in crops if he got paid at all, and you with never more than one decent go-to-church dress." Stepping away, Mitch gave his mother the once-over, from the plaid shirt—his late father's—that came to her knees, to the rolled-up dungarees, white cotton socks, and brown, loosely laced hiking boots with their tongues standing straight up. Sliding his jaw and a smile to one side, he returned his gaze to the plane as it taxied toward them.

"Luckily for Dad, you weren't a slave to fashion."

Thwack!

"Ow!" Rubbing the back of his head where his mother had rapped him with her knuckles, Mitch turned toward her. "You know, for a midget, you've got guts. Whatever happened to that thick skin of yours?"

"In the first place, if you want to be a politician you can't call people midgets, even if they are. You got to say that they're vertically challenged."

"I don't want to be a politician. Therefore"—Mitch

said as he bent over and kissed Lou on the part down the center of her hair—*"you* are a midget."

Making slits of her piercing blue eyes, Lou pushed up her sleeves and then put up her dukes.

"But a right mighty one," Mitch said, holding up his palms in feigned self-defense. With a wink and grin, he lowered his hands. "Just not a well-dressed one."

Planting her hands on her waist, fingers pointing down, Lou returned Mitch's scrutiny. "Doesn't look to me like Tommy Hilfiger dressed *you* today."

Reflexively, Mitch glanced down at his jeans and T-shirt, then looked askance at his mother. "What do you know about designers like Tommy—"

"You forget," Lou replied, folding her arms. *"I've* been to Paducah."

Cupping his hand over his mouth, Mitch wrestled a guffaw back down to his belly. "Forgive me," he said, his expression deadpan. "I'd forgotten about your travels abroad."

"No need to get smart-alecky." Lou punctuated her reply with a small-fisted sock to Mitch's abdomen. "Ooo-ah," she said, shaking out her hand.

Mitch forced a grin from his lips, grabbed his mother's hand, and exaggeratedly planted a kiss on her knuckles. "Sorry to have caused you pain, ma'am."

"Cut that out!" Lou snatched her hand from Mitch's grasp. "Besides, you're thirty-five years too late with your amends. You come into the world breech, you know. And naked, just like ever'body else. So, don't be preachin' to me from no fashion bible by the name of *Vogue.*" She pinned a puzzled look on her son. "Why are clothes and such suddenly so important, anyway?"

Cocking his head to one side, Mitch gazed intently at the small, silent jet. The door now stood open, and an attendant was lowering stairs to the tarmac. Any moment, his world would appear. "Sarah Jane," he replied. "When she turns twelve this fall, she gets to decide whether she wants to stay here with me or move to Atlanta with Ellie. I'll die if I lose her, Lou, and yet . . ." He heaved a sigh, his chest aching as the breath left his body. "I know she needs a mother."

"Then she doesn't need Ellie." Lou snorted. "Leavin' Perfection and a good man mighta been stupid, but walking out on her own child was unnatural. On top of that, she has the nerve to call up out of the blue nearly five years later and ask if Sarah Jane can come visit with her in that mansion she puts on airs about. You shoulda said no to her right then and there."

Though his anger was meant for a woman who lived hundreds of miles away, Mitch turned his expression of it on his mother. "Don't you think I wanted to?" He gazed back at the plane. "But I knew Sarah was getting to the age when she'd need a woman to teach her all the things I never could. Womanly things."

Lou looked down the length of her body. Then, propping her fists on her waist, she glowered at Mitch. "What am I? A kangaroo?"

Smiling, Mitch rubbed the top of her head. "You, LouAnn, are one *hell* of a woman. But as fascinating as it is to watch you dress a squirrel, I think Sarah Jane's more interested in learning how to dress for Bobby Ray Jordan.

Lou batted away Mitch's hand, then smoothed down the hair he'd mussed. "Don't be askin' *me* to encourage her. She's too young to be moonin' after a boy."

Hands in his back pockets, Mitch circled behind his mother. "So I guess you've been lying all these years about how you fell in love with Dad when you were both in the first grade."

Reaching across her chest, Lou cuffed her son's arm.

As she rubbed her knuckles, Mitch tugged a grin from the corners of his mouth. "You know, Lou, if you keep this up, you're going to get me arrested for elder abuse."

"And you'll deserve it, accusin' your own mother of

tellin' tales." Gazing up at the sky, Lou slid her fingers from the base of her throat upward to her chin. "What if I did take one look at your daddy over the modelin' clay and decide that he was the fella for me? Least I had pride enough not to go traipsin' after him, tryin' to get him to notice me."

"That's not the way Dad used to tell it," Mitch replied, never taking his sight from the door of the plane, wondering what was delaying Sarah, praying it wasn't illness or injury. "By his account, every time he went casting for mud puppies he'd find you waiting, offering to bait his hook for him. From the moment he saw you dig into a can of slugs, he used to say, he was as hooked as any catfish ever was."

With a toss of her head, Lou stroked her long braid. "Like I said, I do have my charms." Her brows shirring, she shifted her gaze to Mitch. "But like *you* said, Sarah Jane's probably not keen on imitatin' them. Still, she's got too much of Perfection in her to think that Ellie, with her glued-on nails and phony baloney blow-up doll breasts, has anythin' to teach her about being a real woman."

Mitch snapped a wide-eyed look at the diminutive, suddenly not quite so down-home woman at his side. *"Blow-up doll?* Paducah can't have changed that much."

"Course not. I learned about *them* from watching *Inside Politics.*"

A smile ruckling one side of his face, Mitch returned his gaze to the jet. "You know, Lou, you may have just convinced me to enter politics, after all." Lou attempted a yank on his earlobe, but anticipating it, Mitch dodged to his left. "Uh-uh-uh," he said, wagging a finger. Then he pulled her to his side, dangling his hand over her shoulder. "Listen, whatever you and I think of Ellie, she's still Sarah Jane's mother."

"And you're her father!" Lou reached up and squeezed her son's hand. "And I've never seen a man do for a child the way you've done for Sarah Jane, Mitch. Where was Ellie when that little girl got the chicken pox, and the time she sprained her ankle, or when she just plain needed help with her homework?" She smacked the back of his hand. "Don't you worry, son. Sarah Jane knows doin' from talkin'. When it comes time for her to choose, she won't have to think twice about stayin' on with her daddy."

Though etched-in lines bracketed his mother's eyes, Mitch saw in their blue intensity the ageless faith that had never wavered, never failed to rally him when self-doubt circled him like buzzards. But he was beginning to think there were some forces not even the indomitable LouAnn Ballard could help him believe into submission.

"I wish I could share your confidence," he said. "But Sarah won't be choosing just between Ellie and me." Mitch looked around him, at the gentle green hills in the distance. Miles beyond their slopes thick with tall pines, the Ohio River meandered southwest toward the Mississippi. And in between the hills and the river lay the town that—except for the years he'd studied in Louisville—he'd lived in all his life. With its broad, tree-shaded streets, skyline dense with steeples, and Greek Revival courthouse dominating its square, it looked much as it did in photographs taken a hundred years ago. That, he'd always thought, was Perfection's greatest charm.

And now, as he focused once more on the luxury jet, his biggest worry.

"Lou, for once I'm going to talk politics with you," Mitch began, sliding his fingers into his back pockets. "In a race against Atlanta, I'm not sure Perfection can win the vote of a twelve-year-old girl. Not after all she's seen of what the opponent's offering her."

Lou huffed. "Such as?"

"Restaurants where the waiters wear tuxedos, and

the menus are printed on parchment instead of on chalkboards."

"The cooks must get right bored serving up the same things day after day. And as I always say, a bored cook is a bad cook." Lou kicked away a cinder. "What else?"

"Shopping malls three stories high, like the one Sarah couldn't stop talking about after her last trip."

"We just got ourselves a Wal-Mart, didn't we?"

"Uh-huh. Twenty miles away, and in the next county, where *they* didn't just lose their biggest employer."

"Somebody will come along and set up shop in the old furniture factory. You'll see," Lou replied. "In the meantime, drivin' to Henderson County and seein' how the rest of the world lives is a real"—pausing in thought, she snapped her fingers—"learnin' experience!"

"Just like on The Discovery Channel, huh?" Mitch snorted, imagining his mother demanding, with her final breath, to be buried with her satellite dish. Affectionately, he hooked his arm around her neck. "Thanks, Lou. But in my job, I have to take a good hard look at the facts, and the facts as I see them"—he drew a deep breath, then let it go all at once—"point to Sarah's leaving me.

Lou stamped her foot. "You hush, Mitch Ballard!"

"For the love of Crazy Horse, Lou," he shouted, hopping on one foot while holding the other. "I don't mind your going your one-sixteenth Native American on me, but do you have to do a war dance all over my insteps?"

"When you forget your heritage," she said, shaking a finger in his face, "yes!"

"My heritage. We're talking your great-great-grandfather, Man of the Village People here, right?" As always when speaking of his ancestor, an erstwhile mayor of Perfection, Mitch suppressed the urge to thrust his hands over his head and break into a chorus of "YMCA."

"*And* the Ballards, especially MacDuff. Without him and my great-great-grandfather, there wouldn't *be* a Perfection. The two of them would be downright ashamed of you now, the way you've lost faith in Sarah Jane. In your own blood!"

"Have you forgotten that Sarah is Ellie's blood, too?"

"Maybe so, but she's got your heart, Mitch. She knows the glitter from the gold, all right, because you taught her. I don't care what she's seen in Atlanta. Nothin's going to change her. She belongs to Perfection, I'm tellin' you, and in Perfection she'll stay."

"Look, don't you think I want to believe—" Suddenly, Mitch caught sight of a leggy redhead in the doorway of the jet. Wearing a suit—short yellow jacket and even shorter skirt—and chunky high heels, she nevertheless looked small and slight for a grown woman. As she nuzzled a little brown-and-white dog, she gazed around the tarmac, and when she spied Mitch, she thrust her hand in the air and waved.

"If I'da known Ellie was going to be on the plane," Lou said, folding her arms and turning her back to the jet, "I'da stayed home and finished workin' on your transmission."

Taking a step forward, Mitch took a harder look at the sophisticated creature walking toward him, the little dog trotting beside her on the lead she now held. Shortly, his jaw dropped.

"Then you would have wasted a good snubbing, Lou," he said. "That wasn't Ellie you saw just now."

Her thick, still dark brows gathered, Lou slowly turned back around. "Great Spirit," she murmured. "Sarah Jane!"

TWO

"This is going to be terrific," Zoe said, relaxing her grip on the steering wheel as she strengthened her determination to forge on to Perfection. "That's what it's going to be, terrific."

When not one member of her family responded, not even Bruno, she peered in her rearview mirror. Toby sat in one corner of the backseat, staring blankly out the window, and Bink in the opposite corner, doing the same. Bruno stood on his hind legs, gazing out the rear window as though longing for the hydrant he'd left behind. Biting her lip, Zoe looked over at her father, who was busy writing. Probably a letter to Mrs. Cooperschmidt, she thought, the third he'd written to the hussy since they'd left Chicago this morning. Exasperated, Zoe hit the wheel with the palm of her hand.

"Will somebody please say something? I feel like I'm driving a hearse."

"Okay, Mom," Toby said. "I'll say something."

"Great!" Taking a deep breath, Zoe fueled a grin. "What's on your mind, sweetie?"

A long pause, then, "Are we lost?"

Zoe's grin imploded. "Are you doubting *moi*, especially after the hours I spent memorizing the map?"

"Not *me*, Mom. *Bruno*. And he doesn't really doubt

you. He was just wondering why we passed that farm back there for the seventy-hundred millionth time."

"Did not," Bink said.

"Did too!"

"All farms look alike, Toby. A house, a barn, some cows." Bink gave a foghorn-at-sea moan. "My life is over."

Hearing Bruno whimper, Zoe looked in the mirror and saw the dog slaver agreement on Bink's cheek. "Traitor," she muttered. "Bianca, your life is hardly over. You haven't even seen Perfection."

Grabbing Bruno, Toby cradled the terrier in his lap. "Mom, Bruno and me don't want to be Perfectionists."

Jabbing his letter with the point of his pen, Harvey loudly punctuated Toby's remark. "Me, either."

"That, Dad, is something you'll never have to worry about." Briefly taking her gaze off the two-lane country road, Zoe looked around at her family. "What's the matter with all of you? I thought you wanted to live in a house."

"In a house, yes," Bink said. "On another planet, no."

Zoe sighed. "Correct me if I'm wrong, but we entered Kentucky some time ago, and have yet to sight a single alien."

"Just my luck," Harvey said. "They're all married."

"Dad, please. You're not helping the situation."

"It's beyond help." Peeling a stamp off a roll, Harvey pounded it onto the corner of an envelope. "And probably beyond cable TV."

"We're renting a house," Zoe shot back, "I'm sure we can rent a dish."

"We can't rent friends." Propping her feet on the back of the seat, Bink sank into a sulk. "I miss Tina already."

"I'm sure you do, honey. But . . ." Zoe paused, noticing that the farm she was now passing did indeed look like one she'd passed a few miles back, before she'd taken several turns. Sure, she'd studied the map, but she was beginning to suspect that whoever made the map hadn't studied the roads. If she didn't see a sign for Perfection soon, she decided, she'd stop at the next farm and ask for directions. "You led me to believe you wouldn't mind leaving Tina. You said *I* was the one who was afraid of change."

"Mother, moving to some hick town where everyone walks around barefoot and all the men carry jugs of moonlight—"

"Moonshine."

"And all the women smoke corncob pipes isn't change. It's insanity!"

Mouth agape, Zoe shot a backward glance at her daughter. "Bianca Laurence, where did you learn such stereotypes? Don't tell me. From Tina, who got them from her mother's copy of *Kentuckians Are Weird: Avoid Them.*"

Zoe grinned, expecting at least a few tension-easing chuckles, if not an outbreak of laughter. Instead, the atmosphere inside the small sedan grew quieter and more taut. "On second thought, please do tell where you got those ridiculous notions."

Bink hesitated. "Do I have to?"

"Yes, you have—"

Harvey cleared his throat. "Next mailbox you see, Zoe, pull over."

"Dad, please don't interrupt when—"

"I want to get this letter off to Mrs. Cooperschmidt today."

"We're on a backwoods country road! I haven't seen a gas station for fifty miles, let alone a—" From the corners of her eyes, Zoe funneled a suspicious look at her father in the rearview mirror. "Da-a-ad? What do you know about this?"

"About what?"

"You know what. Bink's Hatfield and McCoy image of Kentuckians."

"Poppy said if we were going to move to Kentucky, we should search it."

Puzzling, Zoe met Toby's gaze in the mirror. "Search it? Oh, you mean *re*-search it." She looked at her father. "Why Dad, what a wonderful idea. Did you go to the library?"

"No, to the video store," Bink said.

"All right! Travelogues." Zoe beamed approval at Harvey. "But," she said, her expression suddenly clouding, "I can't imagine a travel video reinforcing false stereotypes. What was the name of it?"

Harvey scratched the back of his head. "I forget. But it was a real good tape."

"Poppy's right, Mom," Bink said. Then, casting a conspiratorial glance at Toby that Zoe caught in the mirror, she giggled. "I think the title had something to do with lords or earls."

"Earls? Ah, earls." Zoe looked back at Harvey through the slits she'd made of her eyes. "You rented *The Dukes of Hazzard,* didn't you?"

"Certainly not." Harvey sniffed. "I rented *The Best of the Dukes of Hazzard.*"

"That does it!" Jerking the wheel to the right, Zoe pulled onto the shoulder of the road. "Everybody out of the car."

"Huh?"

"Moth-er!"

"Mrs. Cooperschmidt tried to tell me you'd lost your mind."

"Yap!"

"You, too, Bruno. Out!"

Thirty seconds later, Zoe was pacing before the troops she'd lined up on the shoulder of the road behind her car.

"For months, the lot of you campaigned to get me to move out of our apartment and into a house. We needed a yard for Bruno and Toby. A washer and dryer of our own. Freedom from Warden Farnsworth. But that's not all." She clasped her hands behind her. "Bink, you said I needed to take a chance. Well, I took a huge one, because I wanted us all to have the kind of life we could never find in the city, or even in the suburbs. A life without the fear of crime and pollution, and of being dragged off in shackles for breaking some petty regulation."

Sensing she was on a roll, Zoe clamped one hand over her heart. With the other, she pointed heavenward. "I wanted us to find America, the real America, where neighbor greets neighbor over the backyard fence, and no one who seeks to borrow a cup of sugar is turned away . . . sugarless. Where a man can still pull himself up by the sweat of his brow—" Seeing her audience exchange wide-eyed looks, she figured she was at least making an impression, and forged on. "Where it's who you are, and not who you know, that matters. I wanted you to know that out here in"—she gazed searchingly around the rural landscape—"flyover country, this is still the land of the free, and the home of the brave!" Lowering her hand, she lowered her voice. "And God bless America." She bowed her head.

Silence. Then, "I hope this is also the land of Triple A."

Looking up, Zoe leveled a quizzical look at her father. "*What* are you talking about?"

Four heads, three human and one canine, turned toward the car.

Frowning, Zoe turned her whole body toward it. Her eyes ballooning, she inhaled sharply. "Dad," she said, quickly taking her father's arm, "I know you can't even drive—"

"Never needed to," he snapped. "Living in the city."

Zoe pinched the bridge of her nose. "But you *do* know how to change a tire, don't you? I mean, aren't men born knowing how to do that?"

"Sure. Just like you women are born knowing how to whip up a soufflé."

Bink threw her hands in the air. "M-o-o-o-m, you can't even scramble an egg. We're going to die out here!"

"Bianca, must you be so dramatic?" Gazing into the distance, Zoe pointed her finger at the sky. "As President Roosevelt said, 'All we have to fear is fear itself.' " Taking her family in with her gaze, she clapped her hands. "Now, if we all just pull together on this, I'm sure we'll be on the road again in no time."

After what seemed an endless amount of time, the three Laurences, Harvey, Bruno, a jack, a tire iron, and an inflatable spare tire sat on the shoulder of the road.

"Mom, Bruno says he's hungry."

"He's got a nerve." Zoe gazed down at Toby. "His appetite got us into this mess." Smiling softly, she hugged her son to her, patting the top of his golden brown mop of hair and standing the cowlick above his forehead on end. "Help's bound to come along soon. And soon after that, we'll get to Perfection." *I hope.* "You know, right in the center of town there's a wonderful, old-fashioned ice cream parlor, and before we even look for our house I'm going to treat us all to the thickest, maltiest chocolate malteds—" Glimpsing a car in the distance, Zoe scrambled to her feet. "Come on, gang. Help me flag this guy down."

Jumping up, the others joined Zoe in creating a roadside circus with Bruno in the center ring, flipping somersaults.

The car sped past, its horn honking as arms hanging out the windows waved.

"You were right, Zoe," Harvey said, wiping dust from his eyes. "People around here sure are friendly."

"That makes the third car that's passed without stopping." Zoe heaved a sigh. "I think we'd better start walking," she said, heading to the car to lock up.

"Wait, Mom," Bink called. "Someone else is coming."

As the others struck up a chorus of shouts and whistles, Zoe glanced over her shoulder, spotting a pickup—a glittering, black, monster pickup with blacked-out windows and headlamps. And, if she wasn't mistaken, bright orange, yellow, and red flames licking up and over its hood. "Everybody back in the car! Something tells me that whoever this guy is, we don't want him to stop."

"Mom?"

"What *is* it Toby?" Zoe demanded, hauling the boy, who was hauling Bruno toward the car.

"He stopped."

Pulling up, Zoe turned around and stared at the truck only a satanic cult leader would be caught dead in. Spreading her arms wide, she gathered her family in her embrace. "Dad," she said in a low tense voice, "even though you did it for Mrs. Cooperschmidt, I'm glad you got into shape."

"I've got news for you," Harvey whispered out the side of his mouth. "Those were only one pound weights. I painted on the zeroes."

Zoe winced. "Oo-kay. Bruno, you still hungry, boy?"

Yawning, the terrier curled up and went to sleep.

"Don't worry, Mom," Toby said. "The only thing we have to fear is fear itself."

Zoe looked down at her son. "I hope FDR meant that for Republicans, too, because that's what we are."

Toby's mouth formed a small *o*. "Go-o-o-sh."

As the door on the driver's side of the truck opened, the family drew itself into a huddle. "Mom?"

Zoe met Bink's big brown gaze. "What is it, baby?"

"No matter what happens, I just want you to know that I'm proud of you for taking a chance.

Zoe smiled softly, with eyes gone moist. Pressing Bink's head to her shoulder, she kissed the top of it. Then, promising that she was through taking chances, she prayed that the western boot and muscular lower leg clad in jeans now visible below the truck door weren't the prologue to two beefy arms wielding a chain saw.

As the door swung back to half-shut, Zoe held her breath. When she saw that the man who was walking toward her carried no chain saw, she would have liked to sigh with relief. But she couldn't, because he *was* armed, with a pistol of a smile cocked and aiming straight at her heart. Not that his smile alone couldn't slay her, but above it were two startling blue eyes that conjured the sound of arrows flying from bows trained on her defenses. His hair was thick, straight, shiny, and black, and Zoe envied the breeze playfully fingering it. But she gave nature credit for styling sense. She, too, would have angled a few strands into a rakish brim above one eye. The look was right for his attire, she thought, traveling her gaze down the length of him—a good six-foot three, by her estimation, all of it solid and sleek in a second skin of jeans and black T-shirt. *Sleeveless* T-shirt that slowly commanded her gaze to traverse the jut of his shoulders to the taut gleaming mounds of his thick upper arms. They kept bearing down on her, those shoulders and arms, getting broader and thicker. And deadlier. She stood entranced, helpless as road kill to stop staring at them.

"Looks like y'all have got some trouble," he said.

At the sound of his voice, its edge honed just the right amount by a slow drawl, Zoe gazed up into his eyes. Way up. He stood at least six-*four*, she recalculated, every inch of him setting off warnings in every inch of her. He was Jack all over again, not in appearance, but in effect—the kind of man who tripped her security alarm and then with the right tilt of his head and the wrong look in his eye, could hypnotize her into shutting it down.

But not this time. Stepping out in front of her family,

she folded her arms across her chest. "And you just know it, too, don'tcha, buddy?"

Cocking his head to one side, Mitch shaped his gaze at the woman—a Midwesterner, judging from her flat tones—into a question of his own. Three, actually. Was she married? If so, to the white-haired guy who'd just come to her side? The absence of a ring on the third finger of her left hand led him to conclude that the answer to both questions was no. But the answer to the third—What the hell was *that* she'd said?—defied his deductive skills.

Funny, he thought, *she looks normal.* In fact, as he'd approached her, she'd looked better than normal. Standing tall and slender in yellow slacks that invited him to imagine a pair of long, lean legs—the coltish kind that, despite his resistance, brought out the stallion in him—she'd roused his curiosity. Okay, so she'd roused more than his curiosity, which was why he had to know more than she'd already shown him: that her rampant chestnut hair flamed beneath the sun, making him ache to scorch his fingers on it. That her eyes were as green as springtime in Kentucky and just as stormy, flashing like sheet lightning above the roiling waters of the Ohio, warning of a force he couldn't tame. And that if he were smart, he'd get back in the truck, burn rubber, and never look back.

Of course, he'd never claimed to be smart, at least not about women, especially the kind he just had to pursue the way other men chase tornadoes. The long-legged, high-spirited, downright ornery kind. Like Ms. Stranded Motorist, here.

And, lest he forget, like Ellie. He'd chased that red-headed cyclone to the altar, only to wind up in divorce court, where she'd reduced him, emotionally and financially, to rubble. Actually, he hadn't gotten off half-bad, considering he'd have surrendered a lung if she'd wanted one in exchange for Sarah Jane. Still, he'd learned his lesson. Whenever he met a woman who scented the air with electricity—as this one did—and made the hairs on the back of his neck stand up—as they were doing now—he didn't have to think twice before running for cover. As he should now, leaving this green-eyed twister to blow through some other guy's life.

Except that she had two kids, an old man, and a zoned-out dog depending on her. While he might leave *her* to fate, he couldn't in good conscience strand the others. Shifting his weight to one side, he slid his hands into his back pockets.

"Look, lady, I don't know what you're talking about, and I don't want to know. Just tell me, do you need help or not?"

She certainly did, Zoe thought, because the burn she felt on her cheeks had less to do with this stranger's abruptness than the expanse of chest beneath his tautly stretched shirt. *Wow.*

Wow, Zoe? Wow is what you say when you see the Grand Canyon or Niagara Falls, not some guy's pectoral landscape, even if it just may be the eighth wonder of the world. Unless . . . unless you've been kidding yourself that you don't miss being with a man. You know, your hands just roaming all over his good-looking territory. Okay—gorgeous. Okay! So she missed being with a man. She'd get over it, in about thirty seconds, after she'd sent Mr. Roadside Assistance on his way. Figuring there was no crime in expressing a hope, she said, "I'm expecting a tow truck."

"And I'm expecting Heather Locklear, but I'm not holding my breath." Harvey nudged Zoe toward the stranger. "Tell the man what's wrong with the car. It's too technical for me."

Clenching her fists, Zoe dug her nails into the palms of her hands. It was either that, or commit patricide. "Yah, well, basically, what we have here is a flat tire. My father—I use the term loosely—and I got the jack to work just fine. Just not within two feet of the car."

"Harvey Beck." Beaming, Harvey offered his hand to the younger man, who accepted it. "I'm a lover, not a mechanic."

Zoe whipped around, thrusting a finger in Harvey's face. "You promised when we left Chicago. Your best behavior, remember?"

Harvey slapped his forehead. "You're right, Zoe. Forgive me." Taking her by the arm, he hauled her toward the stranger. "This is my daughter, Zoe Laurence."

Zoe's head fell back. "Dad, I didn't mean that you should introduce—"

"And my grandchildren, Bink and Toby," Harvey added, indicating the children.

Woof!

Zoe gazed down at the terrier, who was still prostrate. "And Bruno, the Formerly Hyper."

Squatting, Mitch scratched the scruff of the terrier's neck. "How'ya doing, fella?"

Toby stepped forward. "He's homesick for Chicago," he said, staring into the stranger's eyes. They smiled gently back at Toby, Zoe noticed.

"Well, I can certainly understand that. Home's a pretty important place."

"Our dad didn't think so."

"Bianca!" Zoe turned a fiercely remonstrative look on her daughter.

"Mother, you're in denial again," Bink said. Then, taking Toby by the hand and Bruno by the leash, she led the pair to a spot halfway between the two vehicles, where she sat them down.

Her fingers splayed across her cheek, Zoe stared after Bink in stunned amazement. "I don't know what to say. I've taught her to always be honest and open, but lately I get the feeling I'm living with Oprah."

Mitch rose. "You don't have to explain. I have a daughter her age, eleven going on thirty-five. Most days I can handle it, but others—" He shook his head. "She scares the bejesus out of me."

He has a daughter? That meant the odds were good, Zoe calculated, that he also had a wife. And *that* meant she could let him change her tire, after all, because she didn't have to fear he'd also change her resolve to remain manless. Life was good again. She chuckled softly. "I know exactly what you mean. I've had conversations with Bink that felt like shock therapy. Must be nice to be able to turn your daughter over to your wife when your knees start knocking."

"Not married, at least not anymore." Mitch swallowed the bitter taste in his mouth. "And the last thing I'd ever do is voluntarily turn Sarah Jane over to her mother. I've had sole custody of her since she was six." He gave a soft laugh. "Actually, I think it's been the other way around." Pushing his fear of losing Sarah to the back of his mind, he summoned a smile to accompany the hand he found himself extending to Zoe Green Eyes, who was even prettier when she relaxed. "Now that we've been on Oprah together, I'm Mitch Ballard."

Mitch Ballard, and you're not married, at least not anymore. Along with her heart, Zoe's gaze sank, landing on Mitch's hand. Like him, it was big and beautiful, broad across prominent knuckles, and the back of it was fluted with strong sinews. Long fingers tapered to meticulous, rounded tips. She'd always thought that a man's hand said a lot about his character, and this man's spoke volumes. What fascinated Zoe was what his hand told her about herself: that she wanted to feel the backs of his fingers graze her cheek, and his palm caress her throat and—

"The man's just offering a handshake, Zoe, not marriage." Harvey grabbed his daughter's hand and extended it toward Mitch. "You gotta coax her. She's gone sour on men."

Zoe closed her eyes. *God, please just open up the earth and let it swallow me whole. I said* whole, *didn't I?* she thought, suddenly feeling her hand slip into something warm, sure and gentle—like Mitch Ballard's hand, which she didn't have to see to recognize. She looked into his eyes.

He looked into hers. "Well now, I'm right sorry to hear that."

Zoe inhaled deeply, noticing how different Kentucky's air smelled from Chicago's—so woody, so exhilarating, so masculine—and yet it made her feel so feminine. "You are?"

Did he say he was sorry? He couldn't have said he was sorry, Mitch thought. Learning that Zoe Laurence was off men was the best news he'd heard all day, considering that he couldn't stop staring at her, even now, the way he once hadn't been able to take his eyes off an approaching storm long past the time he should have found shelter. He couldn't let go of her hand, either, its fingers so soft and slender that he wondered how they would feel combing his hair, raking his back. Yeah, the way he'd once just had to know the feel of an eighty-mile-per-hour wind, and had gotten himself knocked cold by a trash can.

He snatched his hand back. "I meant I was sorry to hear you had a bad experience."

Zoe stood stunned, staring at her still extended hand. Nope, it wasn't on fire. Maybe he was given to spasms. Maybe she needed to get her family the heck out of there. "Speaking of bad experiences . . ." she said, glancing back at her car listing on the side of the road.

"Right." Mitch waved a "C'mon over," at the truck. "Don't worry. Lou will have you on your way in no time."

"Lou?" Zoe cast a wary look at the cultmobile. "Who's Lou?"

Mitch ran the back of his thumb along the cocked side of his grin. "Owner of that truck you've been eyeing as if the devil might jump out of it any minute."

Envisioning the devil—a bearded, greasy-haired, three hundred pounder with an expanse of bare pot-belly protruding between his dirty T-shirt and jeans— Zoe started toward the children. She never reached them, having stopped dead in her tracks at the sight of an amazingly short lumberjack with an even more amazingly full bust hopping down from the cab and marching toward her. Lou was a woman, and not the least satanic-looking.

Zoe turned a puzzled look on Mitch.

"You may not believe this," he said, "but that's somebody's mother. Mine."

Zoe gaped at him. "You mean you're going to make your own mother change a tire? What kind of a son are you?"

"The kind that knows I'd punch him in the chops if he tried to stop me," Lou said. Holding her hand out to Zoe, she started the introductions that con-cluded with Harvey. "Couldn't get the hang of tire changin', that right, Harv? Well, c'mon. I'll show you how."

As Lou walked toward the sedan, Harvey stood in place, arms folded, grumbling.

Pausing, Lou looked over her shoulder. "We got all the trees we need in Kentucky, Harv. Now make your-self useful and go on over there and fetch me that jack and tire iron."

"Okay, Lou," Harvey replied, and did as com-manded.

Gaping at her father, Zoe finger-combed her hair back from her forehead. "And she didn't even ask right."

"How's that?"

Zoe turned a bland look on Mitch. "Don't pay any attention to me." *My husband didn't. My father doesn't. No reason why you should.* Besides, she wasn't about to quote *Men Are Weird: Deal with It* to the enemy.

Mitch laid his head to one side. "Give me something easy to do, Zoe."

Okay, stop tilting your head at that angle, the one that makes my heart do back handsprings. And don't think I don't know a line when I hear one, even when it's drawled so low and slow that it drips like honey off those crazy lips of yours.

"Isn't standing by while your mother does the heavy lifting easy enough for you?"

Mitch recoiled, not from Zoe's retort—he liked a woman with a tangy tongue—but from his own stupidity. He couldn't believe he'd actually handed her a line, or what must sure as hell have sounded like one, a really dumb one. Only, he'd meant it. He could easier ignore a vision from heaven than Zoe Laurence. Come to think of it, that's what she looked like, with her raked-back hair streaking red and gold, blinding his eyes to everything but her; her smooth, tawny skin, tempting his hands; her succulent lips bringing moisture to his mouth. And oh yeah, her long, doe lashes tugging his heart.

He tore his gaze from her. He had to, or he might do worse than say something stupid—like taking her in his arms. To keep them out of trouble, he set them akimbo at his sides. "Look, if you won't be wanting me for anything, I'll just head back to the truck."

With her gaze, Zoe mapped the elegant line of his shoulders, the sensual curves of his bare biceps, the lithe spread of his long fingers on his slim hips. *Who said I don't want you? I just don't need you.* "Sounds like a good plan," she said, looking about for the children. When she found them, her eyes popped. "Plans have changed," she cried, dashing past him.

"Daddy! Get Chauncey!"

Hearing Sarah Jane's cry, Mitch turned and saw her running from the truck toward the Cavalier King Charles Spaniel Ellie had given her, fifteen hundred dollars worth of bribe and lapdog now scuffling with a Boston terrier that could take him with one paw tied behind his back. As he made for the tangle of snarling dogs, Mitch had all he could do to keep from yelling, "Go, Bruno!"

"You get that nasty ole mutt off my Chauncey," Sarah Jane shouted at Bink.

"Bruno's not a mutt, you nasty ole girl," Bink shot back.

Mitch and Zoe each picked up a dog. "Sarah Jane, you apologize," Mitch said.

"You, too, Bianca," Zoe added, petting her pooch comfortingly and thinking that if the girl with the coppery curls and the bad attitude were *her* daughter, she wouldn't have to worry about her knees knocking. She'd be on them, praying. "Just because somebody's rude to you doesn't give you the right to be rude in return."

Stroking the head of the dog in his arms, Mitch frowned at Zoe. "Did I just hear you call my daughter rude?"

"Not unless her name is Somebody."

"But that's what you meant."

Zoe shrugged. "If the shoe fits—"

"It's only one of a pair. Seems to me the other one belongs to your daughter."

"I don't think so. Your daughter's the one who let her sorry excuse for a dog get away from her."

"Yeah, well, he may not be Rin Tin Tin, but at least he's not vicious, like your mutt."

Zoe gritted her teeth. "If Bruno were vicious, I'd have sicced him on you the minute you stepped out of that truck. Lord knows, I wanted—"

"You're all ready to boogie, Zoe," Lou said.

Zoe looked down at the small woman who had a large presence, then up at Harvey standing beside her. Each sported a black smudge alongside the nose and mouth—on opposite sides, she noticed, as though one had rubbed off on the other. "Boogie?"

With the back of her hand, Lou slapped Harvey's

shoulder. "Harv and I just finished putting on the spare." Her smile was white against the grease stains. "He's a real fast learner, your dad."

"That's because you're such a good teacher, Lou," Harvey said, wiping his hands on a rag.

"And school's out!" Glowering at Zoe, Mitch took his mother by the arm. "Take Sarah Jane and get in the truck."

"But, son—"

"You, too, Dad," Zoe said, glowering back at Mitch. "Take Toby and Bink and get in the car." She shifted her gaze at Harvey. "And I don't care if I didn't ask the right way, or make you feel needed, just do it!"

Clamping his hands over his ears, Harvey sang, "I can't hear you."

"Aw, let's humor the young 'uns, Harv," Lou said. "Besides, the sooner we get started the sooner we can go out on our date."

"I hear you, Lou," Harvey replied. Then he herded his grandchildren to the car as Lou walked Sarah Jane to the truck.

Mitch and Zoe met each other's thunderstruck gazes. *"Date?"* Each made a beeline for his vehicle.

Tearing open the back door and holding the dog out to Toby, Zoe fixed Harvey in her sights. "Dad, you hardly know that woman. How could you—"

"Mo-o-om!"

"Toby, I'm talking to Poppy. Please just take Bruno."

"I can't, Mom."

"Why not?"

"Because this isn't Bruno."

Zoe looked down at the brown-and-white toy spaniel, then back at the truck. Mitch was well on his way to her with Bruno under his arm. She met him halfway between her car and his truck where, staring each other down like boxers before the bell, they exchanged animals.

"I'll take Chauncey, Daddy." Reappearing, Sarah

Jane commandeered her pet from her father, his gaze still locked on Zoe's. Sarah tugged his arm. "Coming?" She waited for Mitch to reply. He didn't. "Daddy! Come. *Now!*"

Mitch gaped at Sarah Jane. She'd never barked orders at him before, and though he wasn't sure where she'd gotten the notion that she could, he had a pretty good idea—actually, a pretty gruesome image of Ellie and the poor dufus she was henpecking now. Correction. Rich dufus. As he was about to warn Sarah to never again confuse him with her lapdog, he heard a voice tinged with a distinctly smart-butt, big city tone.

"*Coo*-wal. Military training. Every man ought to have it, I always say."

"You got that right," Mitch said. Bending down, he hastened Sarah to the truck. Then, straightening to his impressive height, he speared Zoe with a steel-blue gaze. "It's good preparation for marriage."

Zoe pretzled her arms. "From which you, no doubt, were dishonorably discharged."

Giving Mitch a limp salute that turned into a back-handed dismissal, she pivoted on her heel and marched toward her car, only to recall that before she'd discovered she had a flat, before she'd discovered Mitch Ballard's shameless good looks, shamelessly spoiled daughter, and shameful attitude, she'd discovered she was lost. While her pride balked at the very notion of asking him for directions, her fuel gauge, when last checked, indicated she couldn't afford to pass that farm for the seventy-*first* hundred millionth time.

Taking a deep breath, she turned around. "Hey!"

Mitch halted, giving Zoe a good long look at his back. He had a name, and it wasn't "Hey." Flattening his hands inside the front pockets of his jeans and slapping on a cocksure, good-ole-boy grin guaranteed to infuriate a big city woman, he slowly angled toward her. "Now that's more like it, *darlin'*. Hey, yourself."

"Dar—" Just in time, Zoe backed away from Mitch Ballard's bait. She'd be darned if she'd let him get her goat with a Dixie head pat. No, he was going to have to try harder than that. Not that she didn't give him credit for the grin every woman wants to slap off a man's face, but it was too obviously manufactured—as was his mistaking her deliberately rude call for a Mayberry hello.

But that gaze of his, now that was something else. Like a blue bullet. She could feel its hot penetration right down to her toes. The worst part about it was that, unlike his grin and his condescension, it was uncalculated, unaware of its effect. She could have sworn he honestly didn't know its power to strip a woman of her defenses. And sure as her name was Zoe Laurence, she wasn't going to be the one to tell him. No, she was going to get her directions and get the heck out of his sight. She plastered on a false, sickeningly sweet smile of her own.

"I can see we have a language barrier. Let me see, how to put this?" She started her hands talking. "I . . . am . . . look-ing for . . . Per-fec-tion."

First, Mitch thought, she'd called to him like she was calling hogs. Now, she was talking to him as if he were five gallons short of a full tank. And the fact that he *was*—nearly blurting that if she wanted to find perfection, all she had to do was look in the mirror—was no excuse. Mercy, but the woman was asking for it. He faced her, grinning and spreading his hands wide. "You've found it."

Zoe's breath caught. What colossal ego. What colossal pecs. *Yes, but,* "I meant the town of Perfection."

"So did I," Mitch replied. Stepping to the shoulder of the road, he pushed aside overhanging branches, revealing a sign. "You're just inside the town limits."

Still holding Bruno, Zoe walked to the sign. "Perfection. Population 2,020—give or"—she looked up at Mitch—"take a few?"

"Saves money on signs," he said, letting go of the branch and facing her.

Zoe couldn't help chuckling. "I'm going to like living in a town that's as thrifty as all that."

Mitch frowned. *"You're* moving to Perfection?"

"Assuming I ever find it. You have a problem with that?" Wagging her head, Zoe stepped back. "Oh, no. Don't tell me you're one of the two thousand and twenty, give or take a few?"

"Okay, but you're gonna feel real bad when you hear what Lou does to me for not being truthful."

"Apparently, she's not quite so insistent on your also being modest. How long have you been waiting for some unsuspecting woman to ask directions to Perfection so you could tell her it was her lucky day?"

Taking a deep breath, Mitch propped his hands on his waist. "I'm still waiting. But as soon as I find the female who doesn't automatically suspect a man of one thing or another, I'll let you know."

"Oh, *would* you? I'd just love to find out what planet she's been living on, where men don't automatically prey on women. Oo!" Zoe stamped her foot.

Mitch heard thunder. Peering deeply into Zoe's flashing eyes, he saw reflected the howling clash of his own emotions, of want and need and fear, the fear of a woman tearing up his life. Again. "I've been praying, all right," he said, "that my daughter won't grow up to be a man user like her mother." He stepped closer. "Or a man hater like you."

Zoe raised her hand to deliver a slap, but under the icy glare of this sudden glacier of a man, she froze, all but her tongue. "No wonder you're not married anymore."

Mitch reached for her shoulders, his hands hovering near, as though he wanted to pull her to him. Breathing hard, he lowered his lips to hers, lips no less tempting for belonging to an ice goddess, no less capable of stoking the fires deep inside him. He felt the flames lap closer to his heart, thawing it just enough so that when his hurt wanted to remind her that she, too, had a failed marriage in her past, his heart told him to say something else. "I guess I deserved that, Zoe. I had no right to accuse you of man hating. I don't even know you."

Zoe stared at his lips, puzzled by the unexpectedly warm words they'd just uttered, not to mention the incinerator they'd just lit in her core. She was still a young woman, but standing so near the geography of this man, she suddenly understood what her mother had felt when going from one of her "Arctic spells" to one of her "Florida moments." Worse, she must have entered Ballard's Bermuda Triangle and lost all sense of inner direction, because she actually heard herself ask, "Would you like to—get to know me, I mean?"

Mitch paused, waiting for his breath to return. "That's a real tempting invitation, ma'am," he whispered, then abruptly shot to his full height, as though gripped by an unseen force. "Of course, it all depends."

"Depends?" Zoe murmured, floating in the ether of Mitch's hard-scrubbed, masculine scent and soft-spoken "ma'am." "On what?"

"On whether or not your hound lets go of my arm. Because if he doesn't, I'll see he's thrown in the county pound!"

Zoe snapped her gaze downward. "Bruno!" Instantly, the terrier released Mitch's arm, licked it, then nuzzled his head between Zoe's breasts. "There, you see? He's harmless." Nevertheless, she stole a glance at Mitch's arm and sighed with relief at finding no tooth marks. "I'm sure he was just trying to make friends with you."

"I can't wait to hear you tell that to the folks at Animal Control."

Zoe turned Bruno away from Mitch. "Does that mean you intend to report him?"

Though Mitch scowled at the little dog, he silently thanked him. After all, Bruno had stopped him in the nick of time, before Mitch had done something stupid, like responding to Zoe's invitation with one of his own, to dinner tonight. Hadn't Sarah Jane clearly shown that she resented every woman he so much as spoke to? With the question of his continuing custody of Sarah soon to be hers to decide, he must have been out of his mind to give Zoe Laurence a second thought, to give Sarah the least cause to claim he no longer loved her, cause to go off to Atlanta to live with Ellie. Heaving a sigh, he looked up at Zoe, at the lovely, tough-tender riddle of her, and regretted that he would never know what made her laugh, or cry. Or what might send her seeking the shelter of his arms. Strong as that regret was, however, it couldn't overcome his fear of alienating Sarah. He stepped back.

"Let's just say, Ms. Laurence, that you've been warned."

"I see," Zoe said, quivering with humiliation over the rejection she knew Mitch Ballard had just handed her even as she blamed herself for it. She was a city girl, for pete's sake! On the streets of Chicago, she would never have even made eye contact with a strange man. But she'd allowed herself to be disarmed by the gentle green hills of Kentucky and the muscular terrain of one blue-eyed, slow-talking Southern male.

Disarmed, but not defenseless. "In that case, Mr. Ballard, I have a feeling this town won't be big enough for both of us." Setting Bruno down, she turned and headed for her car. Then she stopped and, over her shoulder, flung a gauntlet of a gaze at Mitch's feet. "And *I* intend to stay."

THREE

Flanked by her family, Zoe sat on a high-backed stool in Cousin Tilly's Ice Cream Emporium, the old-fashioned, candy stripe soda shop that was exactly as she remembered it, like a set in a Judy Garland musical. *Well, perhaps not exactly,* she thought, gazing about as she waited for the double chocolate malted Cousin Tilly herself was concocting with huge scoops of her smooth, homemade ice cream. Unless her memory was as artificial as technicolor, the place had faded into a resemblance of the photograph she'd taken of it when she and Jack had visited years ago—the washed out photograph she'd cut into little pieces the day she'd discovered that over time and by a variety of means he'd gambled away every last cent of their house down payment. Until the day she died, she'd never forgive him for that, for stealing their future, and the children's. Most of all, the children's.

But you're here, now, Zoe, she reminded herself as she ran her palms lovingly over the counter, worn here, marred with glass rings there, yet still—she happily noted—carved everywhere with the initials of long-ago sweethearts. *You and Dad and the children are here in Perfection.* And, as she'd told that odious Mitch Ballard, they were here to stay.

But are you, Zoe? When she'd driven over a crest and saw Perfection spread before her eyes, she'd been de-

lighted to find it unchanged. And relieved to find it
so. Though she'd never admitted it to herself until that
moment, all the way from Chicago she'd worried that
instead of holding true to the idyllic image she'd created for her family, the town would have descended
into the nightmarish, honky-tonk Pottersville, minus
good ole George Bailey. But no. Neon signs and adult
bookstores, multiplex theaters and cappuccino bars
had yet to paint Perfection with colors that were garish
or indecent, cold or ridiculously foreign. On the other
hand, a good coat of paint was exactly what it appeared
to need. The gleaming white of the steeples had
peeled to gray. The shop doors along Liberty Avenue
in the heart of town stood weathered, splintering. And
outside those doors, men and women in threadbare
denim stood idle, or shuffled along the sidewalks, pausing to peer in storefront windows but rarely going in
to buy. Cars and pickup trucks cruised the avenue, but
few pulled into one of the many empty parking spaces
that lined it. Zoe got the feeling that since she'd last
been there, the place had lost all sense of purpose.

But surely, things couldn't be as dismal as all that,
not when Cousin Tilly could still serve up chocolate
malts piled with mountains of real whipped cream and
topped with plump maraschino cherries, like the ones
she'd just now set before them. Or maybe they could.
Completely unlike the chatty, jocular woman Zoe recalled, Tilly had plunked the malts down with the silent
surliness of a hash house waitress. Slipping her straw
from its paper wrapper and inserting it in the malt—so
thick she knew her jaws were going to ache drawing
it up—Zoe puzzled over the incident. Perhaps Tilly had
reason to be wary of strangers; nearly everyone did
these days, even in small towns. Then perhaps all Zoe
had to do was to convince Tilly that she wasn't really
a stranger. Watching Tilly clean the rear counter, she
smiled and said, "I don't imagine you remember me,

because it was so long ago, but I was here once before."

"So?"

"Well, I—" Zoe gulped in astonishment. Tilly had insulted her not just in word but in deed, not bothering to look at her, not even in the mirror over the counter. "I just thought you'd like to know that for years, I've been looking forward to coming back."

"You made it just in time, then. Another month and you'd have found an out-of-business sign on those doors."

Zoe's jaw dropped. "But . . . *why?*"

At last, Tilly met Zoe's gaze in the mirror. "Yogrit."

Zoe glanced from side to side, expecting to catch a fat old hound out the corner of her eye as it shambled toward Tilly in response to her word. When none materialized, she said, "I beg your pardon?"

"You've got eyes, haven't you?" Tilly flung her towel on the counter. Then turning around, she propped, her hands on hips so ample that her white ruffled apron looked doll-size in comparison. "Can't you see y'all have the place to yourselves?"

In the mirror, Zoe scanned the deserted parlor behind her, not for the first time. She had indeed thought it strange, given the heat of the day and that school was out for the summer, to walk in and take her pick of any seat. "I just thought everyone must be down at the river, fishing or swimming."

"All day?"

"You mean nobody's been in here but us? I don't understand."

"I already told you. *Yogrit.*" Tilly uttered the word with such forceful contempt that her peaked white waitress's cap slipped over one eye. With a huff and a bobby pin that she split open with her teeth, she anchored the cap while continuing her explanation.

"It's like this. Half of this fool town is determined to go to heaven skinny—like maybe the Lord will reward them with not having to clean the loos—so they drive on over to Owensboro for that pitiful low-fat yogrit that I can't make 'cause I can't afford the equipment. And the reason I can't afford it is because the other half of Perfection has been out of work since the furniture factory shut down a couple of years back."

That explained why Perfection appeared so down on its luck, Zoe thought. It *was* down, so low that it no longer could support local institutions like this one. "But, couldn't you get a loan from a bank?"

"*A* bank? Perfection's only got but one, and ever since it got bought by some bigger bank somewheres that sent in a passel of mocha capaseeno drinkers to run it, you're lucky if they give you a calendar." Leaning her elbows on the counter, she looked directly into Zoe's eyes. "I'm not giving up any secrets when I tell you that a skunk's a more welcome sight around here than one of them out of town bankers."

"Hey, Mom. You don't smell like a skunk, and you work at—*mmh-hmmm.*"

Knowing Toby and what was bound to follow his "Hey, Mom," Zoe had jumped off her stool and clamped her hand over his mouth. She chuckled nervously. "Yes, yes, I do work hard at smelling good, son. It's so sweet of you to notice. Now drink your malt." After sticking his straw in his mouth, she returned to her seat and met Tilly's astonished gaze. "He gets distracted and doesn't, you know, eat as he should. I have to keep him focused."

"On a chocolate malt?"

"Malts, spinach. They're all the same to him when his little mind's going." Swallowing hard, she brought her own malt closer. "So . . . Tilly. I'm sure you don't really have anything . . . personal against bankers, do you?"

"Oh, no?" Tilly wrapped her hand around Zoe's malted just as Zoe was about to draw her first long-awaited sip. "Do you know what I'd do if I was to find out you was a banker?"

Zoe shook her head.

Tilly shook Zoe's malted out in the sink behind her.

"That's pretty personal," Zoe said, hearing taps as her taste buds committed suicide. She glanced at her family's malteds, which quickly disappeared as their owners swiveled away from her. With a whimper, she slumped over the counter. How was she going to withstand the townspeople turning their backs to her, in the grocery, in the library, on the street? How would the children survive the taunts the local kids were bound to hurl at them? *Hey you, Laurences! You're ugly, and your mother's a banker!* How was she going to get out of her lease on the house?

"Slu-u-urp!"

Zoe sat up and swiveled toward the adjacent stool. "You know, it's not as though I haven't stressed the importance of table manners to you kids."

"And it's caused me no end of stress, I can tell you," Harvey replied.

"Dad, please," Zoe said, laying her hand on his arm. "Try to set an example for the chil . . . Correction. A *good* example for the children."

"Poppy *is* a good example, Mom. Of a man in search of his lost youth."

Zoe looked over her left shoulder, coming nose to nose with Bink. "Thank you, Dr. Freud."

"Dr. Fraud, you mean," Harvey said, leaning over the counter and gazing past Zoe at his granddaughter. "I'll have you know, young lady, that I'm not in search of my youth. Because I never lost it, not all of it, anyway. Just ask that pretty LouAnn Ballard. I've got a darn strong feeling that if I'da told her I was ten years younger than I am, she would have believed me. *Slu-u-urp!*"

Bink cupped her hands around Zoe's ear. "I think what Poppy's feeling is brain freeze."

"I heard that," Harvey said around his straw.

Sidling a smile, Zoe shifted her gaze to her dad. His short spiky hair, small, oval shades, and sunlamp tan did lend a certain golden years hipness to his appearance. "Okay, five years younger, but that's my final offer."

"Good, because that's what I finally admitted to after Lou punched me in the shoulder and said, 'Forty-eight. That's a good one, Harv.' "

"You *told* her you were forty-eight? That would have made you what? Fourteen when I was born?"

Harvey leaned close to Zoe, giving her a nudge. "They didn't hand out you know whats in school back then."

Zoe pressed her fingertips to the brain freeze between her eyes. "Dad, LouAnn Ballard is obviously nobody's fool. Whatever made you think she would buy such a story?"

"Mrs. Cooperschmidt did."

"Of course, she did!" Zoe threw her hands in the air. "If you'd fixed *my* garbage disposal, I'd have told you you look Mel Gibson."

"Funny, that's exactly who Lou said I reminded her of, after she told me she goes for men with a sense of humor and I asked her if she'd like to go dancing with one tonight." Harvey grinned. "Pretty smooth, huh?"

Recalling that her father had made a date with LouAnn Ballard, Zoe frowned. Not that she wasn't grateful that he'd apparently ceased pining for Mrs. Cooperschmidt and was showing interest in a woman closer to his own age, even his real age. But why did that woman have to be Mitch Ballard's mother? "Well, brace yourself, Romeo," she said, "because according to her son, she also goes *at* men who have a problem telling the truth."

"Gosh," Bink interjected. "When does she get time to eat?"

Mother and daughter giggled and snorted. "Seriously, Bink," Zoe said, appearing not the least serious. "I'm concerned about your grandfather. When Mrs. Ballard finds out he lied about his age, she might go after him with that tire iron she's so handy with."

"Don't worry, Mom. Poppy can always blame it on Alzheimer's."

"*Alzheimer's?* Wisenheimer's more like it!" Harvey pounded his fist on the counter. "Zoe, is this how you're raising your daughter, to disrespect her elders?"

Zoe gaped at him. "This from a man who refused to give his seat to an eighty-five-year-old woman on the bus?"

"I was only thinking of her safety. The seat was broken."

"It was also next to Mrs. Cooperschmidt's." Heaving a breath, Zoe looked at Bink. "Your grandfather's right. Alzheimer's is nothing to joke about."

Bink lowered her eyes. "Sorry, Poppy."

"No, no, kid. Don't be so quick to put on the sackcloth and ashes." Harvey got down from his stool and crossed behind Zoe to Bink. "It's a tough world, and you gotta stand up for yourself. Your mother's raising you to be too nice."

Bink stared unblinkingly at Harvey, then looked at her mother. "Mom, it isn't healthy for a child to get conflicting messages from the adults in her life."

Zoe didn't hear her. Her face propped on her fist, she sat fiddling with the paper from the straw that had vanished along with her malted. Abruptly, she spun around to Harvey. "I really don't understand how you could tell that LouAnn Ballard is a woman under all that plaid and grease, much less an attractive one."

Harvey's cheeks pleated in a grin. "The same way you could tell Mitch Ballard is a hunk. By ogling."

"Yeah, Mom, you sure did ogle," Bink added, giving Zoe a pat on the arm.

Openmouthed, Zoe gazed from one to the other of

her accusers, then shimmied her shoulders. "I did no such thing."

"Mom, it's okay to look, but if I were you I wouldn't get my hopes up."

"Hopes?" Her knit brows evidencing her peeved perplexity, Zoe propped her fists on her waist. "Of what?"

"Of double-dating with Lou and me," Harvey said.

"Yeah, Mom. You're not Mitch Ballard's type."

"I couldn't care less whether or not—" Zoe squinted querulously at Bink. "What do you think his type is?"

"You know, Mom. Small brain and big—"

"Bianca!"

"Hair, Mom. I was just going to say the type with big hair."

Reflexively, Zoe combed her loose waves away from her face and found herself imagining what she would look like with Dolly Parton curls. Like Dolly the Sheep, she decided, which served her right for even wondering whether Mitch Ballard had found her attractive. Lifting Bink's chin, she peered into her eyes. "Haven't I warned you not to make snap judgments about people? Even though I think the man is an egotistical bore, it took me ten whole minutes to come to that conclusion. And as much as I do dislike him, I have to say I don't think he's shallow, not the way he loves his daughter."

"That's exactly what I'm talking about, Mom," Bink replied. "She's scary, that Sarah Jane, and any man who could be fooled by her can't know the first thing about women."

Zoe dropped her hand into her lap. "The fact that he *has* a daughter, daughter dear, proves that he knows the *first* thing."

"Yeah, but he never gets past that to the second thing."

"Which is?"

"Don't make a woman feel like the only thing you care about is the first thing."

Smiling, Zoe cupped Bink's cheek. "Sometimes I wonder why I worry so much about you." She arched a brow at her father. "You're taking notes, I hope."

"I'm taking notice of the time," Harvey replied, glancing at his watch and then showing it to Zoe. "Movers oughta be at the house soon."

"And we still have to pick up the key from the realtor," Zoe added, collecting her purse and covering the check, minus the charge for the malted she never got to drink. "Let's go, kids."

"Better make that *kid*, Mom. Toby's gone."

Zoe looked to her left, past Bink, to the stool where Toby should have been sitting, drinking his malted. That was gone, too, along with the glass it had come in. Concerned, she nevertheless saw no reason to panic. Like most young children, Toby loved to hole up in small spaces, where he felt safe. Once, he'd outsmarted three mall security guards and taken ten years off her life by hiding under their very noses, inside a crammed clothes carousel. She'd made him promise to never, ever, wander away again, explaining that if she ever lost him, she'd lose her mind. He'd said he understood, and she'd believed him. Since that incident, he'd limited his disappearances to the broom closet, and only after taping a note to the door, his gawky, sometimes backward letters announcing his whereabouts.

"Toby, honey, come on out. It's time to go now. We have to pick up the key to our house before the real estate office closes. Don't you want to see your new room?"

No answer. Where was he hiding?

"And the swing set the real estate man said was in the backyard?"

Still no answer.

Sending a half-puzzled, half-worried look to her father, Zoe asked him to check the men's room, then began a search of her own, under tables, behind curtains, discovering only dust.

"Toby Laurence," she called, hearing the frayed edges of her voice. "Come out this instant!" Finally, glancing at the counter and figuring he had to be scrunched up on a shelf behind it, she said, "I'm going to count to three. One, two . . ." She rounded back of it. "Three," she whispered. He wasn't there.

"He's not in the washroom," Harvey said.

Zoe clutched her throat. "Dad, I'm really frightened, now. Where could he be?"

"Take it easy, Zoe. He can't have gone far." Scratching the back of his head, Harvey stared out the window. "I've got it," he said, then snapped his gaze at Zoe. "It's about time for the kid's nap, isn't it? He probably went back to the car for a snooze."

"I'll bet he did go to the car, Mom," Bink said, "but not to take a nap. He said Bruno told him he wanted a malted, too. Remember?"

"And *I* said that a double chocolate malted was the last thing I'd ever buy that four-legged front for a tapeworm." Zoe gave a soft laugh. "That little devil, sneaking away to share his malt with . . . Oh, dear God." She pressed her palm against her stomach, suddenly sick with the realization that Toby would have to cross to the other side of busy Liberty Street to get to Bruno.

Praying she wouldn't hear the screech of tires before she could reach him, Zoe dashed out the door and into the street, heedless of horns blaring at her own reckless disregard of traffic. She knew that even if he'd managed to cross safely, he would have found the car locked. She prayed he'd have stayed put. Short, panicky moments later, she knew that prayer had been in vain. When she reached the car—the only one parked along the curb—the only recognition awaiting her was Bruno's as he stood yapping at her through the crack she'd left open for him in the rear passenger window.

A scream of fear lodged in her throat as, for the

first time, she allowed herself to think the unthinkable, the unbearable—that someone had stolen her child. Standing on the walk, she tented the gaze she once again sent up the street, frantically willing it to produce a little boy wearing a Chicago Bears T-shirt and sipping chocolate malt. But her will wasn't enough to conjure up Toby, not even to keep tears from stinging her eyes.

A woman approached, a plastic grocery bag in each hand. Zoe grabbed her arm. "Excuse me, have you seen—"

"Lose something?"

Her heart thudding to a stop at the sound of a familiar male voice behind her, Zoe let go of the woman, who gave her a strange look and then walked on. Zoe whipped around to see standing before her both heaven—Toby—and hell—Mitch Ballard, firmly holding her son's small hand in his large one. Rushing at Toby, who held the malt glass precariously in his right hand, she pulled him from Mitch's grasp. "Do you have any idea of the scare you gave me?"

"I—I promised Bruno I'd share my treat with him, and you said to never break a promise unless it was for a real good reason."

Squatting, she gently squeezed his little arms. "But you promised *me* something, Toby, that you'd never go off by yourself again."

"Oh yeah. Guess I forgot." Toby lowered his eyes, feathering his apple cheeks with long, heart-melting lashes. "I'm sorry if you lost your marbles."

Zoe's shoulders slumped on a long sigh that expressed mixed urges—to laugh, to turn Toby over her knee, to faint. Woozy, she closed her eyes and lowered her head to her cold fingertips. Suddenly, she felt a sure hand clasp her upper arm and draw her effortlessly to her feet. She swayed.

Mitch took hold of her other arm and turned her toward him. "Take a deep breath," he said softly, but firmly.

Zoe did as he ordered, and again, when he told her to take another, deeper breath. Slowly opening her eyes, she met his, so like two blue bolts of lightning, they instantly shocked her back to her senses. "I'm all right now," she said.

"Good," Mitch replied, letting go of her arms and folding his own. "Because there are a few things you need told."

Who said lightning doesn't strike the same place twice? Zoe thought. "Really? Well it just so happens, there are a few things I'd love for you to tell me, like—"

"Mom, I'm sleepy."

Zoe gazed down at Toby, his small mouth yawning and his eyelids fluttering closed. Unlocking the car, she helped him into the backseat. Keeping what was left of the malted, she fully intended to enjoy it as soon as she dealt with Mitch Ballard. Holding the rear door open between them, she said, "What were you doing with—"

"Oh, no, no questions. Not until you hear what I have to say."

"I'd suggest we toss a coin to see who passes and who receives, but I hate all forms of gambling, so I'll just choose. I choose me. Now, *what* were you doing with my son?"

Turning his gaze aside, Mitch snorted. "Maybe you city types can ignore a kid who's having a hard time crossing the street, but hereabouts, we help him. At least Toby had sense enough to try crossing at the corner half a block back, which is more than I can say for his mother. And I don't just mean that jaywalking stunt that nearly got you killed a minute ago."

Zoe's already frayed nerves snapped. Slamming the car door shut, she rushed at Mitch. "What exactly *do* you mean?"

"Exactly? Sure you can handle it?"

"Oh, I don't know. I've survived divorce, destitution,

and my mother's death. Do you think I can handle something as insignificant as your opinion?"

"The question is whether or not you can handle Toby." He leaned one shoulder toward her. "How hard can it be for one grown woman to keep track of one little boy?"

Zoe's gaze riveted itself to the sight of that big, bare, brazen expanse of taut skin over hard muscle and corded vein. No wonder she'd felt like a feather on the end of a crane when he lifted her to her feet. She could feel safe with arms like that to surround her, she thought, provided she could be sure she was the only woman they ever needed to hold—the one thing she could never be sure of again with any man.

"You're right," she said, looking up at Mitch, waving the malted in the air. "You'd think I'd have learned from his father that you just can't trust a male not to stray."

Cocking one hip, Mitch hooked his thumbs over his belt. "Could be there's truth in that, Zoe, about it being in a man's nature to wander. Guess that's why it's always so much harder to understand a woman walking out on a husband and child who love her."

"Ah, the old double"—Zoe broke off, resenting the hitch in his stance that had thrown a hitch in her concentration—"standard," she blurted. "Boys will be boys, and women will be unforgivable."

Unexpectedly, Zoe saw Mitch's two slashes of black eyebrow knit, then his gaze lower by degrees. "And unforgettable," she heard him murmur, arrested by the unmistakable sorrow in his tone. *He's not so different from Toby,* she thought, *in his need to hide.* To hole up in the cramped confines of the bitterness he'd earlier expressed toward his ex-wife, and shut out the truth. That he still loved her.

"Hey, Mitch. How's my favorite fella?"

Looking over her shoulder, Zoe saw a mass of long blonde hair pass by on a pair of legs in shorts that advertised they knew the fine distinction between just plain plump and juicy.

"Hey, Lila," Mitch said, craning his neck and following the woman, Zoe noticed, with a gaze that took a freight elevator from the backs of her slim ankles to her topmost blonde curl. "How's it going with you?"

Zoe's eyes grew wide as she watched Lila cast a look at Mitch that could have reeled in Moby Dick. "Can't complain, unless it's about you not callin' lately."

"Who says I haven't called, Sugar? Your line's always busy."

"In that case, I'm going to order that call waitin' the minute I get home," Lila replied. "And the call I'll be waitin' on is yours." Wiggling her fingers beside a dazzling, pink-frosted smile, she wiggled away.

Must be cozy, Zoe thought. *Mitch in a closet with painful memories of his lost love and 130 pounds of instant amnesia.* "Well, I'm sure you're anxious to get home and check for a dial tone, so—"

"Hold on, Zoe."

Seeing Mitch draw up that slim, thrust hip and walk toward her, Zoe drew her defenses in tight, tighter still when he stopped at her side, leaned over, cupped her shoulder, and gazed her a blue streak that made her pulse go wild and her inhibitions go missing.

"Keep a closer watch on the boy from now on, okay?"

Zoe went speechless. Judging from her brief— though it couldn't have been brief enough—encounter with Sarah Jane, he was in no position to tell her how to parent. But by the time she'd found the words to tell him so, he was striding away.

"Wait just a darn minute," she called, beckoning him back with Toby's malted. "I don't have to take—"

"Okay, Mom *I'll* take the glass back to Cousin Tilly's," Bink said, appearing and disappearing and, in-between, swiping the malted from Zoe's hand.

Zoe looked down at her fingers, still curved but now empty. Her chin quivered. She sniffled. "Da-a-a-ddy."

"Oh, boy, there's gonna be a hot time in the ole town tonight," Harvey said, coming up beside Zoe. Winking naughtily, he nudged her arm. "Do you think Lou's the type to kiss on the first date?"

Zoe snorted softly, at herself. When would she finally get it into her head that, although she'd grown up with both parents, she'd been raised by a single mother? "I wouldn't know, Dad, but I'm sure you'll make every attempt to find out."

"Yes indeed," Harvey said, tugging on the ends of an imaginary bow tie. "Before I married your mother, the gals didn't call me Marvy Harvey for nothing."

Zoe looked aside, her stomach suddenly queasy for the second time that day. "Dad," she said, placing her hands on her waist, her fingers pointing down, "you know I've never interfered in your personal life, but if I were to ask you not to get involved with LouAnn Ballard, would you promise not to see her after tonight?"

Harvey gazed up the street, in Mitch's direction. "You really go for the guy, don't you, Zoe?"

Zoe sent her gaze after Harvey's, where, to her great dismay, it honed in on Mitch like a heat-seeking missile. "I hardly know the man," she replied testily. "Then again, I have every reason to believe that behind all that smug arrogance and strutting ego, there's more of the same."

"Wow, you really *have* got it bad."

"Grrrr!" Unclenching her fists, Zoe lowered her imploring gaze from the sky overhead. "Just forget I asked, okay? Only, if you do go on seeing the woman, don't expect me to welcome her into the house. Speaking of which," she began, seeing Bink return. Then glancing at her watch, mindful that she had to pick up the key before the realty office closed, she added,

"Would you all please sit in the car now so we don't have to sleep in it later?"

"I found this on the windshield, Mom," Bink said, handing Zoe a pink slip of paper before sliding into the backseat.

Stepping toward the curb and around to the driver's side, Zoe read the slip. "A parking ticket?" She looked around. "Where's the sign? Does anybody see a sign? There's no bleeping sign!"

"Oh, it blew away in a storm two years ago."

Zoe shifted her gaze to her left, at the straw-hatted man—a ringer for Mayberry's barber, Floyd—peering over her shoulder. "And the town still hasn't replaced it?"

"Oh my, no. No money for printin' up signs to tell folks what they already know.

"And what would that—*pitooey!*" A cloud of dirt and grit and if she wasn't mistaken, candy wrappers, engulfed Zoe as, too late, she paid heed to the hum of the heavy equipment that had just passed by. Clearing the air with her hand, she looked at the man, his eyes concealed by the layer of dust on his glasses. "Don't bother. I think I know what the sign said."

"Yes. Oh yes, indeed." The man pointed his finger in the air. "Times may be hard, but that's one thing we still do—clean the streets the third Wednesday of every month, after four in the p.m."

With an incredulous laugh, Zoe threw her hands up, ticket and all. "This is perfect, just perfect."

"Oh, no, miss. This is Perfection." Doffing his hat to her, the man walked off, stumbling up the curb he apparently couldn't see through the lenses he apparently hadn't thought to wipe.

"Careful there, Mayor."

Zoe looked on as a police officer appeared in time to catch the little man's arm. *Mayor?* Pop-eyed, she mouthed the word. She had a word for the cop, too, several, in fact. She rushed at him, waving the ticket. "Are you responsible for this?"

"No, ma'am," he said, stone-faced. "The credit for that parking violation is all yours."

Something about the way this well-muscled arm of the law cocked his head and said "ma'am" struck Zoe as familiar, but then, she'd been a *C.H.I.P.S* fan when she was a kid. She still grew teary eyed whenever she recalled the day she'd left her youth and innocence behind forever, the day she'd discovered that Erik Estrada couldn't act.

And the six feet plus inches of humorlessness in uniform standing in front of her apparently couldn't act rationally. "How can you give me a ticket when there's no sign posted? And if you say you're just doing your job, so help me, I'll scream."

He cracked a smile. "Everybody thinks cops talk like they do on TV."

Zoe smiled back. Maybe she could talk him into tearing up the ticket, after all. "They don't?"

His smile vanished behind granite. "Yes, ma'am, we do. That's because the law's the law."

She was too tired to scream, Zoe thought, or to argue, and even if she weren't, she couldn't waste another minute getting to the real estate office. "Well, we'll just see about that. In court," she said. Stalking to the driver's door, she tore it open, then paused. "By the way, what's your name?"

"Ballard. It's on your ticket."

Thunderstruck, Zoe watched him unchain a bicycle from a lamppost and pedal away. "Why *wouldn't* it be on my ticket?" she said, gritting her teeth, getting into the car, and grinding the ignition. "It's already in my worst nightmare."

Mitch drew to an abrupt halt in front of Wick's Hardware, two blocks from where he'd left Zoe, and three from Lou's truck. Until this moment, he hadn't realized that he was headed in the wrong direction, though he wasn't exactly surprised at the discovery. As Lou had reminded him earlier, he'd come into the world headed the wrong way, and, as he reminded himself now, he'd had trouble getting his bearings ever since.

Except around Sarah Jane. She'd been his compass, his true north. He couldn't navigate through life without her, stay on course the way a man with half a brain does when he has a child depending on him. That was why he'd had to stop bringing his dates home to meet her, because she'd gone haywire, like a compass needle in a magnetic field. He'd tried to reassure her that no woman could ever take her place in his heart, and though she'd said she understood, she'd sulked. And if there was one thing he couldn't take, it was her sulks. Eventually, he'd had no choice but to stop dating altogether.

No choice a moment ago but to give Zoe Laurence the impression that he was interested in Lila Garnett. Lila! *The* talkingest, single most annoying female he'd ever met. Once, a few months back, he'd asked her to have barbecue with him at Jake's Feed Store next to the courthouse. Lou had been in Paducah and Sarah in Atlanta, his brother Matt at the police academy, and Mike on his honeymoon. His friends now had wives, too, wives who didn't trust them not to participate in whatever hell they imagined divorced men raised. After five nights of sitting in front of the TV and pulling his dinner out of a sack—there hadn't seemed much point in cooking for himself—all he'd wanted was someone who didn't look like a cable sports announcer to talk to over his meal. Someone he could share his day with, who could share hers.

If only he'd known Lila was an electrolysist before he'd called her. Talk about a hairy evening. The more she'd shared her day, the sleepier he'd gotten. He'd even nodded off once, when she'd gone to powder her nose. Noses. He'd been seeing double by then. He wasn't much of a drinker, but the only explanation he could think of was that he'd had one beer too many. The worst part was when she'd driven them back to her house. And brought him another beer. Then she stopped talking and started rubbing his thigh.

Not that he remembered what had happened between the time she'd started in on his thigh and the time she'd brought him a breakfast of black coffee and dry toast in bed. All he knew was that ever since, the only place he could be sure he wouldn't run into her, wiggling those fingers at him and calling him her favorite fella, was the library. So, with three month's worth of the musty smell of old books up his nose, what did he do? Lead her to believe he'd been trying to call her.

Thank God she'd come along when she did, though, Mitch thought, so he could lead Zoe to believe it, too. Flattening his hands inside the front pockets of his jeans and heading back toward Lou's truck, he recalled that he'd known full well what he'd been up to, walking Toby across the street and to his mother's car—aside from making sure the boy didn't get himself hurt. He'd been hoping he'd find Zoe there, just as he had, frantically searching for her son. And hoping that she'd be so grateful to him for looking after the boy that she'd forget that really dandy first impression he must have made and throw her arms around his neck, and press her soft cheek to his. And that then, feeling her tremble with the aftershocks of her emotions, he could hold her close, steeping himself in her fragrance, and maybe even stroke his palm over the shimmer of her hair as he whispered, "Shh, Zoe. Everything's all right, now. I'm here."

Of course, she hadn't been at all grateful, and even though she *had* gone understandably faint, when he'd lifted her to her feet had he taken her in his arms, told her to lean on him all she liked? Ne-e-e-w. He'd told her to take a deep breath. Two, no less. Then, what had he done? Practically accused her of child neglect. *Oh, very good, Mitch,* he remembered thinking at the time. *You really know how to sweep a woman off her feet. Why didn't you just push her in front of that street cleaner coming up behind you?* Then, just as he'd been about to say, "Look, I don't know why it is that every time I get near you I act like a jerk, because I'm really not one most of the time, so will you please let me start over? How 'bout Saturday night?" Lila had come along.

Lila had come along and called him her favorite fella, and reminded him that as long as Sarah Jane had yet to decide whether she was going to live with Ellie or him, he couldn't be anyone's favorite fella but his daughter's. Letting Zoe think he was involved with Lila just seemed easier than explaining the situation with Sarah, because he just knew that if ever he got to talk to the woman—share his day, his loneliness, share hers—he'd be headed off again in the wrong direction, away from Sarah Jane.

The only solution was to avoid Zoe Laurence. And *that,* he thought as climbed into Lou's truck, shoving aside the twenty-five dollar bag of designer dog food Sarah had insisted was the only brand Chauncey would eat, could be a problem. He had the feeling that Zoe liked to read, though he'd never been around a woman who smelled less like a library than she did. *Great.* How was he going to avoid two women at the same time, he wondered as he pulled away from the curb, when the place he was sure to avoid the one was also the place he could bet on running into the other? At this rate, he'd be spending the rest of his life going from home to work, work to home, like a parolee wearing a monitor.

At this rate, he thought, passing the old furniture factory on the outskirts of town, *you'll be spending the night in St. Louis.* After checking his mirrors, he made a hard turn, back toward town and the house he shared with Lou and Sarah Jane. One of these days, he thought, he was going to start in the right direction. And with his luck, run head on into Zoe Laurence.

FOUR

With the moving van containing their belongings
parked behind them, Zoe and clan stood on the sidewalk in front of 222 Magnolia Street, assessing the
house that Zoe had leased sight unseen.

"Somebody say something."

At her mother's request, Bink looped her arm
through Zoe's. "It looks . . . interesting."

"If you're interested in condemned properties."
Harvey sent a sidelong what-have-you-gotten-us-into-
now look at his daughter.

Zoe stepped closer to the two-story house with the
wraparound porch that the agent had described as a
charming example of Queen Anne period architec-
ture. Unfortunately, he hadn't also mentioned that it
looked old enough to have been built when Queen
Anne reigned. Summoning good cheer for the children's sake, she said, "You know, it must have been
really beautiful, once. I'll bet we can get the landlord
to pay for the materials to fix it up, and even give us
a break on our rent if we do the work ourselves."

"What you mean, 'we'?" Harvey asked. "I've lived
in apartments all my life. The only screwdriver I know
what to do with comes in a glass."

Grabbing his hand, Zoe made broad up and down
strokes with it. "Surely, even you can figure out what

to do with a paintbrush. That's all the place really needs, a little paint."

"And shingles," Harvey replied.

"And grass," Toby put in.

"And we don't even know what's missing on the inside yet!" Bink folded her arms tightly. "Mother, are you sure they have indoor plumbing in Kentucky?"

"Hmm, no." Zoe forced a laugh. "But we'll soon find out, won't we?"

"Not soon enough," Harvey shot back.

Zoe's shoulders slumped at the reminder that they'd arrived at the realty office to discover their agent had flown to Denver on a family emergency—with the only house key in his pocket. At least he'd sworn on his great Uncle Jonah's grave that he'd overnight it. "Well, we can't get in until tomorrow, so we'll just have to make the best of a bad situation. Look at it this way— how much worse can things get?"

"Okay, Mrs. Laurence, I got it all figured out, what keeping my men an extra day is going to cost you. Up front."

Zoe looked down at the numbers on the clipboard that Pete, "the man who makes your move complete," had shoved under her nose. He should have had the decency to also waft smelling salts. "But my move isn't complete."

"Right, and if you want me to finish the job, I gotta get paid up front. Either that, or I dump your stuff on the sidewalk."

Zoe wrote a check, figuring that before it bounced she'd get the realty office to reimburse her for an expense that was rightfully its own. As Pete drove off, she gathered the children to her sides. "Chins up, guys. *Now* things can't possibly get—"

The thrum of a hot rod engine vibrated from farther up the street. "Worse," Zoe said, her pinched gaze going to the source of the sound, an approaching pickup—an iridescent black monster pickup with tinted windows and orange flames streaking along the sides and over the hood.

"Looks like one of us is being followed," Harvey said. "Sure hope it's me."

"Either that, or Mr. Mom wants to make sure I'm keeping an eye on Toby."

Zoe, Bink, and Harvey stood with their arms about each other's waists, and Toby stood with his arms around Bruno's belly, watching the truck near. They watched it pass. They watched it turn into the driveway alongside the house catty-corner to theirs. The door opened, and a leg that was long, hard, and all too familiar to Zoe showed itself.

"Now *this* is what I call interesting," Harvey said.

Her heart racing, Zoe kept a tight focus on Mitch as he walked up to the front door of the house, a sack slung under one arm. "He's probably just visiting friends."

"Probably," Harvey replied. "He must have unusual friends, though, if they like their guests to bring dog chow instead of a six-pack. Now, dog chow *and* a six-pack—"

"Hush, Dad," Zoe said, scooching down and pulling the children down with her. "I don't want him to see us." Like a mother duck, she led them waddling to her sedan for cover, then peeked over the rear fender and saw Mitch stop outside the door to sort through his keys. "Don't say it," she begged, squeezing Harvey's arm. "Don't even think it."

Suddenly, the front door of the house flew open. Chauncey, Sarah Jane's Cavalier King Charles Spaniel, flew past Mitch. Sarah Jane flew after Chauncey.

"Okay, Zoe, I won't think that Mitch lives across the street from us," Harvey whispered. "But while I'm at it, would you mind if I also didn't think that Lou lives there, too?"

"Mother, you promised things couldn't get worse! I'm not going to be able to stand it, living on the same

street as that horrid, disgusting Sarah Jane Ballard."
Bink shot to her feet. "How could you do this to me?"

"To *you?*"

"Yeah, and to Bruno," Toby said, shooting up with
the terrier. "That Chauncey is hard, and cussing, too."

Zoe gazed from her children, who were looking at
her as though she'd just sentenced them to eating
brussels sprouts every night for the rest of their lives,
to the man standing in the yard across the street. *What
about to me? How am I going to stand living on the same
street as that hard and cussingly handsome Mitch Ballard?*

"Bruno! Come back!"

As though she were watching a fast-forwarding video,
Zoe saw Bruno, his leash streaming behind him,
charge across the street at Chauncey. From behind the
car, Toby charged after Bruno. Zoe started after Toby,
shouting at him to stop. Tires screeched, sucking the
air out of Zoe. When she lowered her trembling hands
from her eyes, she saw only a huge Dodge Ram pickup
at a standstill. A dead standstill. On legs she couldn't
feel, she ran toward the truck, but just as she reached
it, it slowly pulled away. The fast-forwarding ended,
and Zoe saw Mitch, as though in a frozen frame, with
Toby safely tucked under his arm. The gaze he leveled
at her was nothing short of prosecutorial.

Swallowing a lump of more fear, anger, and chagrin
than she'd ever known in one hour, let alone one day,
Zoe started toward him. "Thank you," she said breath-
ily, and reached for Toby.

Holding up his left hand, Mitch turned the boy away
from her. "I'm not sure I ought to give him back to
you. I'm not sure you *deserve* to have him back."

Zoe jerked backward, feeling as though she'd been
slapped. Given what Jack had put her through, she
wasn't unaccustomed to the feeling, nor to the way
every smack had only served to stiffen her spine.

"Give . . . me . . . my . . . son."

"What's all the commotion?" LouAnn Ballard, her

face smudged with grease, suddenly appeared at Mitch's side, wiping her hands on an oily rag. "Anybody hurt?"

"No," Mitch replied, his gaze remaining locked on Zoe. "At least not yet."

Incensed, Zoe again reached for Toby, but Mitch blocked her move.

"Oh, thank goodness." Lou pressed her hand over her heart. "When I heard brakes squealin', I was sure I'd find Sarah Jane lyin' in the—" LouAnn blinked hard at Zoe, as though just then recognizing her. "Well, goodness gracious. What are you doing— Where's Harv?"

"Here I am, Lulu!"

Zoe turned to her father, who was coming up behind her. *"Lulu?"*

Pushing past her, Harvey took Lou's hand between both of his. "I just knew it! We're gonna be neighbors," he said, pointing to the house behind him. "And you know what they say, don't you, Lou? 'Love Thy Neighbor'?"

"Well, for gosh sakes. I heard someone had finally rented the old Jenks's place, but I couldn't imagine anyone being that dim-witted." Lou chucked Harvey on the shoulder. "You need any tools, Harv, you just come see me."

"In that case, have you got a lock pick?" Harvey explained his family's predicament. "I'm sure not looking forward to sleeping in a motel tonight."

"I've got a better idea, Harv. You all are going to—"

"Get your ugly dog off my Chauncey!"

"Can't you see I'm trying!" Bink shouted back at Sarah Jane as the two girls struggled to disentangle the snarling animals. "Do you think I want him to get fleas?"

"I'm warning you," Zoe said, her teeth gritted and her fist aimed at Mitch's nose. "Give me back my son."

"So you can lose him again? I don't think so, woman."

"Don't you call my mom names!" Kicking wildly, Toby beat his fist on Mitch's back. "You're a bad man, and I hate you!"

LouAnn Ballard smiled up at Harvey Beck. "As I was sayin', y'all can spend the night with us."

"Lulu," Harvey replied, smiling back, "I can't think of anything my family and I would like better."

Sticking out her elbow, LouAnn offered Harvey her arm. "Zoe," she called over her shoulder as she walked Harvey toward the house, "you help Mitch with dinner while Harv helps me work on Mitch's transmission."

Stupefied, Zoe looked at Mitch. At the moment, he looked like the kind of man who preferred his meat raw. *"You're* cooking dinner?"

Sending glinting shards of blue ice at her with his gaze, Mitch thrust Toby into her arms. "No problem," he replied. Then he bent and picked up the twenty-pound bag of dog food he'd dropped when he snatched the boy from the truck's path. Rising, he gave her a crooked smile. "We've got plenty."

However clear Mitch had made it that she and her family weren't welcome in his home, the dinner he whipped up for them was as far from dog food as Kentucky was from Italy—Tuscany, to be specific. That was the Italian region whose cuisine he'd served, starting with Portobello mushrooms sautéed in olive oil and balsamic vinegar with provolone cheese melted on top. Thin slices of tender beef encrusted with black pepper and a side dish of delicate white beans with fresh, sautéed spinach comprised the entrée. Dessert was a scrumptious egg custard laced with marsala wine that Sarah Jane had declared her favorite, though she informed her father that, "At the Italian restaurant in

Atlanta where Mom and The Donald take me, the Zuppa inglese is served with fresh berries."

She'd also unintentionally informed Zoe of the reason for the spread that was standard fare in Pisa but was probably nothing short of exotic in Perfection: Mitch's ex-wife. *Unforgettable,* he'd murmured earlier in the day, and had left no doubt in Zoe's mind that he'd been thinking of Sarah Jane's mother. Just as she had no doubt now that he was competing for her with another man, hoping that Sarah would relate his culinary feats to the woman. But did he really think he could compete with—

"The *Donald?*" Zoe queried, halting her dessert spoon midway to her mouth. "Your mother is seeing Donald Trump?"

"Of course not," Sarah Jane replied, looking at Zoe as though she had the IQ of the custard. "His name is Charles, but Mom and I call him The Donald because he's rich and says his S's funny."

How cruel, Zoe thought. Apparently, LouAnn thought so, too, because Zoe witnessed her leveling a look at her son that challenged him to admonish his daughter. After meeting his mother's gaze, Mitch looked at Sarah, a scowl darkening his expression. His lips parted, he raised a finger at the child. Then, on a sigh, he reached for the dessert bowl. "How about another helping, baby?" he asked, and—without waiting for a reply—spooned one into her dish.

Across the table, which Zoe had set—the lone and obviously begrudged contribution Mitch had allowed her to make to the meal—Zoe and Bink exchanged surreptitious glances. Bink's said that there was no way she would sleep under the same roof as Sarah Jane Ballard, and Zoe's replied, *Don't blame me. This is all your grandfather's doing.* First chance she got, she promised herself, she was going to kill him.

"You know, Mitch," Harvey began, "a man never stops worrying about his little girl, not even after she's grown and has children of her own." He put his arm around Zoe, who gazed suspiciously down at his hand on her shoulder as she raised her coffee cup. "And I'm worried right now about my baby, here. After that long drive down from Chicago she looks kinda pale to me. So how about taking her out for some fresh air, showing her the town?"

Zoe sprayed instant cappuccino into her cup.

"You just leave the cleanup to me," Harvey continued. "In our house, the cook doesn't do the dishes."

Dabbing her mouth with the corner of her napkin, Zoe squeezed off green-eyed bullets at Harvey. *Oh yeah?* she thought. First chance she got, she'd kill him. Since when, she wanted to ask, had she ever been his baby? When had that business about the cook not cleaning up ever been the rule in their house? And even if it were, *when* had Harvey Beck *ever* abided by the rules? *Duh, Zoe.* When he discovered that a rule, however pulled from thin air, could help him get his hands into a dishpan along with LouAnn Ballard's. "Dad, I'm sure Mitch has plans for the evening. Maybe he has to work."

"He's taking the rest of this week off," LouAnn said. "Now, skedaddle, you two. You both look like you've just seen that portrait Dick Clark's just gotta have in his attic."

Yep, Mitch thought, first chance he got he was going to strangle Lou. First, she'd invited total strangers—well, strangers, anyway—into the house when she knew he'd been looking forward all week to being with Sarah Jane. Of course, she had every right to do so, considering that the house was hers. All he could afford was a seedy apartment on the outskirts of town, not the kind of home he wanted for his daughter. So, in exchange for affordable rent, the right to tinker with his car whenever she wanted, and the cooking—which he'd done when he was married and actually enjoyed—Lou had taken Sarah and him in. But why she'd taken away the excuse he'd planned to give for disappearing for the rest of the night—that he had to prepare for work—was beyond him.

No, it wasn't. Beneath those WD-40 stained overalls beat the heart of God's gift to single women, the mother of a single man. No matter that a woman might look like last year's Derby winner, or make conversation as bright as an old horseshoe, just as long as she was breathing, and passed her blood test. The problem now was that the only thing equine about the woman Lou had hurled in his path were those long, coltish legs of hers. And her spunk. Mitch could have laughed out loud when Zoe had planted that tiny fist of hers under his nose and demanded her son back. *Could* have, if the least funny sight to him in the world weren't a careless mother. And though she didn't look the type—like Ellie, too busy keeping an eye out for a rich man to keep an eye on her daughter—what else could he conclude after she'd let her son slip away from her for the second time in one day?

But this is good, Mitch thought, *if not for the Laurence kids, for me.* He recalled the day he'd come home from work and discovered Ellie had left two-year-old Sarah Jane alone in the tub while she'd sat watching one of those shopping networks. He'd been beyond furious, so disgusted with Ellie he couldn't bear to look at her. And when she'd tried making it up to him the only way she knew how, he'd turned away from her touch in revulsion. He should find Zoe Laurence equally repulsive now—those full, peachy brown lips of hers, those soft, not too big and not too small mounds beneath her T-shirt—a complete turn-off.

Okay, Plan B. Flinging his napkin on the table, he stood and glared down at Zoe. "You ready?" He was going to give her a tour of Perfection that would guarantee that before her movers could unload so much as themselves from the their van tomorrow, she'd order them back to Chicago. And, taking off behind them, she'd restore order to his life.

As Mitch climbed in behind the wheel of Lou's high pickup, Zoe reached up and opened the passenger door for herself. She looked at the seat, which was roughly level with her breasts, then at the running board, then at the hand grip on the door frame. She placed her left foot on the running board and, hoisting herself up, tried backing in, but her left buttock kept slipping off the seat. Then she planted her right foot on the running board, but couldn't clear her left from behind it. Finally, she tried going in headfirst, kneeling on the board and stretching her arms across the seat. Now all she needed to do was establish toeholds on the board, one set of toes at a time.

"Need help?"

You wouldn't happen to have an elevator handy? "No . . . ugh . . . doing just fine." Turning her right knee out, she got her right foot on the board, performing half a dandy plié. Then, pushing off that foot, she executed a lovely châiné turn, hoisting herself into the cab and landing on her back.

Her upturned green eyes met a blue put-down.

"This isn't hard. It's like mounting a horse."

"Well, why didn't you say so?" Zoe turned herself onto her elbows. "Of course, I've never mounted a horse. But . . ." Laboriously, she backed out of the cab and slid to the pavement. After stretching the kinks out of her spine, she rubbed her palms together. "I know I can do—Aa-a-a-a!"

Two large hands, planted firmly on her bottom, had catapulted her into the truck. As she righted herself, the door at her side slammed shut. Mitch got back in beside her, threw the gearshift into reverse, and tore out of the driveway.

Sucking in her cheek, Zoe leaned against the door

and folded her arms. "Was that part of the tour, or will there be an extra charge?"

He ought to pay *her,* Mitch thought. What a sweet tush the woman had. What a sour view of the county he was going to give her. "No charge," he replied, then twisted a grin at her. "But when it comes time to get down, for a nominal fee I've got this parachute . . ." His mouth suddenly going from grinning to grim, he said, "And speaking of harnesses—"

"What do you think you're doing?" As Mitch's long, taut arm reached across her body, Zoe flattened herself against the seat back.

He pulled down her seat belt. "Buckle up," he ordered.

"Why?" Zoe asked as she inserted the metal clasp in the buckle. "Is it going to be a bumpy night?"

Mitch glanced from the road to Zoe. Her hair wilded about her head on a breeze that provoked him with traces of her scent. Her skin glowed, and her lips were plump following her exertion getting into the cab, which even now was thick with the heat of the day. Yeah, all in all he'd say it was going to be a hell of a bumpy night, because he was going to have a hell of a time keeping his hands off her.

"You can let me know when it's over," he replied in a growl, then rammed the shift into a higher gear. The big truck thrust forward. Zoe's head jerked back.

And as she gazed at Mitch Ballard, his black hair spiking wildly in the wind, his arm on the gearshift, one long, tense muscle matching its power to the power of the engine, Zoe's heart lurched. Any woman who could prefer a limousine and a man who said his S's funny to Mitch Ballard riding roughshod over 300 horsepower must be out of her mind.

Am I out of my mind, Zoe asked herself several hours later, *or did I just get the Beer Bellies, Pork Bellies, and*

Underbellies Tour of Winsome County, Kentucky? Providing obviously knowledgeable commentary, Mitch had whooshed her past every brawling back road dive in a thirty-mile radius. She felt as if she'd been on a drive-by shooting spree mapped out by the Board of Health. But if he thought a few roach motels were going to scare her away from Perfection, he had another think coming. As he wheeled the huge truck back onto the main road, she folded her arms and propped her feet on the dashboard. "So, where are we going next?"

Mitch frowned at her. The way he'd had it figured, by now she was supposed to be begging him to take her back to the house so she could get a good night's sleep before starting back to Chicago in the morning. "Haven't you seen enough?"

"Oooo, I don't know. I haven't seen the bus station yet."

Mitch couldn't help the smile that quirked his lips. There had to be more he could do to help her decide to leave Perfection. "I just wanted you to see what you're getting into."

"I'm not getting into one of those booths in the window of Booger's Place, I can tell you that."

To himself, Mitch said, *Yes! I've got her on the run, now.* To Zoe, he said, "Well, there you go!"

"No-o-o, I don't," Zoe shot back, with a wag of her head. "Of course, if I wear one pair of jeans for about a year without washing them, then maybe I'll feel properly dressed."

At her undisguised disgust for Booger's—the place that, truth be told, probably sent him more business than the other joints combined—Mitch hid a triumphant grin. "Try not to feel too disillusioned," he said with feigned empathy. "You city types can't help it if you're clueless when it comes to small town life. All you know is what you've learned from TV. You expect to find Aunt Bea and Opie everywhere you look."

"I've already run into Floyd the barber and Barney Fife."

Mitch slid her a Sheriff Taylor look of bemused comprehension. "So you've met Mayor Ballard and my brother Matt."

"Hmm, yes indeed." Zoe gave him a querulous look. "Did you say Mayor *Ballard*?"

"He's a cousin, several times removed."

"Maybe he ought to be removed from office if he allows places like Booger's to operate."

"It brings in revenue."

"And rodents." Zoe shivered. "And as for your brother, he gives a whole new meaning to the term 'the spirit of the law.' He believes in no parking signs that nobody can see." Puckering her lips, she reached into her purse and brandished the ticket Matt Ballard had given her.

Mitch's gaze caught on Zoe's fleshy, glistening, succulent mouth. He shifted to ease the sudden bind of his jeans. "I wish you wouldn't do that."

Zoe slanted a querulous look at him, wondering why he was looking at her as if he were allergic to peanuts and she'd just threatened to open a jar of Skippy. "Yeah? Well, I wish your brother hadn't done *this*," she replied, and stuffed the ticket back in her purse. "Judging from your familiarity with the graffiti in the men's room at Booger's, I gather you don't share his devotion to law and order. Or spelling." She gazed out the window, at the world going to silhouette against the darkening sky. "But then, the minute I saw you I pegged you for a black sheep."

"Stupid and smelly?"

Zoe whipped her gaze around and met Mitch's, which glinted like the barrel of a gun. His trigger of a grin was cocked, and capable of blowing a hole in her defenses. *No. More like armed and dangerous.* She laughed out of the side of her mouth. "Sounds like grounds for divorce."

"Nah." As he turned the truck off the road leading back to town, Mitch's voice turned dusky, like the sky. "Ellie wouldn't have cared if I'd smelled like a whole herd of sheep, just as long as she could have clipped me for diamonds and furs and a house so big she could go for years without bumping into me—unless, of course, she wanted something." After bringing the truck to a stop, he turned to Zoe, extending his arm along the back of the seat. "How about you? What brought your happily ever after to an unhappy end?"

Looking down, Zoe flicked a piece of lint off her knee. "Another woman."

Mitch's eyes narrowed in doubt as his raised fingers hovered behind her neck, aching to stroke that delicate column, then to sift the tresses that beckoned in the dim light with a cool, clay-colored earthiness. Reining in his touch and his yearning, he rested his face on his fist. "Either he was blind, or the woman kidnapped him."

Zoe snapped her gaze up at him, both it and her heart perplexed by his indirect compliment—indirect and disarming, unlike whistles and shouts of "Great bod, baby," which, for all their blatancy, were easier to ignore. She stroked the back of her neck, where she'd imagined his fingers doing the same only a moment ago and then delving through her hair. She shook off the shiver that ran down her spine, and the fantasy that could only lead her down a path she'd sworn she'd never go down again with any man.

"In a way, she did kidnap him." She sat up straight and cupped her hands in her lap. "Her name was Lady Luck, and if you don't mind, I'd rather not talk about it."

"So who asked you?" After all, he had troubles of his own, Mitch thought. Like a woman sitting beside him he was dying to kiss so she'd know that as far as he was concerned, the promise of aces in every hand could never trump those luscious lips of hers. He popped his door handle. "You coming?"

Still rankling at his most recent outburst of rudeness, Zoe shot him a distinctly hostile look. "Are you sure you're asking *now?*"

Mitch heaved a sigh. "Come on," he said. And with a single kick, he swung the door wide.

Leaning forward, Zoe peered out the windshield at the building looming in the distance, large and lifeless. No, not entirely lifeless. Haunted. She pulled the handle on her door. "Where are we?"

Standing on the pavement, his hands planted on his hips, Mitch gazed across at her. "No tour of Perfection would be complete without a stop at the old furniture factory."

Or a stroll along the banks of the Ohio, especially at sunset, when the sky shames art, and artifice yields to gently rippling waters, the green smell of moist leaves, and the whispers of the wind. When a man rediscovers awe, and what really matters to him. The daughter whose hand he holds. The woman he wants to hold, needs to hold. A woman he wouldn't have to buy, like Ellie, but who'd buy his babying her every now and then. A woman like Zoe Laurence?

Whom Sarah Jane would never accept. That was why, instead of strolling the banks of the Ohio with Zoe tonight, cupping her face in his hands and plundering her mouth for the sweet pleasures he craved, he was going to scare her the hell out of town with a walking tour of the old furniture factory. Assuming she was ever going to get down from the truck. He watched her slowly swivel her legs out of the cab and then warily study her descent.

"Look, just stay where you are," he said, holding up his hand. "I can't afford to get sued."

As she watched him come round the front of the truck, Zoe recalled how Mitch had helped her into it. "No thanks! I can—"

In a swift, seamless motion, he slid one arm under her knees and the other around her waist, and lifted her out of the cab.

"Manage," she whispered on the little breath he'd left her. With her arms around his neck, she met his level gaze, unable to discern its color but shatteringly aware of its heat. And met the nearness of his lips, like pillows redolent of a heady mix of man and marsala wine. She wanted to punch them. "I suppose there's a nominal fee for this, too."

"That depends," Mitch said, hefting her in his arms. "I charge by the pound."

Zoe scrunched up a smile. "In that case, I'm not sure I can afford your services."

Mitch folded her, bringing her lips even closer to his and creating a heat so palpable that with their next breaths it was bound to spark lightning. "No problem," he murmured. "I'll make you a loan."

At his unwitting allusion to her profession, Zoe pulled back. She was a loan officer and, as Cousin Tilly had informed her, the townspeople hated loan officers, which was probably just as well. If Mitch hadn't inadvertently reminded her that she was a banker, she would have behaved in a very wanton way, turning her head and trying his lips on for size, and probably crying, "I'll take them! What else have you got?" Never mind. Whatever he had, she'd take that, too.

What she needed to take, she told herself, was a sobriety test. Better yet, the veil. She'd have to rely on her scars to steel her willpower.

"I avoid borrowing," she said. "It took me years to work my way out of the debt Jack left me."

"Jack, huh?" *Jackass.* Which was exactly what *he* would be, Mitch thought, if he didn't put her down. Now. "Okay, then, this is the end of the line," he said as he set her on her feet. "After all, neither a borrower nor a lender be, right?"

Lender? Zoe squeezed out a mirthless titter. "Right."

"Especially a lender," Mitch added, taking her by the arm and starting her toward the deserted factory across the parking lot that had been overtaken by weeds.

Zoe's heart picked up the pace of her growing apprehension. "Why *especially* a lender?"

"You'll see."

When Mitch pulled her toward a pair of wide, darkened windows that appeared terrifyingly like the blank stare of death, she jerked her arm from his grasp. "See what?"

Mitch raised one of the windows, then turned to her. "How a town dies, and who struck the fatal blow."

Zoe hesitated, afraid of the answer to the question she nevertheless uttered. "Who?"

With ease, Mitch cleared the window ledge, then turned and reached out to Zoe. Lifting her beneath her arms, he hauled her inside. "I'll tell you who," he said, peering down at her through the shadows, his thumbs still slanting over the tops of her breasts. "The out of town scrooges who took over the bank and put this place out of business when they called the loan on it, that's who."

Zoe was already weak from the touch of his palms to the sides of her breasts. Now she went limp. "Oh, *that* who."

She pushed away from him, stepping farther into the shell of the once thriving business, hiding the secret of her profession in the shadows of machinery rising ghostlike around her. The place was indeed haunted—by failure, both corporate and personal. When corporations failed, the toll was always personal, especially on those men and women who lost their livelihoods, as half of Perfection had when this factory had shut down. Still, she thought as she ran her finger through the dust layered on a workbench, the bank must have had a sound economic reason for calling

the loan, though she doubted she could convince
Mitch or any of the other townspeople of that.

At the sudden, shocking realization that the only
person she really wanted to convince that bankers
weren't sadistic—that *she* certainly wasn't—was Mitch,
Zoe came to a halt. The man was rude, arrogant, apparently a frequent patron of every stop-and-sock dive
in the county, so why the heck should she care what
he, of all people, thought of *her?*

Because he was a rude, arrogant, apparently brawling hunk who could melt her bones with a look. So
what was she doing alone in the dark with him? Turning, she made her way back through the shadows to
the place where she'd left him.

He wasn't there.

She called his name.

He didn't answer.

She walked toward the end of the building opposite
the one she'd already explored, each step a blind ven-
ture into what increasingly felt like a graveyard.

"Mitch?"

Her voice was hoarse with the struggle inside her
between reason and mindless terror. At the moment,
reason was winning, assuring her that it made no sense
for him to abandon her in this crypt.

But then, why had he given her the creepy-crawly
tour of Winsome County? Why, she thought, her heart
now pounding, had she gotten into that truck with
him in the first place, when everything about the man
shouted *Stranger Danger?* Whoever said 'timing is everything' sure knew what he was talking about. She'd arrived in Perfection in time for the debut of its first
serial killer.

Certain she'd heard movement behind her, Zoe
froze. "Is anybody there?" *Brilliant, Zoe. In the movies,
does anybody ever answer that question?* Suddenly, something swooped down at her head and plucked at her
hair. She screamed, clasping her arms over her head,

then ran forward—into something silky and suffocating. A stocking! He was gagging her with a nylon stocking. She screamed more shrilly, shredding away at the stocking with her nails. "Oh! Oh, God!"

"Zoe!"

"No, get away from me!"

Evading Zoe's flailing arms in the dark, Mitch grabbed her from behind, restraining her and holding her tightly against him. "What is it, baby? Tell me what happened."

Zoe grew quiet, so quiet she could hear Mitch breathing in her ear. Leaning her head back, she slanted her gaze up at his, feeling more than seeing its intense concern.

"You called me 'baby'." *The way you called Sarah 'baby'. Tenderly, indulgently, protectively.*

He had, Mitch realized just then. And judging from her body, stilled and pressed against him inside the circle of his arms, and the sudden sinew of trust in her murmur, she'd liked hearing the term as much as he'd liked saying it. Taking her by the shoulders, he turned her toward him. "Are you all right?"

Zoe flattened her hands against his solid chest, somehow knowing it to be a shield between her and whatever had attempted to harm her. She gazed up at him. "I am now that you're here."

Mitch curled his fingers around hers. That was the nicest thing a woman had ever said to him. "Why did you scream?"

Zoe told him about the stocking.

Spreading one hand across her back and drawing her into him, Mitch reached into the darkness behind her. Then he wrapped her tightly in both arms, clasping his hands at her waist and resting his chin atop her head. "If you ever find the spider who spun that web, see if you can get her to make me a pair of socks. I go through socks like you wouldn't believe."

With a soft laugh at her overactive imagination, Zoe

lifted her chin. "Now I know what to get you for Christmas."

Mitch took a deep breath, expanding his chest into the palms of her hands. Oh man, why did he have to be a slave to habit, wearing a shirt day in, day out? "I was hoping you wouldn't be here that long."

"Ah, light dawns." Zoe flexed her fingers over his pecs and wondered if men got implants, too—of rock. "Was that the reason for the Fright Night Tour of Winsome County?"

The way he was holding her, the way her hips fitted to his, made Mitch want to move. Dance. Slow dance. And there was only one song to slow dance to. The melody started in his head, then traveled to his feet, impelling them to weave a circle. Hips swaying, he pressed his forehead to hers. "I was desperate. My doctor says I have to give up sweet things."

Zoe smiled. Then, closing her eyes, she sent her inner gaze to his thighs, pulsing against hers to the beat of a song she couldn't hear. "What are we dancing to?"

Mitch knew, but he wasn't telling. She'd laugh. He raised her right hand in his left, meshing their fingers. "Guess."

Pressing her temple to his cheek, Zoe inhaled deeply of its scent, which was both warm and dangerous. " 'La Bamba'?"

Eyes closed, Mitch rubbed his cheek against the side of her head. "I knew I couldn't fool you."

"No, but you nearly frightened me to death, leaving me alone." She gazed up at him, making out little but the strong line of his jaw. "Where'd you go?"

"I went looking for one of the unfinished pieces the company left behind, to show you the workmanship of folks who're now on unemployment." He leaned back, pressing Zoe onto the hard plane he'd made of his body. "But then you had to go and scream at a cobweb—"

"And whatever dive-bombed me and flew off with a chunk of my hair." Zoe rested securely against his arm as he eased her backward. "What do you think it could have been?"

"Some kind of bird. This place is loaded with nests." Shuffling to a stop, Mitch thrust his hands along either side of her head, combing her hair back from her face. He savored its luxurious texture.

"Then . . ." Her heart thumping, Zoe closed her eyes as she clasped his wrists. "I was really safe all the time?"

"I wouldn't say that . . . exactly." Locating her mouth with his thumb, Mitch parted her lips, grazed her teeth.

Moaning, Zoe turned her head to one side, scraping her teeth over the pad of his thumb. Then she took it into her mouth and circled the tip of her tongue around it.

Mitch pulled her hard against him, forcing her head back. He flicked his tongue up her neck, now a torch.

They both felt the heat, heard the sizzle.

Then, lightning struck.

FIVE

Lying on an abandoned sofa somewhere in a warm recess of the factory, upholstered head to toe with Mitch Ballard, Zoe opened her mouth to his deepening kiss. "Mmm, I see what you mean about the quality of the workmanship," she said between fiery licks of his tongue, as wicked as those flames on the Ballard Satanmobile pickup. She had no doubt he was going to consume her. And take her straight to—

"Heaven." A word was one too many when a man was starving, Mitch thought, and the woman spread beneath him was a feast. He delved his tongue back into Zoe's mouth, hungry for more of her. He pulled back, panting. "Oh God, Zoe, you taste like heaven." Like a lava flow, Mitch coursed his touch down the slope of her shoulder, over the peak of her breast, the swell of her hip. "You *feel* like heaven."

"Do I?" Zoe pulled his shirt out of his jeans and up his back. Then, with her palms, she traced the V-shaped thrust of his torso, the line of his shoulders. "Well, to me, *this* feels like sin."

"What about this?" Pushing up on his hands, Mitch pressed the straining shaft beneath his jeans against her pelvis.

Arching, digging her fingers into his upper arms, Zoe whimpered. "I was wrong. *That* definitely feels like sin."

"And this?" Leaning to one side, Mitch yanked her shirt out of her slacks and then slid his hand beneath it and under her breast, lifting it. Lowering his head, he took as much of the soft mound as he could into his mouth, swirling his tongue over the center. Then he pulled away, exposing his brand to the cool air. Tortured by the unbearably pleasurable tingle he'd created, Zoe saw starbursts. She drew her knees up around his hips. "Now *that* feels like *The 1812 Overture* when Mrs. McIntyre takes Regina Elizabeth to the sitter's."

With his fingers curled around her bra strap, poised to slide it off her shoulder, Mitch froze. "Say again?"

"When we lived in my apartment in the city, that was the only time I could blast my stereo. Those cannons just shatter me."

Mitch cocked a grin. "Well, if it's cannons you like—"

"Hold your fire!"

Off his guard, Mitch rolled off the sofa at Zoe's shove.

Turning onto her side, Zoe peered down at him. "Ooo, are you okay?"

Braced on his elbows, Mitch looked up at her. "No problem. Happens all the time. Never to me, but I'm sure it happens."

Zoe reached down to him. "Look, can you see my hand?"

"I see it. But don't read too much into that. I've seen hands before."

"I mean, will you take it?"

"Why, don't you want it?"

Zoe tsked. "I'm offering to help you get back up."

Mitch gazed down his torso to the swell below his belt buckle. "I'm still up from the last time you helped me, darlin'."

Zoe bit the corner of her lower lip. She was "darlin' " again, which meant he thought she was anything but. "Please, Mitch. I want to explain."

"Hey, forget it." Sitting up, Mitch dangled his hands over his knees. "You suddenly remembered you have to rotate your tires. I understand."

Zoe withdrew her hand. "No you don't. Because what I suddenly remembered is that I have an eleven-year-old daughter." Swinging her legs off the sofa, she stuffed her hands underneath the cushion, where they couldn't get into trouble. "And I can't expect her to practice restraint when she's old enough to date if I'm not willing to practice it myself."

"When will she be old enough to date?"

"When she's thirty-seven."

So swiftly she had no time to resist, Mitch pulled her into his arms and cradled her across his lap. Peering down at her, he grazed her cheek with the backs of his fingers. "That gives you a good twenty-six years."

Oh, Zoe. You want him. You know you do. You've been so long without a man, and that was fine, until now. Until Mitch, who makes you more than hungry for his touch, his kiss, who makes you feel as though you'll die without them. "If you don't kiss me this minute, that shove off the sofa will seem like a ride on a merry-go-round." Reaching up, she pressed her palm to his cheek. "Don't ask me why, because I never thought I'd say this to a man again, but I need you, Mitch Ballard."

Zoe, Zoe. You strike words like matches and light fires in me, fires that make me feel alive again. Like a man again. And it's been so long since I've felt like a man, because it's been so long since a woman said she needed me. A woman like you. But then— "I've never known a woman could be like you, Zoe Laurence. Feel like you. I never knew I could want a woman the way I want—" Out of breath, out of control, Mitch crushed her to him. Devouring her mouth, plying the curves and hollows of her body, he glutted his senses with the flavor, the feel, the scent of her.

He's skinning me alive, Zoe thought as he tugged a bra strap off her shoulder, and then, pulling the cup down, molded her breast, raked his thumb over her nipple. *He's stripping away my scarred memories, my hardened will, layer by layer getting closer to my heart. And I don't even know the man, don't even know the man, don't even—*

"Ow!" Letting go of Zoe, Mitch shot up, startled more than hurt by a sudden blow to the back of his head.

Gasping for breath, Zoe scrambled off his lap. On her hands and knees, she backed away from him, dragging the purse she'd managed to grab and clobber him with. "I'm sorry Mitch, I can't . . . I won't . . ." Getting to her feet, she ran heedlessly into the darkness, bumping into unseen obstacles, knocking over unknown objects, crying out with pain, physical and emotional—and moral. *Or more to the point,* she thought, *immoral.*

"Zoe!"

Hearing Mitch's call only made her run faster and more recklessly. She stumbled over something, breaking her fall with her hands. They ground into a mixture of some kind of grit, probably sawdust and wood shavings.

"Zoe, wait. You'll hurt yourself."

"I already have." Righting herself, she plucked splinters from her palms that, while painful, were not the cause of the hot tears streaming down her cheeks. Or of her murmuring, "I've behaved like a—Oh, God. I can't say the word." But she could think it, and did. *Tramp.* Sick to her soul, she fled, praying she would find the window through which they'd entered the building before Mitch could find her. Before he could force her to look into his eyes and see her reflection, the reflection of a woman who'd lost her self-respect.

"Zoe, *please.*" Coming to a stop, Mitch rubbed the sore spot on the back of his head. Too bad he couldn't do the same for the one in his heart. Only Zoe could heal that pain. But first, he had to find her. "I just want to talk with you, Zoe."

"No way. I'm not participating in any activity that involves your mouth."

Scraping his teeth over his lower lip, bursting lingering buds of Zoe's flavor, Mitch inhaled sharply. "I'll keep my back to you, and my hands in my pockets," he said, starting in the direction of her voice. "I promise."

And where do you suggest I keep my hands while I'm staring at that tight rear end of yours? "I have a better idea," she said, finding her way along what felt like metal shelving. "Do you have e-mail?"

Mitch turned in a circle. Her voice was now coming at him in tinny echoes, making it harder for him to pinpoint her location. "Not *on* me."

And what a dangerous place to be that was, Zoe thought, pulling herself along by the edges of the shelves. "Tell you what. As soon as I get my phone installed, I'll send you my—"

Crash.

At the deafening clatter of a metal avalanche, Mitch cringed. The bad news was that Zoe might be pinned beneath a ton of debris. The good news was that he definitely knew where to find her. But, he thought as he took off, his heart pounding like a kettledrum, would he find her conscious? Alive? "Zoe, can you hear—"

"Don't come any closer!"

"Damn it, woman, it just sounded like the end of the world, and you expect me to stay—Whoa-oa-oa!" Mitch hydroplaned across the floor, his feet thickly coated with a substance that was wet, sticky, and noxious. His eyes stung, and his nostrils flared under the assault of rising fumes. Arms flying and upper body rocking, he fought to keep from diving face first into the brimstone Zoe had unleashed. He would have won the battle, too, if Zoe hadn't also unleashed those long legs of hers. "Ugh!"

Zoe stood leveraged against the shelf she'd backed into when she'd accidentally pulled down a bin of cans containing what smelled like varnish. Her hands dripping with goo, her shirt spattered with it—her legs, too, and stretched out in front of her—she looked down at Mitch. "You can't say—"

"That you didn't warn me?" His hands and knees swirling in furniture finish, Mitch looked up at Zoe. "Oh, but I can. I can say anything I want to, because—" Sliding sideways to a shelf, he grabbed on to a support and pulled himself up. Then, shoving off with his hands, he skated to Zoe. "Because I'm bigger than you." He pinned her against the shelf. "And you're going to listen to every word I have to say. Only, not here." Clamping one hand around her upper arm and pinching his nose with the other, he hauled her onto dry floor, then to the window.

"Let go of me!"

"Not until you hear me out."

As Zoe's shoes sloshed, tears sifted through her lashes. "Please, Mitch. I don't think I want to hear that Booger can always use a good table dancer." *Not that you'll think any better of me when you find out what I really do for a living.*

Before the open window, Mitch swung her around to him. *"What* are you talking about?" He held up his varnished hand. "Never mind. I forgot *I'm* doing the talking." He scooped her up and pitched her out the window. And nearly pitched himself on his head. Tearing his sticky grip from her clothing, he dragged his lower half over the window sill. "Oh, no you don't," he said, grabbing Zoe's wrist as she made for the truck.

Rounding on him, Zoe dug in her heels as she attempted to twist from his hold. "You're hurting me, Mitch."

"If you'd stop squirming—"

"I mean with words. I can't bear to talk about . . . I've never done anything like . . ." Her energy spent, Zoe stilled, except for her shoulders shaking on silent sobs. "I'm so ashamed. Please let me go. I just want to go somewhere and die."

"Fine. Just do me a favor and leave room for me." Mitch pulled her against him. "Because I'll die if you don't let me tell you how sorry I am. Nothing happened on that sofa, Zoe, except that I behaved like a complete jerk." Lowering his eyes, he shook his head. "Lord, what you must think of me."

"What *I* must think of . . . But—"

"Shh. Let me finish while I still have the courage." With his gaze, Mitch limned the aura of soft moonlight around her lovely head. Peering into her eyes, he winced at the pain he saw in them, the pain he'd inflicted. "Zoe, you have nothing to be ashamed of. You were frightened. I held you. Things got out of control. Please don't think I don't know you're not the kind of woman who—" He let out a breath. "Well, who's run out her odometer. A man just has to look at you to see that." He gave a shake of his head and a shrug of his shoulders. "I don't know what got into me. Lonely as I get sometimes, I'm not the kind of man who goes in for joyriding."

For a moment, seeing the oh-so-alone look in his eyes, Zoe believed him. *Nearly.* "Does Lila know that?"

Mitch's shoulders slumped. "Zoe, believe me, I'd like to know what Lila knows. The truth is, I had one date with her, and my memory of it is a little foggy. Actually, I have no memory of it at all after that last beer at her place."

"That could certainly never happen to *me.*" Zoe cocked a hip and a grin. "I drink Scotch."

Mitch smiled at her. Then, leaning down, he pressed a kiss to her cheek. "You're quite a lady—you know that, Zoe Laurence?"

Zoe stood hushed by Mitch's light, sweet, undemanding kiss that had nevertheless awakened her need for soft intimacy as powerfully as his touch had aroused her demand for savage pleasure. Having betrayed herself by letting the latter loose, she renewed her vow to contain both urges. Despite Mitch's excusing her behavior, she pledged to prevent a future loss of her self-respect and her self-reliance. Never again would she risk a man's playing roulette with her heart, or her finances.

Flinging one hand in the air, she laughed dismissively. "It's a tough job, but somebody's got to do it."

"Yeah, but do you have to do it with a sledgehammer? What do you keep in that purse of yours, anyway?"

"The usual. Wallet, makeup, comb. *War and Peace.*"

"Well, we've had the war. How about some peace?" With his curved forefinger, Mitch lifted her chin. "Will you forgive me, Zoe?"

Refusing to chance her gaze or her lips meeting his, Zoe looked away. "There's nothing to forgive."

Mitch turned her face to his. "Do it anyway, so I can sleep tonight."

She hesitated. Why should *he* sleep tonight when she would lie awake, remembering his kiss? "Sure," she said curtly, and with resentment. "You're forgiven." *But not for possessing a gaze that makes me want to know you, and a mouth that makes me want to give myself to you. And arms that make me want to stay forever sheltered by their warmth and strength.*

"Thanks," Mitch said, lowering his hand. "And thanks for that hit on the head. It reminded me that I have a daughter, too. And if she ever suspects I've so much as *thought* of kissing you or any other woman tonight—Whooeee! Can that girl ever throw a hissy fit."

"Excuse me?" Fitting her hands on her hips, Zoe wiggled her fingers. "Are you telling me that the real rea-

son you wanted to stop doing what we were doing was because your *daughter* wouldn't like it?"

Mitch jerked back. "What happened to the restraint you said you had to practice on account of *your* daughter?"

"That's different. I do that voluntarily, to set an example of responsible behavior, not because I'm scared Bink will throw a fit."

Mitch thrust his fingers into Zoe's hair. As he tilted her head back, his gaze seared hers. "I am *not* afraid of Sarah Jane. I realize the truth may not interest you, but I have to be very careful how I handle her until she turns—"

"My stomach," Zoe said, gazing away, then back. "It just turns my stomach the way I believed you when you said you'd acted like a jerk, that you'd practically taken advantage of me, good girl that I am. That Lila had taken advantage of you, angel that *you* are!" Her tone segued from sarcastic to accusatory. "Were they *all* lies?"

Mitch grabbed hanks of her hair. "Was it a lie when you said you needed me?"

Zoe's heart tripped over her own words—words she wished she could take back, no matter how much she'd meant them at the time she'd spoken them. "I know what I don't need. I don't need to hear that when my father told you to take me for a spin, you took him literally. That you would have gone 'joyriding' with me in a heartbeat if it hadn't been for an eleven-year-old girl who, in my humble opinion, could use a good paddling!"

"Like your son could use a leash?"

Zoe gasped. "Oooof!" Smacking her hands against his chest, she shoved away. "Ow!" She gritted her teeth. "Kindly let go of my hair. Now."

"I can't."

"I'm warning you, I have a hair-trigger knee."

"And I have hairy hands."

"What?"

Mitch tried prying his palms off her head.

"Stop it! You're pulling my hair out!"

"As much as the idea appeals to me, I'm not doing it on purpose. In fact, you could say I'm stuck on you."

"Oh, no!" Instinct commanding her to reach for her hair, Zoe tore her palms from Mitch's chest.

"Yeow!"

Zoe huffed perturbedly. *"What* is *your* problem?"

His tongue lying along his bottom teeth, Mitch sniffed. "If you look down, I think you'll find that my shirt is stuck to your hands."

Lowering her gaze, Zoe confirmed Mitch's theory. "Oooo. I'll bet you have a hairy chest, too."

"Had," Mitch said, looking up through watery eyes and wondering what it was about him that attracted women who were into hair removal. "The correct word is *had."*

Spreading her fingers, Zoe patted what she deemed a growth pattern over his pecs.

"I didn't get it from The Hair Club for Men, Zoe."

"No, I don't suppose I can press it back—" Her eyes ballooning with panic, Zoe shifted her gaze from side to side, at Mitch's wrists, at the ends of which were his hands, glued to her hair. "Um, are you by any chance . . . mad?"

"Why should I be mad?" Mitch asked, drumming his fingertips on her head.

"You *are* mad. The question is, are you a lot mad, or just a teensy mad?"

Mitch ceased drumming. "You're wrong, Zoe. I don't get mad."

Zoe squeezed her eyes shut. "Don't tell me. You get even?"

"No-o-o-o. Revenge is a waste of time and energy."

Breathing a sigh, Zoe smiled up at him. "Boy, have you got that right."

"Yeah, a real waste, darlin'."

Darlin'? Zoe gulped.

Mitch stood swirling his fingers around her head, figuring he was giving her a new kind of permanent wave. Then, abruptly, he squared his face with hers. "What I believe in, when I'm looking pain in the eye, is biting the bullet, making quick work of it."

Zoe wrinkled her nose. "Like . . . like when you were a kid and had to remove a Band-Aid?"

"Now isn't that somethin', the way you read my mind? Darlin'." He snorted. "Yeah, I'd always just rip those dudes right off."

Zoe whimpered. "I always preferred the soak-and-peel method, myself. It only takes a few days."

"Yeah, but we don't have warm water *or* a few days. If we don't get home soon, your father's going to come after me with a shotgun."

"You don't know my father. If we don't get home soon, you might have to go after *him* with a shotgun."

Mitch's gaze narrowed. "*Your* father is after *my* mother?"

"Well, I'd say the feeling is mutual. He may not have been able to keep his eyes off her rear axle, but I got the distinct impression she wouldn't mind checking out his piston assembly."

"Why didn't you say something sooner?" Tilting his head, he looked aside. "Great. At this very minute your father might be giving my mother a hand-rubbed finish, and I'm miles away getting shellacked by you."

"*To* me, you mean. And *I'm* not the one who took a freefall into the varnish."

"And I suppose I'm the one who knocked it over in the first place?"

"In the *first* place, it wasn't *my* idea to come here."

Their legs entwined, Mitch and Zoe held their breath as they held each other's gazes. Mitch breathed first, unwanted desire torquing his belly as it rubbed against Zoe's. "I . . . I think our shirts are stuck together now, too."

Zoe had held her breath too long. She needed to draw deeply to replenish her lungs, so much that her breasts strained against Mitch's chest, the hot sensation sieving molten, unwelcome desire into her core. "What do we do now?"

For a moment, Mitch thought he'd find it easier to remove his fingers from her hair than his gaze from her lips as they glistened in the moonlight. He bowed toward them. Then, catching a whiff of varnish on a breeze, recalling his and Zoe's predicament and how they'd gotten into it, he straightened. "We dance."

Tucking in her chin, Zoe peered up at him. "Dance."

"We two-step, to be exact, over to the truck, where there's a can I meant to refill with gas for the lawn mower. I think there's just enough left in it to unglue us." Mitch outlined his plan in detail, starting with how Zoe was going to dampen the rag stuffed in the can's spout with gasoline, then apply it to his hands, dissolving the varnish and freeing his hold of her head. "You ready?"

Zoe nodded, flinching at the tug on her hair. "Ready."

Mitch raised his left foot, aimed it at the truck, then set it down. "This might be a good time for me to ask whether you smoke?"

Zoe ground her jaw to one side. "No, but I think I could start any time now."

"Well, I wouldn't commence just this minute, if I were you." Mitch shook out one leg, then the other. "Okay. You ready?"

"I'm ready!"

"One, two . . . 'Goin' to the Big D, don't mean Dallas. I cain't believe what the judge had to tell us. I got the Jeep, she got the palace. Goin' to the—' "

"Stop!"

Halfway to the truck, Mitch brought an end to his rendition of the Mark Chestnut classic and his feet together. "Don't you like country music? It takes an unvarnished look at life, you know. I thought it might inspire us."

Zoe inverted a smile. "I'll choose my own inspiration, if you don't mind." She raised her right foot. "You ready?"

"I'm ready. You ready?"

"I'm ready! One, two . . . 'I'm gonna wash that man right outta my hair . . .' "

Mitch threw his head back. " 'Goin' to the Big D . . .' "

By the time they reached the truck, laughter as well as shellac glued them to each other. "You know," Zoe said, catching her breath, "those were some nifty chassés you did getting over here."

"Thanks, but don't tell the guys at Booger's. I've got a reputation to protect." Mitch prompted another round of laughter, then, "You were pretty light on your feet yourself, and while carrying quite a tune."

"I played Nellie Forbush in my high school's production of *South Pacific*."

"Yeah? When I was in high school, I played hookey at least once a week." Their laughs entwined. Then, soberly, Mitch gazed into her eyes. "All in all, I guess we don't have very much in common."

"Oh, I don't know about that," Zoe replied, wanting to run her hands up and down his forearms, stopping them before they could glom on to more of his hair. "We're both single parents." Her gaze went to his mouth like metal to a magnet. Her breathing quickened. She parted her lips. She watched his come closer . . . closer. "And I, for one, want to stay that way," she said, pulling her head back, feeling the loss of his solid warmth. "What about you?"

Mitch shuddered with a breath of acute frustration—and extreme reality. Whatever else he was, he was still small town, and whatever Zoe thought she could become, she'd always be big city. Like Ellie wanted to be. And, as with Ellie, he'd never be able to make her stay. He couldn't even try. Not with Sarah

Jane watching, disapproving. "I don't have much choice, not if I want to keep my daughter."

"*Keep* her?"

Mitch explained the choice awaiting Sarah on her twelfth birthday, and the heartbreak awaiting him if she chose to live with Ellie and Charles.

Zoe recalled Sarah Jane's remark that the dessert Mitch had made especially for her was good, but not as good as the one she could get in Atlanta. She remembered, too, Mitch's reluctance to admonish her for ridiculing her stepfather. "She's holding it over your head, too. You know that, don't you? Manipulating you into letting her do and say whatever she pleases. You're even letting her dictate how you should live your life."

"I know." Mitch's voice dropped low, as low as he felt. "But what would *you* do?"

In her mind's eye, Zoe saw Jack, wearing a Santa suit and carrying a sack.

I finally made that killing, Zoe, he said. *Now I want custody of the kids, and I can get it, too. When the judge asks them who they'd rather live with, do you really believe they'll choose you and your budgets and savings accounts over all this?* Grinning malevolently, he reached into his sack and hauled out gifts, which he hurled through the air. Nintendos, CDs, cellular phones. His "Ho! Ho! Ho!" was a far from merry laugh on her. He reached into his bag of goodies again and produced a bicycle, a go-cart, a pony!

Zoe shut her eyes, shutting out the nightmare, the purely manufactured, nevertheless paralyzing fear of losing her children to their father. "I . . . I'm not sure what I'd do," she replied, looking at Mitch. "All I know is that I want you out of my hair"—*and my system*—"now. I don't want to be the reason Sarah Jane throws a tantrum tonight." *Not tonight. Not ever.*

That's too bad, Mitch thought, because suddenly he couldn't think of a better reason. "Fine," he snapped, though he wasn't just angry at Zoe. No, he was angry at Ellie, the city of Atlanta, the damned deserted furniture factory, the falsely named Progress and Pride National Bank, his busted car, his low income.

Himself.

And yes, at Zoe, too, for being everything a man could want, but—for a man who was lucky just to pay his bills each month and still add a little something to his daughter's college fund—everything he could never have. She'd made it clear she'd learned her lesson, having gambled once before on a loser. And no matter how he looked at himself, that's what he was: a loser. He'd lost his wife. He'd probably lose his daughter. And now he was about to lose his hold on the only woman who had ever made him feel like a man, if only for a moment. No—like a hero.

It was definitely bullet-biting time.

"Let's get this over with, okay? The gas can's over there." He directed Zoe to its location in the truck bed. Shortly afterward, his hands reeking of gasoline, he said, "Well, I'm out of your hair."

I wish, Zoe thought, already missing his touch. "We'd better go. You ready?"

Gazing down at Zoe Laurence, her face—*that* face, the one a man realizes he's been searching for all his life—Mitchell Lee Ballard decided he was damned tired of being a loser. "Hell no, woman," he said, the words rumbling. Enfolding Zoe tightly in his arms, he turned her and touched his lips to hers like flame to a wick.

Scorched, Zoe fought for release until, like a candle, she radiated light as she was consumed by fire. And what she saw in the light was the match that had torched her, *her* match, body, mind, and soul. Mitch Ballard.

A dangerous man.

When he knew he'd claimed her, however briefly,

Mitch swept her back onto her feet. *"Now,* I'm ready. Ma'am."

Ma'am? Earlier, when he'd drawled the word, Zoe had heard an invitation to explore the mysterious rituals that govern relationships between men and women in the South. Now, she heard a curt dismissal. Dousing the fire he'd lit inside her, snuffing the light, and reminding herself that an end to this infatuation was, after all, what she wanted, she said, "I was ready hours ago." Heading for the passenger side of the truck, she pulled away from him.

And went nowhere.

Together, they looked down to where they were joined like Siamese twins, by their shirts.

"I'll get the gas can," Mitch said. Reaching into the truck bed, he retrieved the can, pulled the rag from the spout, and handed it to Zoe. "Hold this while I pour." He hoisted the can over his shoulder like a jug of corn liquor.

Zoe looked dubiously at the spout, poised to give them a high octane shower. "Wouldn't it be better if we put the rag on the ground and I sprinkled it, like we did before?"

"Look, I've got things under control. Just do as I tell you and hold the rag under the spout."

Do as he told her? If he wanted to call her *ma'am,* Zoe thought, then *he* could just take orders from *her.* She waved the rag in front of his eyes, then flung it to the ground.

Mitch looked down and saw not a rag, but a gauntlet. "One of us is going to pick that up, and it's not going to be me."

"Then I can't imagine who."

"Maybe I can help." Intending to pull her down to her knees, Mitch grabbed her arm.

In a move she'd learned in a self-defense class, Zoe threw off his hand and jabbed her fingers beneath one of his ribs.

Seeing Mitch's eyes glaze over with pain, Zoe covered her mouth. "Oooo, I'm so sorry."

"No problem. Happens all the—" Mitch pitched forward.

The spout tipped downward.

"Oh, Lord!" Mitch shot up and off Zoe. Joining her white-eyed gaze to his, he looked down at the puddle between their feet. Shaking out the can, he increased it by a drop. The last drop. "I'll take the good news, darlin'. The operation was a success."

Zoe held her shirt away from her body. "But the patient's condition is highly flammable."

"Make that both patients." Crossing his arms, Mitch grabbed fistsful of his shirt.

"What are you doing?"

"What do you think?" He stripped off his shirt, tossed it and the empty can into the truck bed. Then, pulling out a blanket, he held it out to Zoe. "You can cover up with this."

Confronted with Mitch's bare and utterly monumental chest, Zoe made what she considered to be a responsible choice. In place of her hands, she let her hungry gaze roam up sleek ab rows, over hard if patchy pectoral blocks, and along oh, miles, of shoulder range. She started tucking her shirt back into her slacks. "No thanks. I'll stay like this."

Mitch's gaze slowly skimmed down her torso and up again. "Personally, I think you'd do just fine in Booger's wet T-shirt contest, but the fumes from that shirt will knock us both out before we get there."

With a snort, Zoe snatched the blanket from him and took concealment behind the tailgate. "I suppose you're an expert at judging that kind of event."

Poised to climb behind the wheel, Mitch paused and smiled. "Just the opposite. Seems like I'm the one who's always coming before one judge or another."

"Hah. I can believe that!" Zoe rolled her eyes, then rolled her bra and shirt into a ball and hurled them into the back of the truck. Drawing the blanket tightly around her, she stalked to the cab and yanked open the door. This time, she perched both heels on the running board, wedging herself in the doorway, and tried backing in.

Mitch just shook his head at her. Stretching across the seat, he wrapped his arm around her waist and hauled her inside.

Nestled in the crook of his arm, Zoe looked up at him. Black strands raked his forehead; a dark stubble textured the lower half of his face. In between, his eyes reflected light but hinted at depth, or perhaps destiny. "I guess this is where I say, 'Thanks for the lift.' "

Mitch ran his gaze over Zoe's luscious shoulders, then arrowed to the tops of plump half-moons rising above the tightly secured blanket. Such softness, such refuge. Such a long time since he'd been offered or taken any, that he could remember. One thing he knew for sure, with Zoe Laurence he'd want to remember. "And where I say, 'my pleasure, ma'am.' "

That 'ma'am' *was pure honey. And honey comes from bees, and you, Zoe Laurence, are allergic to bee stings.* She sat up and faced forward. "I'd better put my seat belt on."

Back behind the wheel, his key in the ignition and his heart in his throat because this was the last time Zoe would ever sit beside him, the last time he could pretend she was his girl, Mitch looked over at her. "You ready?"

Click. "Ready. You?"

"Ready." Mitch pulled on the lights and turned the key. The engine sputtered, coughed, then died. He leaned forward, scanned the instrument panel, then sat back. "Unfortunately, darlin', the truck's not ready." He faced Zoe. "Maybe if we wring our shirts out in the gas tank—"

"Nice try, Ballard. But nobody runs out of gas any-more."

"Yeah, I know. Zoe . . . do you think it could be a miracle?"

Zoe looked at Mitch. Then, leaning forward, she looked at the gas gauge, then at Mitch. "I don't believe this." She sat up and stared unblinkingly out the windshield. "We're out of gas." Grinding her jaw to one side, she scratched her bare skin above the wool blanket. She was allergic to wool, too. "We're really out of gas."

"Not exactly," Mitch said, bracing his outstretched arms against the wheel. "We're twelve miles from the nearest gas station, and we're out of gas."

Clawing at her abdomen, reaching behind her to scratch her back, Zoe looked at Mitch and saw trouble, stripped to the waist. "Update. We're miles from help, you're half-naked, I'm about to crawl out of my skin, and—"

"We're out of gas," they said in unison.

"If you'd listened to me," Zoe said, "there'd still be gas in that can."

"If you'd listened to me, you mean. But no, you had to go and throw down that rag."

"You're right. I should have stuffed it in your mouth."

"Fine, blame it on me." Mitch kicked open his door. "All I know, darlin', is things can't possibly get worse."

Zoe stopped scratching. "I really wish you hadn't said that."

SIX

"I can't believe you don't have a cell phone." Scratching her back with a branch she'd picked up along the side of the road, Zoe trudged beside Mitch. "Or at least a two-way radio."

"You mean like 'Breaker! Breaker! Big Daddy, here. What's your handle, Sugar Buns?' " Mitch kicked a chunk of gravel up the shoulder of the road. "So, how many times did you see *Smoky and the Bandit* when you were a kid?"

"Please. I was into *C.H.I.P.S.* You know, clean-cut, law and order types keeping the streets safe from sickos who lure women to abandoned factories and then take off their shirts and claim they've run out of gas?"

Scooping up a handful of gravel, Mitch hurled a chunk up the deserted, two-lane road back to town. "How many times do I have to tell you I just didn't pay attention to the warning light?" *Because I couldn't take my eyes off you.* "And as far as being into law-and-order guys, don't make me laugh. You were into Erik Estrada, period." He underhanded another stone, sending it clacking along the pavement. "Come on, Zoe, the guy couldn't act his way out of my Aunt Tilly's soda shop."

Zoe drew to a halt, the blanket entangling her legs and nearly tripping her. "Tilly is your aunt?"

"She's my dad's sister." Mitch glanced over his

shoulder at Zoe. "And Toby's right. She makes a great chocolate malted."

Behind his back, Zoe scrunched her face up, sticking the tip of her tongue out at him. "I'll have to try one sometime."

Mitch turned and walked backward, his thumbs hooked in the waist of his jeans. "Better make it quick," he said, and told Zoe what she already knew, that Tilly was going out of business because the new bankers had refused her an improvement loan. "Talking to one of them is like getting one of those automated phone answering systems. You hear a voice, but nobody's listening. All they know is what they're programmed to know, their precious ratios and risk averages. About people, they know zip." He pitched the last stone over Zoe's head. "Glad I don't have to get into bed with one of them at night. Must be like trying to warm up to a snake."

Zoe cringed. "Or a skunk," she muttered, recalling how Tilly had said the town regarded bankers.

"Nah. Skunks are warm-blooded."

"Oh." Zoe felt her heart sink as low as Mitch's estimation of her—professionally, at least. She knew she was going to have tell him the truth now, before someone else found out about her, and did. Sure, he'd look at her and see a reptile, but if she waited, he'd see a coward. More importantly, she'd feel like one. Besides, she was making entirely too much of what he thought of her, considering that she wanted to strangle him for the mess she was in—the blanket, for instance. *Brother, would I love to wring his neck,* she thought as she scratched her own. As long as she didn't have to get within twelve feet of his big, beautiful body and the sometimes grown man, sometimes little boy lost, look in his eyes.

All the more reason to expose herself—*poor choice of words, Zoe.* She sighed. *Reveal. Repulse the man with the truth.* "Mitch," she began, looking at the branch as she dangled it in front of her, "there's something I have to tell you. Well, I don't *have* to tell you, but I'd like to. Actually, I won't like it at all, but—"

"All right!" Mitch thrust a fist triumphantly in the air. "You are *saved*, woman." *And I'm saved from having to spend another minute alone with you, wanting to throttle that stubborn neck of yours. Just plain wanting you.*

With a start, Zoe looked up. "Uh, maybe you should hear what I have to say, first."

Slipping the small flat flashlight he'd taken with him from the truck from his pocket, Mitch bounded to the middle of the road. "Maybe you should do something with your hair. This could be Erik Estrada." He switched on the flashlight and waved it over his head.

Zoe turned and shaded her eyes from approaching high beams. A moment later, a white Jeep Cherokee pulled to a stop along the shoulder. Taking Zoe's arm, Mitch shepherded her to the vehicle's passenger side. The window slid down. A provocative scent wafted from inside the SUV. Then a woman appeared in the light Mitch shone on her. Zoe saw a striking brunette wearing a royal blue jacket that was both feminine and businesslike.

The woman curled her long polished nails over the sill. "I *thought* that was Mrs. Ballard's truck I saw as I passed the old factory," she said, her gaze at Mitch's muscled torso appreciative, Zoe observed.

Her assessment of Zoe, however, appeared less certain. And who could blame her? Zoe knew that—hair spiked with varnish and smelling of gasoline, shoulders bare except for her purse strap, wrapped in what looked and felt like steel wool and carrying a forked branch—she must look, at best, like a crazed douser.

"Are you all right, Mr. Ballard?"

To Zoe, the woman sounded more East Coast than Western Kentucky, and unnecessarily alarmed, at least over Mitch's welfare. "As you can plainly see," she began, casting the branch aside and folding her arms, "he did manage to untie himself before I could set him on fire."

The woman blinked. "I beg your pardon?"

Mitch slanted a perturbed look at Zoe. "I'll do the talking, if you don't mind."

Turning down the corners of her mouth, Zoe shrugged as if to say, "So talk."

"Thank you." Mitch put the flashlight back in his pocket. Leaning against the door frame, he bent toward the woman, opened his mouth, closed it, then let out a sigh. "I'm not sure *what* to say."

"Puh."

At Zoe's editorial comment, Mitch ground his jaw to one side. "I mean, I know how this must look," he said to the brunette, "but we really don't need help." *Not from you.*

Zoe gaped at him. "Excuse me, what happened to *I AM SAVED!?*" Diving at the window, she thrust her hand inside and grabbed the woman's arm as she was about to slide back over to the driver's side. "*Hell*-o. Do I look as if I don't need help?"

The woman gave Zoe a stark, arresting stare. "I assure you, I'm not a psychiatrist."

Sniggering, Mitch withdrew Zoe's arm from inside the car. "Believe me," he said, smirking down at her but speaking to the other woman, "I've got the *problem* under control."

Zoe snatched her arm from his hold. "The way you had the gas can under control?"

Mitch propped his hands on his hips. "Darlin', why I didn't varnish that mouth of yours instead of kissing it, I'll never know."

Beneath arched brows, the woman gazed from Mitch to Zoe and back. "Oh, so that's how it is."

"No, that's not how it is!" Zoe elbowed her way in front of Mitch. "Please, *please,* give me a lift back to town. I promise you I'm not crazy. Just a little . . . sticky."

"Well . . . If Mr. Ballard were to change his mind

and come along . . ." Giving him a definitely come-hither look, the brunette hit the switch that unlocked the doors.

"Oh, thank you, thank you." Grabbing the handle, Zoe cracked open the door.

Mitch pressed it shut. "But I'm *not* coming along, darlin'."

"Look, this isn't exactly the interstate. We could end up walking all night." Zoe yanked the door wide and clung to the handle.

Mitch slammed the door. Zoe boomeranged. "Like you said, darlin', you're sticky. We both are. You wouldn't want us to make a mess of the lady's car now, would you?"

"The upholstery can be cleaned," the woman said.

"And I'll even pay the bill." Zoe applied all her strength to opening the door, but was no match for Mitch. With one hand, he kept the door sealed.

"I'm not going, and if I don't go, you don't go." Still gazing down at Zoe, Mitch addressed the brunette. "Isn't that so?"

The woman stammered an indefinite answer.

"Besides," he said, peeling Zoe's fingers off the handle, "she'd have to go out of her way to take you to my house."

"*Your* house?"

"Uh-huh." Mitch looked at the woman in the vehicle, her eyes wide as she tugged the pearls ringing the neckline of her jacket. "That's where she's spending the night."

The woman's gaze raked Zoe with the wrong conclusion, to which Mitch had made certain she jumped. "I see."

"Ooo!" Clutching the sill, Zoe lowered herself to the brunette's eye level. "Believe me, if you saw what I see, you'd see red! Please, you have no idea what I've been through tonight. Don't leave me here with

this . . . this"—she gave Mitch a scathing look—"am-
nesiac!"

The woman bit the inside of her lip. "Well . . ."

"I'll take that as a yes." Zoe darted to the rear door.

"And I'll take that cellphone you've got there,"
Mitch said, grabbing Zoe by the arm as he peered in
at the brunette. "I'll be glad to pay you for the call."

"Don't be silly," the woman replied as she handed
her phone to him through the window. "But you know,
Mr. Ballard, by the time someone gets here, I could
have you at your front door." She tilted her gaze and
a smile up at him. "Are you sure you won't change
your mind?"

Abruptly, Zoe ceased struggling to free herself from
Mitch's grasp. Her mouth dropped open. How did the
woman do that, pout and talk at the same time? Mitch,
apparently, was unimpressed. He answered the
woman's question by punching in a number and, after
giving their location to the party he'd called, he
handed the phone back to her without thanks. Zoe
was beginning to suspect that there were no circum-
stances under which he'd accept a ride from this
woman. But why? And why couldn't he at least let *her*
accept one?

"So who did you call?" she asked him. "A towing
service, or the dry cleaners?"

"The police dispatcher. My brother Matt will be here
in a few minutes." Taking Zoe by the shoulders and
moving her back from the Jeep, he spoke to the brunette. "No reason for you to wait."

"I've got a great one," Zoe called to the woman as
she tried to shimmy out of Mitch's restraint. "I refuse
to be driven through town in the back of a squad car!"

But the brunette had already given Mitch a rueful
smile that said, "Some other time, perhaps," and was
sliding behind the wheel. Appearing not to hear Zoe,
she pulled away.

At that time, Mitch released Zoe, who ran after the

Jeep. "Come back!" She shouted and waved until the vehicle's taillights were two red blips on the horizon. When they disappeared, she turned to Mitch, who was sitting on the shoulder. "Okay. You've got me stumped. What was that all about?"

Hunching forward, his hands dangling over his knees, he looked away. "I just didn't want to take a ride from her."

"No kidding." She waddled to him, raised the blanket above her knees, crossed her legs, and sat down at his side. "Did you have a memory lapse with her, too? Or maybe the trouble is you remember too much?"

Mitch leveled a hard gaze at her. "I wouldn't be seen with the woman," he replied, then skittered to his right. Eight inches from Zoe Laurence was eight inches from disaster. And incredible desire.

"I'd rather be seen with her than in a marked car." Zoe wiggled next to him. "Whatever your problem with her is," she said, clasping his arm, "why couldn't you have let *me* go with her?"

Mitch looked down at her hand, wondering how something so slender and delicate could pack such a wallop to his insides. *Because I didn't want to let you go at all.* "You don't want to be seen with her, either. This is a friendly town, but not to any friend of hers." He widened the space between them from inches to feet.

Zoe narrowed it to nothing. "Why? What's she done?"

"Nothin', darlin', that's the—" Meeting Zoe's gaze, a pool of moonlight, Mitch found he wanted to dive into it, cleanse his soul in it, get born again. And then he wanted to take her in his arms and ask her to share his new life with him and then—"Trouble," he finished. Unable to be so near her and not touch her, Mitch shot up. "Quit following me, will you?" Flattening his hands in his front pockets, he stalked to a position a few yards away and scanned the road for a sign of his brother.

"Oh! What ego!" Clambering to her feet and securing the blanket, Zoe scurried after him. "If I'm following you, it's only because you owe me an answer. My kids are probably scared to death, wondering what happened to me. Thanks to you, that woman is not taking me to them. The least you could do is tell me who I'm not riding with."

Whipping around at her touch to his arm, Mitch bumped into her. To steady her, he grabbed her shoulders. To steady himself, he closed his eyes. But the image of her glistening lips was a still-frame in his mind, the feel of her warm sleek skin an invitation to yet another vision—of a wife to more than make a living for, but to live for, of a mother, a good mother, for Sarah. Despite his ragging her about Toby, he knew Zoe was a good mother. Unlike Ellie, she thought of her children before herself. She just had more weight on those lovely shoulders of hers than they should have to carry. Single-handedly rearing two children—three, counting her father—had to be tough. Suddenly, he wished he could ease her burden, be the kind of man she could turn to, not just when she was spooked by the dark, but when she needed understanding, encouragement. Love. Sex. More love. More—

Yeah, he'd like to be all that to her, and a good father to her kids, too.

But he'd lose his own child in the process. Sarah wouldn't hear of it. For that matter, neither would Zoe. If her ex had taught her one thing, it was to avoid gambling, especially on men. He opened his eyes and let her go, also letting go of his vision of love and laughter. And family. Letting go, too, of a breath.

"You can thank me again, darlin', because the woman I kept you from riding with is the manager of the Progress and Pride National Bank. Her name is—"

"Don't tell me," Zoe said, pressing her hand over her suddenly sick stomach. *I already know it. Constance Martin. My new boss.*

"Have it your way. But I never felt less like playing guessing games."

Mitch kicked a stone away with the heel of his boot, then paced farther up the road. *Where the hell are you, little brother?* He didn't think he could stand it much longer, at least not stand so near someone who had gone in a single day from a stranger to a woman he wanted to make love to, to a woman he wanted to love. And who didn't want his love. He'd never felt closer to any woman, and never lonelier.

She wasn't in the mood for guessing games, either, Zoe thought, so she was glad she didn't have to wonder why Mitch kept distancing himself from her. She already knew. She'd forced him to take the shirt off his back, the way his ex-wife apparently had. No mystery, either, as she'd only now realized, why she'd been following him. Every time he'd moved away from her she'd felt a chill, as though the sun had vanished behind a cloud. No, more than the loss of warmth, she'd felt the loss of . . . companionship. True, companionship was the last thing she'd come to expect from Mitch Ballard, given that their only compatibility appeared to be a sexual one. Sure, they'd bonded, with shellac. And trying to get free of one another, they'd bickered incessantly. Except for when they'd two-stepped, and belted a Broadway and country duet, and dissolved into laughter.

And would she ever forget the way he'd come running to slay her dragons—okay, her cobwebs—and called her "baby," and slow danced her fears away to a tune she couldn't hear but sensed held a deep meaning for him—perhaps for both of them? Strange, but she had the feeling that whatever he valued, she would value. Not things. Certainly not the shirt off his back. Intangibles, like the song in his heart. She only wished she could tell him so.

Zoe couldn't help speculating now, about what they'd be like together, not only as a couple, but as a family. He was a loving father, if understandably over-indulgent at the moment. Bink was getting to the age when she needed a father's love so that she wouldn't later seek it, as perhaps Zoe herself had, from the first man who paid her attention. As for Toby, she could teach him to throw a baseball, and even how to tie a tie, but not how to be a man. And she certainly couldn't rely on her own father to do any of those things. He was too busy being a great lover.

And as for Sarah Jane, perhaps she needed family most of all. She'd had Mitch to herself for so long that she didn't know that he could love others and not love her any less. Zoe knew she'd like to be the woman who would help Sarah to learn that lesson.

She rubbed her forehead. How, in less than twenty-four hours, had she traveled from Chicago to Kentucky, from a confirmed single woman to one who wanted what she'd sworn off? A real marriage, with a man who was a stranger, yet whom she knew better and felt closer to than she ever had her own husband. Life was unpredictable, and cruel. Mitch stood no more than twenty feet from her, but it might as well have been twenty light years. He'd been to the altar, and he wasn't about to make a return trip. Experience wouldn't let him. Neither would his daughter. Neither would hers. Bink hated Sarah Jane.

Zoe dusted off her hands. Guesswork done. Almost. She wondered how long after she reported for work at the end of the month Constance Martin would fire her. Seeing flashing blue lights in the distance, hearing the wail of a siren, Zoe thought they presaged a fitting end to a day that had defied both belief and justice. A day that had brought her a flat tire, a parking ticket, a house that was more nightmare than dream come true, and a man who was, quite simply, a dream—and would never be anything more. She'd never even gotten her malted, either.

"Cheer up, darlin'. This could be—" Mitch broke

off as a police cruiser flew over the crest of a hill and spun around before them. "Yeah. That's Matt. What do you think of his Erik Estrada imitation?"

Zoe rolled her eyes. She thought it was the perfect touch to the perfect ending to her first day in Perfection—and her last. Without the job she would soon lose, she didn't see that she had much choice but to transfer back to Chicago while she had the chance. Tomorrow, she'd simply call her old boss, Violet Pringle, and tell her that the children were incurably homesick and wanted to return to the city. That wouldn't be far from the truth.

Now all she had to do was to tell the children that they wanted to go home.

In the driveway alongside his mother's house, Matt Ballard let Zoe out of the rear of the patrol car. "First, it's a parking violation. Then it's vandalizing abandoned buildings, which I'd still like to book you for except for Mitch swearing that you spilled that shellac by accident." Puffing out his chest and setting his gun belt creaking, he palmed the butt end of the revolver in his side holster. "A word to the wise, little lady. That's how they all start out, pullin' the small jobs, and next thing you hear"—he clicked his tongue—"they're on death row."

Scratching her left shoulder blade, Zoe gazed across the street, at the ruin whose lease she somehow had to get out of. "So that's where we are." Stooping, she gathered the hem of her blanket. "Good night, Officer Ballard. I can't tell you how you made my day, beyond my wildest imaginings." She ducked her head back into the car. "Good night, Father O'Reilly. I'll say a prayer you get your bicycle fixed soon. Yes, it was my first confession in a squad car, too."

As Zoe, shaking her head and muttering, stalked to

the front door, Mitch came around the back of the squad car. "Zoe, wait!"

"Hold on there, big brother." Matt smacked the back of his hand against Mitch's bare chest. "Take my advice and lock up Lou's tool chest tonight. And y'all better lock your doors, too." He looked at Zoe. "There goes a one woman crime spree just waitin' to happen."

Mitch gazed down at his brother's hand, then lifted it from his chest. "Good night, Officer Ballard." An instant later, as Matt pulled away, Mitch bounded over the front porch step, reaching Zoe as she was reaching for the door. "Wait, please," he said, wrapping his fingers around her wrist.

She gazed down at his hold on her. "You wanna cuff me? Didn't you hear the good priest in the car? I'm a new woman."

Mitch gave her a mock frown. "And just when I was getting used to the old one."

"Hmm. Well, both of us have a long drive back to Chicago tomorrow, so if you don't mind, we'll call it a night."

Lowering his gaze, Mitch leaned his shoulder against the doorjamb. "Zoe," he began, uncurling his fingers and then running just one slowly up and down her forearm. He could do this for hours, stroke her all over. "Considering what you've been through today, I don't blame you for wanting to leave Perfection first thing in the morning. But I'd hate thinking you'd left before you really got to know me."

Zoe's eyes narrowed. "What did you say?"

Mitch shot off the jamb. "It! Know *it*. Because . . . it's really a great place to become a family."

Zoe shook her head. "What?"

Mitch looked at her askance. "What *what*?"

"You said Perfection is a great place to become a family."

"Um . . ." Looking past her, he scratched the back of his head. "To become a"—he cleared his throat—

"a close-knit family. Well, at least it used to be." Mitch stepped to the railing, shut his eyes, and took a deep breath. Hurricane Zoe had already blown into his life on her own, but God help him, he was actually inviting her to stay.

"And it could be again, if only those evil bankers would loosen their tight fists." Smoothing away the tingle he'd raised on her skin, not with his touch alone but with his words—she would have sworn he was trying to convince her to stay—Zoe joined him at the railing. "You really love this town, don't you?"

Taken aback by her question, one he'd never really thought about, Mitch gazed querulously down at her and then at the houses lining the opposite side of the street. He knew who lived in every one of them, knew all about them, too. Widow Corbett, who kept flasks of whiskey hidden in her flower beds. Mr. Terwilliker, who lived with his mother. For twenty-five years he'd been in love with Miss Dunaway, the Presbyterian church organist, and she with him, though as far as anybody knew they'd never done more than exchange longing looks during services. And Dave Hardy, who grabbed his lunch pail and left the house at the same time every workday morning so his kids wouldn't know he no longer had any work to go to.

Likely as not, they'd all known about his and Ellie's problems, probably before he did. And after his divorce, they'd nearly consoled him into having to buy bigger pants. In the first week alone, he'd gained five pounds on the dinners they'd asked him to so he wouldn't dwell on "getting dumped," as Widow Corbett had put it.

He smiled gently. "Yeah, I love this town," he said. Then, looking down at Zoe, he gave a sigh of resignation. "But I know it's not for everybody." *'Course, I don't care about everybody. Only you.*

Zoe gazed out, not at a grid of lights in the next high-rise, but at friendly porch lanterns like the one behind them, beside Lou's front door. Instead of blaring horns, she heard crickets cricketing. The air she inhaled wasn't fouled by diesel fumes, but perfumed by magnolia blossoms. "I could get used to it," she said, then turned to Mitch. "If I had a reason to stay." *Like a job.*

Mitch leaned over Zoe, backing her into the post. He latched onto it, his hand above her head, and peered deeply into her eyes. "You mean that?"

Under the onslaught of his gaze, Zoe clutched the post behind her. *No. I'd also like someone to love. Someone who was free to accept my love.* Barely able to breathe, she murmured, "Of course, I do," then ducked beneath his arm, rounded to his left side, and tightly grasped the railing. "I came all the way from Chicago, didn't I, hoping my family and I could make a new start here?"

Mitch laid his hand over hers. "Then you'll stay?"

Zoe stared down at his hand covering hers. Amazing, she thought, how that one small gesture made her feel as secure as if his arms were around her. "You want me to?"

Mitch's heart began to pound. *Oh God, Zoe, how I want you and your kids to stay here with Sarah and me.*

Sarah. "It wouldn't matter if I did," he said. "You know why."

Sarah. Zoe slipped her hand from beneath his and turned away. "And I don't blame you. But that's just as well, because I *can't* stay." *Not if Constance Martin has anything to say about it.*

Mitch turned her to him. "Can't, or won't?"

Zoe hesitated. "Won't." She had her pride.

"I don't believe you. I don't believe you could have kissed me the way you did at the factory if you weren't ready to take a chance. To start living again. To let me make you feel like a woman again." Crushing her to him, Mitch forked his hand along her jaw. "Tell me,

Zoe. If nothing were standing in either of our ways, would you stay?"

She shifted her gaze downward. "As you said, what difference would it make?"

Lifting her chin, Mitch recaptured her sight. "Because I have to know." Slowly, he fanned his fingers across her lips and down her throat. He lowered his mouth to hers. "Tell me."

Zoe parted her lips, not in response to the demand of his words, but to that of her body melded to his.

Mitch opened his mouth hungrily over hers.

Zoe gasped.

The screen door squeaked. "We thought we heard somebody out—Harv, forget lighting another incense stick and come on out here. You've got to see what the cat just drug in." LouAnn Ballard stepped onto the porch, holding the screen door open for Zoe's father. He soon appeared and put his arm around her shoulder. They stood together in silence, their wide-eyed gazes like brush strokes over Mitch and Zoe.

After a long moment, Harvey said, "So, you kids have a good time?"

Zoe's purse slipped over her slumped shoulder. "Gee, Dad, you don't know how relieved I am to hear you weren't worried about me. I was afraid I might be spoiling the good time you've obviously been having."

"That reminds me," Mitch began, taking Harvey's arm from around his mother and replacing it with his own. "Are you all right, Lou?"

"Of course, I'm all right," she said, stepping away from him to Zoe's side. She stroked the mane of hair now cascading over one shoulder. "What did you two come home so early for? Harv and me were just fixin' to listen to my Barry White collection."

Zoe and Mitch exchanged alarmed looks. "Not tonight, Lou," she said, then grabbed Harvey's hand. "Dad, I need to speak to you and the kids right away."

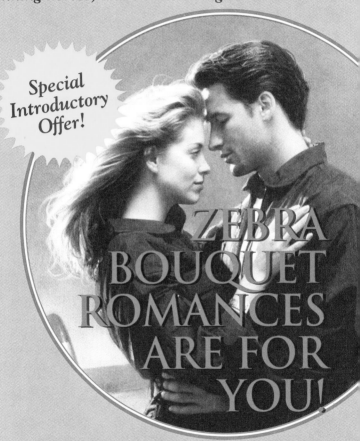

THE PUBLISHERS OF ZEBRA BOUQUET

are making this special offer to lovers of contemporary romances to introduce this exciting new line of novels. Zebra's Bouquet Romances have been praised by critics and authors alike as being of the highest quality and best written romantic fiction available today.

♥

EACH FULL-LENGTH NOVEL

has been written by authors you know and love as well as by up and coming writers that you'll only find with Zebra Bouquet. We'll bring you the newest novels by world famous authors like Vanessa Grant, Judy Gill, Ann Josephson and award winning Suzanne Barrett and Leigh Greenwood—to name just a few. Zebra Bouquet's editors have selected only the very best and highest quality for publication under the Bouquet banner.

♥

YOU'LL BE TREATED

to glamorous settings from Carnavale in Rio, the moneyed high-powered offices of New York's Wall Street, the rugged north coast of British Columbia, and the mountains of North Carolina. Bouquet Romances use these settings to spin tales of star-crossed lovers that are sure to captivate you. These stories will keep you enthralled to the very happy end.

♥

4 FREE NOVELS
As a way to introduce you to these terrific romances, the publishers of Bouquet are offering Zebra Romance readers Four Free Bouquet novels. They are yours for the asking with no obligation to buy a single book. Read them at your leisure. We are sure that after you've read these introductory books you'll want more! (If you do not wish to receive any further Bouquet novels, simply write "cancel" on the invoice and return to us within 10 days.)

SAVE 20% WITH HOME DELIVERY
Each month you'll receive four just published Bouquet Romances. We'll ship them to you as soon as they are printed (you may even get them before the bookstores). You'll have 10 days to preview these exciting novels for Free. If you decide to keep them, you'll be billed the special preferred home subscription price of just $3.20 per book; a total of just $12.80 — that's a savings of 20% off the publisher's price. If for any reason you are not satisfied simply return the novels for full credit, no questions asked. You'll never have to purchase a minimum number of books and you may cancel your subscription at any time.

GET STARTED TODAY –
NO RISK AND NO OBLIGATION

To get your introductory gift of 4 Free Bouquet Romances fill out and mail the enclosed Free Book Certificate today. We'll ship your free selections as soon as we receive this information. Remember that you are under no obligation. This is a risk free offer from the publishers of

Zebra Bouquet Romances.

Check out our website at www.kensingtonbooks.com.

FREE BOOK CERTIFICATE

Yes! I would like to take you up on your offer. Please send me 4 Free Bouquet Romance Novels as my introductory gift. I understand that unless I tell you otherwise, I will then receive the 4 newest Bouquet novels to preview each month Free for 10 days. If I decide to keep them I'll pay the preferred home subscriber's price of just $3.20 each (a total of only $12.80) plus $1.50 for shipping and handling. That's a 20% savings off the publisher's price. I understand that I may return any shipment for full credit no questions asked and I may cancel this subscription at any time with no obligation. Regardless of what I decide to do, the 4 Free introductory novels are mine to keep as Bouquet's gift.

Name _____

Address _____ Apt. _____

City _____ State ____ Zip _____

Telephone ( ) _____

Signature _____

(If under 18, parent or guardian must sign.)

BN030A

For your convenience you may charge your shipments automatically to a Visa or MasterCard so you'll never have to worry about late payments and missing shipments. If you return any shipment we'll credit your account.

Yes, charge my credit card for my "Bouquet Romance" shipments until I tell you otherwise.

☐ Visa ☐ MasterCard

Account Number _____

Expiration Date _____

Signature _____

Orders subject to acceptance by Zebra Home Subscription Service. Terms and Prices subject to change. Offer valid in U.S. only.

If this response card is missing,
call us at 1-888-345-BOOK.

Be sure to visit our website at
www.kensingtonbooks.com

BOUQUET ROMANCE
120 Brighton Road
P.O. BOX 5214
Clifton, New Jersey 07015-5214

Harvey held back. "We put the kids to bed an hour ago."

"That's right," Lou said. "Bink's bunkin' with Sarah Jane and Chauncey—"

"You put the girls in the same room?" Zoe tried to remember if Bink had any sharp objects on her. She asked where Toby was, and learned he was sleeping in the guest room with Bruno. She also learned that she was to sleep with Lou, and Harvey with Mitch. Good. They could all keep an eye on each other, prevent any getting up to satisfy midnight cravings down the hall. "Dad, I can't explain now, but we can't stay here—in Perfection, I mean." She brought her lips to his ear. "I'm pretty sure I no longer have a job."

"Oh, that's too bad, Zoe." Cupping her shoulders, he steadied a heartfelt look into her eyes. "I'm going to miss you and the kids."

"What?"

"Well, there's no reason why *I* can't stay!"

Turning away, Zoe pressed her fingertips to her temples. "Look, I cannot deal with this tonight. I've had a long day." *An incredible day. The kind of day that changes a woman's life. And breaks her heart.* Over her shoulder, she looked at Harvey. "So if you don't mind, I'll just take a shower and go to bed, and we can discuss this in the morning." Opening the door to a squeal that grated on her already jarred nerves, she hurried into the house.

"Zoe!" Mitch pursued her, catching her at the bottom of the stairs.

"Please let go of my arm."

"Not until you tell me. Which is it, Zoe? Can't . . . or won't?"

Zoe stood on the second riser, gripped as much by his question as by his strength. Most of all, by her own sense of simple honesty. "Mitch, has it occurred to you that neither one of us knows what the other does for a living?"

"Zoe, I'll tell you anything you want to know about me." Rising to the step below her, he cupped her cheek in the palm of his hand. "Strange as this sounds, I already know all I need to know about you."

Shaking her head, Zoe shook away his caress. "Not all. And when I do tell you, believe me, you won't want me to stay."

Smiling at her, he placed his hands around her waist. "Now, ma'am, I truly doubt that. But why don't you let me decide for myself?"

Zoe had felt the sweetness of his smile tug her heartstrings, but that subsequent *ma'am* had outright cut them into pieces. She laid her hands on his broad bare shoulders, summoning the courage to look into his eyes. And when she did, she saw something new in them, something in addition to the unmistakable desire she'd had to muster all her willpower to resist. *Liking.* Something she wouldn't be able to resist at all unless she told him in the next ten seconds exactly what she was.

"Mitch, do you remember when I told you not to tell me the name of that woman in the Jeep, and you thought I wanted to play a game? Well—"

"Mom, is that you?"

Together, Mitch and Zoe gazed to the landing at the top of the stairs, where Toby stood, rubbing one eye.

"I'm here, sweetie."

"Bruno can't sleep. He wants you to sing to him."

"All right. Tell him I'll be up in a minute."

"You gotta come now, Mom. He won't say so, but I think he's really scared."

Her hand on the banister, Zoe looked at Mitch. "I have to go."

"I know." He hooked her little finger on his. "I'll see you in the morning."

Zoe met his warm gaze and knew it had to be for the last time. She was running low on willpower, and three quarts down on plain common sense. A sensible woman with two children just didn't allow herself to fall in love with a strange man in one day. "Can't," she said. Reaching the top of the stairs, she looked down at him. "And won't!"

Early the next morning, Zoe looked up from the bathroom sink, where she was washing her hair yet again, trying to remove the residues of varnish and gasoline. "Bianca Laurence, what do you mean you'll never forgive me if we leave Perfection?" She barely whispered, desperate to avoid waking up the rest of the household—specifically, Mitch. "Yesterday you were going to die if you had to live on the same street as Sarah Jane."

"That was before I found out that she's really not evil, Mom, just suffering the insecurities that come with being the product of a broken home. We have a lot in common, though she's a lot more insecure. She was afraid to admit she still slept with her blanket until I brought mine in from the car."

Pausing with her fingers enmeshed in her sudsed hair, Zoe smiled. "Just as I've always said. Be yourself, and things will work out."

"Right, Mom. Did they work out when you told Mitch you're a banker?"

Zoe froze. "Um . . . Oooo! Soap in my eye." She quickly turned on the faucet and splashed her face. "There, that's better," she said a moment later, patting her face with a towel.

"Uh-huh," Bink said, her smile indicating Zoe hadn't fooled her a bit. "Anyway, Sarah and I really *bonded* last night."

Suddenly smelling varnish, Zoe wrinkled her nose. "Couldn't you have just become, oh I don't know, kindred spirits?"

Bink shook her head at her mother. "How about sisters?"

"Sisters? After one sleepover?"

Folding her arms and leaning against the jamb, Bink smiled. "Why not? If you could fall in love with Mitch after one—"

"Bink, where did you ever get the idea—"

"Sarah's window is over the front porch. She was asleep, but I saw the whole thing."

A gong went off in Zoe's head. She pulled Bink inside the bathroom and quietly closed the door. "You saw *what* whole thing?"

"The way you two were looking at each other, and how you almost kissed." Bink patted Zoe's shoulder. "Chill, Mom. I didn't tell Sarah, if that's what you're worried about. The way she feels about her dad, she'd freak. Do you know what she did the last time he had a date? As he was going out the door, she brought him a cup of hot cocoa she told him she'd made all by herself just for him. So, naturally, he drank it. And do you know what was in that cup besides cocoa? Those melatonin tablets you take when you can't sleep because you're worrying about the effects of the culture on Toby and me."

Zoe's jaw dropped. "Why that little . . . did she say who his date was with?"

Bink shrugged. "Lisa or Lola. Something like that."

No wonder he couldn't remember what happened that night. Nothing could have happened. Sarah had slipped him a melatonin Mickey Finn. "I don't care how insecure Sarah is, she was terribly wrong to do that."

"Yeah, I told her. So now you know what you're up against, Mom."

Zoe tipped Bink's chin up, focusing her daughter's gaze on hers. "*I* am not up against Sarah Jane, because despite what you saw last night, I have no interest in her father."

"That's too bad, because, despite that blanket you were wearing, he certainly seemed interested in you."

Leaning one hand on the sink and crossing one foot over the other, Bink gave her mother a highly parental look. "By the way, what *did* happen to your clothes?"

Zoe attempted several versions of the truth, none of them sounding plausible even to her, except for her disastrous encounter with Constance Martin. Bink thought that was just her luck. "Now do you understand why we have to go back to Chicago?"

"But you don't know for sure that your job here is history."

Zoe sighed with exasperation. "Bink, trust me, I know. Now will you please get your things together? Quietly." She turned on the faucet then bent over the basin.

"You know what I think, Mom? I think you're using Ms. Martin as an excuse to run away from Mitch."

Straightening, Zoe turned off the faucet. "Bianca, while I ponder that, would you please tell me if there's a reason why we always seem to have these conversations in the—"

Three small poundings, as if from a tiny fist, came at the door. "I gotta use the bathroom!"

Zoe hurried to the door and opened it. Gazing down at Toby, she pressed her forefinger to her lips. "You'll wake the others." Suddenly, she frowned. "How did you know to get up, much less get dressed?"

" 'Cause Lou promised to take Poppy and me in a real police car to get her truck. And you know what then, huh? We're all goin' fishing." Toby gave her a broad grin, the broadest she'd ever seen on her son's face, so broad and eager she wanted to cry. "And you know what else, Mom? Lou's gonna show me how to bait a hook, with real worms!"

"Eeewww." Bink squinched her features. "That's disgusting."

"Is not."

"Is too."

"Is that Bruno and Chauncey?" Zoe gaped at the

two dogs playfully nuzzling one another, their tongues darting in affectionate licks as they sauntered past her and down the stairs. "I don't believe it."

"It's true, Mom," Toby said. "Bruno told me Chauncey's not as wimpy as he looks. They decided to be brothers. Now can I use the bathroom? Lou and Poppy are waiting for me."

A bit numbly, Zoe ruffled her son's hair. "Sure," she said, suspecting she was agreeing to more than letting him use the bathroom. "And Toby," she added as she stepped into the hall with Bink, "Lou is your elder. You should call her Mrs. Ballard."

"I did, Mom," the boy replied, peeking from behind the door. "But she said if I did it again she'd belt me in the chops."

Her brows raised, Zoe stood staring at the closed door.

Bink yawned. "As long as Toby's going fishing, can I go back to bed?"

Zoe sighed. "Why not?"

"Looks like you're staying, Zoe Laurence. At least for one more day."

At the timbre of Mitch's voice, raw-edged with morning, Zoe whipped around. Her breath caught. He stood leaning one hand against the wall, his long legs crossed. His hair was tousled, adorably, the way Toby's typically was when he awoke, before she slicked it down. She didn't want to slick Mitch's hair down, though. She wanted to rifle through it. His eyes were lidded but sharp, sharp enough to carve out every curve of her body. She drew the flannel robe Lou had loaned her around her throat, grateful that he was at least wearing a shirt. *Nearly* wearing a shirt. The blue pajama top that matched the cobalt color of his eyes gaped open down the center of his chest. The top's buttons were missing, as was her sense of shame. Unabashed, she stared at the broad expanse of his chest, the arrow of hair to his slim waist, visible—navel and all—above low-riding pajama bottoms. The carelessly tied ends of their drawstrings begged to be tugged.

Staring at Mitch, she barely felt Bink's peck on her cheek.

"If you need me later today, Mom, I'll be in town with Sarah. We're going to look for Barenaked Ladies."

"That's nice," Zoe said absently, wondering when, exactly, she'd lost control of her life.

Bink gaped at her mother. "Mom, did you hear what I said?"

"Hmmm." Still staring at Mitch, Zoe waved at Bink over her shoulder. "Have a good time."

Bink looked from her mother to Mitch and back. Then, laughing, she shook her head. "Earth to Mom. You are in major denial."

"Uh-huh. Goodnight, sweetheart." As Bink returned to Sarah's room, Zoe took a step toward Mitch. "I—I hope I didn't wake you."

"No, you didn't." *I lay awake all night, thinking of you.* Mitch met her in the middle of the hall. "Sleep well?"

"Like a baby." *With colic.* A mound of shampoo plopped onto Zoe's nose, and another on her cheek. As she started to wipe them away, Mitch took the corner of the towel from her fingers.

"Here, let me." Taking his time, he gently blotted the dollops and lingered long after they'd vanished. "Do you always look like this in the morning?"

Zoe snapped back to reality at the antidote Mitch had administered for his spell when he'd referred to how she must look sporting a red plaid robe, a suds cap, and no makeup. "Oh my gosh!" Hastily, she wrapped the towel around her head and ran to the bathroom door. "Toby! Mommy really needs to get back in there." Seeing Mitch coming toward her, she jiggled the knob. "Hurry, honey!"

Mitch turned her to him. "I meant, do you always look so adorable in the morning?"

"When I get back to Chicago I'll ask my mirror and let you know."

"You don't have to. I already know you're the fairest in the land."

Zoe gazed up at him, mesmerized. "Really?"

The toilet flushed. He was silent.

Zoe nodded her toweled head. "That's what I figured."

"You're wrong," Mitch said, drawing her closer. "Spend the day with me, Zoe. We'll take it real slow. Get to know each other."

Sounds wonderful, but—"There'd be no point. You need Sarah to stay, and I need to leave, first thing in the morning."

"Hey!" Stepping outside the bathroom, Toby squeezed between Mitch and Zoe and tried forcing them apart. "You okay, Mom?"

Zoe got on one knee before her son. "Yes, I'm all right. But thanks for defending me."

Mitch smoothed back the boy's hair. "And you're right to look out for your mother, son," he said, then looked at Zoe. "That's what a man does when he loves a woman, if she lets him."

Her gaze affixed to Mitch's as Toby wriggled away, Zoe rose.

Mitch reached for her.

She ducked into the bathroom. "Well, this woman's got to finish washing her hair," she said, then closed and locked the door. Pressing her back against it, she exhaled. "And that man right out of it. Once and for all."

SEVEN

"That's right, Pete. I want you to take our things back to Chicago." Zoe spoke on the phone in the Ballards' kitchen, looking everywhere but at Mitch, who was looking at her, his gaze as piercing as the knife he was using to slice the ham steak he'd just fried.

"Want some?" He held up a portion.

Although it looked and smelled delicious and she was starving, Zoe knew better than to sit down at the table with him. One bite of ham and eggs and another refrain of, "We'll take it real slow, Zoe," and there would go all her resolve. Shaking her head no, she turned her back on him. "I know, Pete, my move still won't be complete, and no, I'm not obsessive-compulsive. How much is this going to cost?" A moment later, Zoe closed her eyes. *I'm a masochist.* "Okay, Pete. Yes, I'll page you again if I change my mind, which I won't, but if I do, you have my permission to seal me in a carton and put me in storage."

After she hung up the phone, she went to the counter, poured a mug of coffee, then took it outside onto the screened porch. She stood gazing out at Lou's cheery garden, giving a soft laugh when she realized that it was bordered by old, half-buried car fenders. Lou couldn't be more different from Mrs. Cooperschmidt, nor from Zoe's own mother, who had been as feminine as lace curtains. On the other hand,

Margaret Beck had had a will of iron, and had kept Zoe's father in line with it. Lou had a way with him, too—one uniquely her own. Zoe began to wonder if he wasn't just dallying with Lou, if he'd really meant it when he said he wasn't going back to Chicago with her and the children. And if Bink was serious about never forgiving her if she had to leave Sarah Jane. And after Toby's adventures with Lou, how would he react to the news that he had to say good-bye, forever?

But she was the head of her little clan, Zoe argued to herself. If something was wrong for her, wasn't it also wrong for her family? She wasn't wanted here, or at least she wouldn't be once everyone found out she was a banker. And once they did, then where would she be? Stuck across the street in a house with a leaky roof, wanted by no one but Perfection's finest, Officer Matt Ballard. The wrong Ballard. Yep, she'd be a masochist of the first order, Zoe thought, if she pitched camp in this hamlet.

Then why was she holding her mug so tightly, hoping its warmth would chase the sudden chill of self-doubt from her heart?

"It's hard making decisions alone, especially when they affect your kids. You wonder whether or not you're doing the right thing."

Turning, Zoe saw Mitch standing behind the screen door, his blue eyes like flames. Flames, she reminded herself, burned, and sometimes left scars. "I'm used to it," she said, taking a sip from her mug and not letting on that she'd scorched the tip of her tongue. "Besides, I trust my instincts." She knocked on the plank porch wall. "No major errors yet."

"There's always a first time."

"Yah, but going back to Chicago isn't it." *Is it?* Setting her mug down on the wicker table beside her, she pushed the outer door open and took the steps down to the yard.

Mitch walked onto the porch, sipping coffee and

watching Zoe stroll toward Lou's garden wearing one
of Lou's man-size denim shirts over a pair of cutoff jeans
his mother must have cut with him in mind. Zoe's legs
were just as he'd imagined, long, sleek, coltish. And
cruel. Seemed like they were always taking her away
from him. Tomorrow, for good. He needed a miracle,
one that would make her stay. He really needed to know,
too, why he wanted her to stay bad—aside from the obvious reason, which was that all he'd wanted since he'd
first laid eyes on her was to be bad.

Maybe that was the reason, he thought, that he'd
tried to be bad last night and she'd conked him on
the head with her purse and made them both be
good—the old Challenge Thing. Of course, he'd once
tried feeling the muscles of a lady bodybuilder from
Madisonville, and after she'd flipped him on his back
had he gone back for more? Had Grant surrendered
to Lee? He'd torn up her number.

So, if it wasn't The Challenge Thing, maybe it was
The Respect Thing. Yeah, that was it. She'd so much
as said, *"I'm not that kind,"* which at least made a man
think twice before asking a woman if she'd like to be.
Of course, he hadn't asked that of any woman since
he'd gotten custody of Sarah Jane. Amazing how a man
acquires character when he acquires a daughter. Now,
whenever a woman said she wasn't that kind, the first,
second, and only thing he thought was that she was
the right kind to help raise Sarah. But he knew some
nice women, right here in town—pretty, too—and he'd
never once practiced saying, as he'd done all morning,
"Sarah, baby, you're going to have a stepmom, and a
brother and sister, and we're all going to be one big
happy family, and please stop holding your breath!"

Okay, so he could cross The Challenge and Respect
Things off his list of reasons why he wanted Zoe to
stay. Maybe it was something simpler, like The Ego
Thing. He had to admit, when he'd kissed Zoe and
she'd melted in his arms, and when he'd run to her

rescue and she'd said she felt safe as long as he was near, his heart had swelled. But not his head. He'd learned long ago that a big ego just gave a woman a bigger target.

So, if it wasn't The Challenge Thing, or The Respect or The Ego Thing, what was it about Zoe that wouldn't let go of him, wouldn't let him let go of her? Of course! It was The Mystery Thing. He wanted her to stay so he could find out why it was he wanted her to stay. And if she stayed and he found out, then what? Then, he imagined as he rubbed his forehead, the thing that happens when a woman causes a man to stop making a shred of sense would happen. The All Hell Breaking Loose Thing.

"Excuse me, ma'am. Are these your dogs?"

Seeing the uniformed, County Animal Control officer approach Zoe with Chauncey under one arm and Bruno under the other, Mitch choked on a swig of coffee. He set his mug down next to hers. Then, pushing open the door, he bounded down the steps to the yard. Could be he was about to get his miracle.

Behind dark glasses, the officer looked at him. "Hey, Mitch. I found these two in the front yard. No tags. You know anything about 'em?"

Mitch took the Cavalier from the man. "This one just got back from Atlanta with Sarah Jane. A present from my ex."

"In that case, want me to throw him in the pound?"

"Nah, it's not his fault that I can't afford a gift like him." Mitch patted the top of Chauncey's head, then set the dog on the ground. Straightening, he looked at the officer. "You wouldn't know where I can get a part-time job that pays two hundred thousand a year, would you?"

While staring at the officer—*he* really did look like Erik Estrada—Zoe addressed Mitch. "I'm sure Booger could always use an extra bouncer."

"Bouncer?" The officer gazed from Mitch to Zoe, then back. "What's she talking about?"

Shaking his head, Mitch frowned as if to say "I'll tell you later." "The, uh, Boston terrier is Bruno. He belongs to the lady here. If he clamps down on your arm, don't worry. He's just being friendly."

The officer laughed. "Is that what she told you?"

Ignoring the death threats in Zoe's green eyes, Mitch skewed a smile at her. "Yep."

"Figures," the officer replied. "I heard she denied vandalizing the old furniture factory last night, too."

Zoe gasped. "How did you—? I did no such—" She rushed at Mitch. "Tell him I did no—" Taking a breath, she reminded herself that since she was leaving town in less than twenty-four hours, attempting to complete a sentence, let alone rebuild her reputation, was pointless. She reached out for Bruno. "May I have my dog back now?"

"My pleasure, ma'am," the officer said as he handed Bruno over to her. As she headed back to the house he called, "Hey, where do you think you're going?"

Zoe stopped and looked at the man over her shoulder. "Is there a law in Perfection against parting company without leaving a forwarding address?"

"No, ma'am. But there's one that says that out of doors you have to keep your dog on a leash." From inside his waistband, the officer withdrew a booklet with a pen clipped to it. Removing the pen, he clicked the plunger with his thumb. "I'm going to have to cite you."

Zoe's brows shot up as her lips drew into a tight pucker. "You mean you want to quote me for an article you're doing for the SPCA?"

Looking up from his pad, the officer glanced a "Huh?" at Mitch before meeting Zoe's gaze. "No, ma'am," he said, then returned to writing in his booklet. "But I *will* be reporting your violation to the county district court."

"Court?" After three angry strides, Zoe stepped in front of Mitch and in the officer's bronzed face. "But, I'm going back to Chicago tomorrow. Pete, the man who makes your move complete, told me his self-esteem is depending on me. Can't I just send in a fine?"

The dark-haired agent went on jotting. "Like the one you got for a parking violation?"

Zoe rolled her eyes. Even for a small town, Perfection was circulating news about her with amazing speed. "Exactly."

The officer shook his head. "Not even roughly. You committed a misdemeanor, ma'am."

"Misde—? As in somewhere between taking paper clips home from the office and holding up an armored car?"

"Yes, ma'am. You have to appear before the judge. Spell your name, please."

Zoe huffed. "You mean it isn't on the town's web site?"

"Could be. I haven't checked it out today."

Hoisting Bruno over her shoulder, Zoe began pacing and arguing, offering every rationale she could think of for why she oughtn't to be cited, then threatening to take her case to the mayor, the governor, and finally the Welcome Wagon. As a last resort, she said, "Instead of harassing law-abiding citizens, you could be rounding up hardened criminals. You know, raccoons who go through trashcans and steal credit card numbers? Beavers who build faulty bridges? Surely, somewhere in this county there's a sheep on the lam!" When this last gambit failed, she begrudgingly supplied the information the officer requested.

After a moment, he ripped the yellow copy of the citation from his pad and handed it to Zoe, telling her she'd be notified of the date of her appearance, which would likely be before the end of the month. Then, with a nod for her and a "See ya, buddy" for Mitch, he turned away—to Zoe's astonishment.

She tapped him on the shoulder. "Ex-*cuse* me."

The officer turned back. "Ma'am?"

"Aren't you forgetting something?" Zoe scowled at Mitch. "Like a ticket for your pal, here." Pinning the county agent with a steely squint, she went toe to toe with him. "Or maybe you're just another corrupt dog-catcher."

Sucking in air, Mitch bent over Zoe's shoulder. "I don't think you should have called him that."

Holding the agent with the corner of her gaze, noting the beefy arms he was folding over his chest and the angry bull expression on his face, she said, "What? Corrupt?"

"Dogcatcher. He's very sensitive about his image. Boycotted Walt's Video World when *Lady and the Tramp* came out."

Grrrrr.

Zoe darted her gaze from Bruno to Chauncey to Mitch. "I distinctly heard three different growls."

"He told you," the officer said. "I'm sensitive."

Zoe came to her full height. "Obviously. You couldn't bear to hurt a friend's feelings, which is why I have to keep a date with the judge and Mr. Ballard only has to keep a date to judge Booger's next wet T-shirt contest."

Hands on his slim waist, the officer bore down on her. "For your information, ma'am, Mitch is a man I'm proud to count among my friends. But the reason I didn't cite him is because he didn't break the law, which says that you have to keep your dog on a leash except in your own yard. Now, according to the address you gave me, this isn't your yard." He looked up at Mitch. "I didn't know you judged those contests of Booger's. Does the county prosecutor know about that?"

"Oh, for the love of—" Moving Zoe to one side, Mitch squared off with the other man. "Of course, I don't—"

"County prosecutor?" Pushing the men apart, Zoe shook her finger in Mitch's face. "I knew it! You're on probation . . . O-o-oh, my Lord." One hand under Bruno's butt and the other against her cheek, she started backing toward the house. "I slept under the same roof as a felon . . . my children slept . . . my dog—"

"I am not a—" Mitch grabbed the officer's arm and shoved him toward Zoe. "Will you tell that lunatic that I am not a criminal!"

"That's right, ma'am. I'd stake my name on it."

Halting at the stairs leading to the screened porch, Zoe honed her gaze on the agent. "That reminds me. What *is* your name? If for no other reason, I'd like it for the doll I'm going to be sticking pins in tonight."

The agent looked over his shoulder at Mitch, then back at Zoe. "It's the same as his, ma'am."

Leaning away, Zoe looked at him askance. "Your name is Mitch?"

Mitch threw up his hands. "Zoe, his name is Mike. Mike—"

"Don't tell me!"

Mitch slanted his gaze at Mike. "She likes to play guessing games."

"I *hate* guessing games!" Her chest heaving, she shifted her gaze between the two strapping men. Along with police officer Matt, she realized a moment ago, they would make a great country music trio. "And I'm not real fond of the Ballard Brothers, either." She focused on Mitch. "Isn't there anyone in this town who isn't related to you? No. Don't answer that, either. After I win my case, I'm outta here. No more Perfection. No more Ballards." She backed up the stairs. "Good-bye. Good-bye. I'm going to call my moving man, now, and pray I can afford the therapy sessions he's going to charge me for."

When the screen door slammed shut behind her, Mitch Ballard let loose a broad grin. "Thanks, little brother. You just made me a miracle." Turning, he clamped his hand on Mike's shoulder. "Now all I have to worry about is what I'll do if all hell breaks loose."

A flash of lightning and rain plinking on the roof roused Zoe from the rare sleep that hadn't overtaken her in the last few weeks before she could change out of her work clothes—not her banker's blues, but the jeans and T-shirts she'd destroyed while scrubbing and sanitizing every square inch of 222 Magnolia Street. It wasn't much of a house, she'd admitted to Pete after he'd brought in the first of her household belongings and asked if she wouldn't rather stay in a motel until her court case came up. Of course she would, she'd replied, and she could if only he'd reduce his bill. But since he wouldn't, and she'd already paid a month's rent in advance, until the end of the month this house would be home. And it would be clean. If only it had occurred to her to poke a few more holes in the roof the last time it rained, she thought as she stiffly slipped on her robe and padded downstairs for the necessary buckets, she could have left the cleaning to Mother Nature.

On the other hand, if the place had been immaculate, she thought after placing the last bucket strategically beneath the steady drip in the hall outside Bink's room, she would never have discovered its oddities. Like the border of cabbage roses in her bedroom that only a close look would reveal was upside down. And the light switch in the middle of a dining room wall that, as far she could tell, turned on nothing but curiosity.

On her way to the kitchen for a cup of tea now that her mind was as awake as her body, she stopped in the spacious, high-ceilinged dining room and flipped the switch one more time. No light appeared, and Zoe smiled, realizing that she would have been disappointed if any had. Light would have dispelled the darkness, but also her delight that a small mystery should dwell within her very own house.

Leased house. The reminder, like the useless light switch she now flicked off, served up a larger mystery, one she found less charming than disturbing. As she switched on the hall light and headed to the kitchen, she puzzled over why she was suddenly glad that her finances had left her no choice but to stay in this crazy old place. Why, in only a short, backbreaking spell, she'd become attached to it as she never had to the easily maintained apartment she'd called home for so many years. Why, she already knew the location of the creaks in the floors and the cracks in the walls and lived comfortably with them, as though they were eccentric members of the family she was already beginning to miss.

When she'd spoken to Pete yesterday, she'd told him to stand by, that she would be leaving Perfection in a day or two. This time, she gave him her word. After all, her court case was coming up—she glanced at the clock on her countertop microwave, one of the few items she'd deemed it necessary to unpack—in a little less than six hours. After that, all she'd need was word from Violet Pringle informing her that her request for a transfer back to Chicago had been approved—practically a done deal—and she could leave this house. But a part of her—aside from the part that hated the idea of losing her security deposit for breaking her lease—didn't want to leave this house.

Perhaps, she thought as she placed a mug of water in the microwave, she was merely enjoying the novelty of not having to share her walls, however cracked, with neighbors. And relishing the freedom of being able to listen to music at any hour and any decibel, and to use the washer and dryer, however held together with duct tape, any day of the week. Or perhaps she was only reacting the way any mother would, with joy at watching her little boy romp with his dog in the back-yard, especially after he'd so bravely tried to hide his disappointment that the promised swing set was not only rusty but lacked actual swings. But did that joy alone account for why, when she knew she had no intention of staying beyond her court date, she'd caught herself calculating how she might afford to sur-prise Toby with a brand new set?

As she shaved a sliver from the last of the carrot cake Widow Corbett had brought over yesterday, she wondered if this feeling of belonging in this house, of it belonging to her, was nothing more than the accep-tance that had come with the cakes and pies and whole meals Magnolia Street had visited on her in the past weeks. She hadn't known neighbors anywhere were still what neighbors should be—a little nosy about her, a bit gossipy about one another, but a lot welcoming.

And just plain nice, like Kathy Hardy, whose fried chicken dinner Zoe had appreciated even more after Mrs. Terwilliker told her that Dave Hardy was still out of work following the closing of the furniture factory. Appreciated, and felt guilty about, because she hadn't revealed to Kathy or any of the other neighbors that the job she'd told them she wasn't assured of—not an untruth—was at the bank they blamed for their trou-bles. She'd rationalized that she'd soon be on her way back to Chicago, so why roil friendly waters? But she hadn't told them that, either—that she planned to leave Perfection. She'd accepted their hospitality as though she knew she'd be around long enough to re-ciprocate it.

She quickly discovered, however, that repaying a kindness on Magnolia Street didn't require planning a seven-course dinner months in advance so that her guests could work the event into their schedules. Here, thoughtfulness was as spontaneous as breathing. So, when the Widow Corbett, whose husband had always taken care of their finances, mentioned she couldn't make sense of her checkbook, Zoe found herself offering to straighten it out. And when poor shy Mr. Terwilliker, who'd made her a lovely birdcage, a replica of the Presbyterian church, had told her he'd always dreamed of going to Chicago, she'd helped him to plan a sightseeing tour, though she'd had the feeling he'd never take it. She'd even grown close enough to Kathy Hardy to sense and worry about the strain she and Dave were under. Suggesting that they share a quiet romantic evening at home, she offered to keep their kids overnight. "I owe you," Zoe had insisted when Kathy, obviously delighted, nevertheless maintained that she couldn't impose. After all, Zoe had reasoned, Kathy had voluntarily kept Toby from under her feet so she could get on with her cleaning or just take a leisurely bath.

As Zoe finished her tea, an irony occurred to her, one that brought a smile to her lips. She, Zoe Laurence, the woman who despised debt, had found friendship through it.

Suddenly, her smile faded. Setting her mug down, she realized that in the few weeks she'd lived in Perfection she'd made more friends of neighbors than she had in all the years she'd lived in the Happydale Apartments. So had Bink and Toby. Not only had Bink and Sarah Jane become inseparable, but Sarah had initiated Bink into her circle of giggling eleven-year-old girls who were painting their nails one minute and trading Beanie Babies the next. And Toby was acting so like a typical six-year-old boy, digging up worms with other little boys and scaring little girls with them, that Zoe at last realized how atypical—and lonely—his life in a high-rise must have been. Now that she thought about it, it had been days since he'd last reported having a conversation with Bruno.

What rankled her were the conversations he was apparently having with Mitch Ballard. She was getting a little tired of hearing about Mitch's remote control airplanes, and Mitch's dirt bike, and Mitch's pocket knife that had a gazillion tools on it.

What's the matter, Zoe? she asked herself as she heated water for a second cup of tea, her microwave humming. *Jealous?* Sure. A little. She was no longer everything to Toby. Nor, she supposed, should she expect to be. He wasn't a baby anymore, hadn't been for some time. He needed to look to Mom, but also up to a man. Naturally, the first man who took him to that mysterious place where women didn't reign supreme, or even remind him to put on his sweater, would look ten feet tall. That was why, given that Toby's relationship with Mitch would soon have to end, she regretted having allowed it to begin. Returning to the table with her tea, she recalled how it had.

After dinner one evening, she'd been washing the tall windows in what used to be called a parlor and had seen Toby sitting dejectedly on the curb, his face in his hands. He'd been watching the Hardy driveway next to the Ballards', where Mitch had been playing against Dave and his little boy. After making a shot that she, a Bulls' fan, had recognized as a great dunk, Mitch had spotted Toby. He'd crossed the street, bent over Toby, his hands on his knees, and spoken to him. A moment later, he'd looked up and caught Zoe's gaze on the bright blue hook of his own through the window. She hadn't seen him since the morning she'd walked off with Bruno and the citation his brother had given her, mostly because she'd disciplined herself not to look in the direction of his house, entirely because she'd known exactly what those eyes of his could do to her—break through the brick-hard wall she'd built around her heart as easily as she'd dug through a carton of those airy packing "peanuts" to her microwave. She'd held her breath as, scooting Toby ahead of him, he'd come up the walk to her front door. He'd waited outside while Toby, bursting through the foyer and into the parlor, begged her to let him join Mitch and the Hardys.

She'd hesitated. Strangely, neither Bink's friendship with Sarah Jane, nor her own growing relationship with the surprisingly likable girl, nor her dad's romance with Lou, had inextricably linked her to Mitch the way Toby's going off with the man threatened to. Her instincts had told her not to allow it. But she'd known that her instincts had been selfish. Anyway, besieged by Toby's wide-eyed excitement and his "Ple-e-ease, Mom," how could she have refused him something that, after all, could only do him good? Even now, as she stood at the sink washing her cake plate, she remembered him scampering back to Mitch, shouting, "She said I can!"

She could also remember seeing Mitch across the threshold, and the "Oh, boy!" way he'd grinned at Toby. In her mind she watched him now as she had that evening, captivated by the all boy way he'd played, first against Dave alone while Toby, at his direction, looked attentively on. He'd been rough and tumble, strong and agile, aggressive, competitive. Sneaky. He'd laughed a lot. And then, as he'd taught Toby how to hold the ball and dribble it, and launch it into the air from between his knees, he'd changed from a male into a man. His body language was direct but kind, instructive, and patient. And when he'd lifted Toby up to make a dunk, then sat him on one of his broad shoulders and paraded him in a victory cheer, he'd changed from a man into a dad.

Drying her plate, Zoe wished now, as she had then, that she'd never seen that transformation in Mitch. If she hadn't, every evening, when he sent Toby to ask her permission to join in what she'd learned was a ritual of Magnolia Street dads and sons—and some daughters—she wouldn't have to admit the real reason Toby always looked as though his life depended on her saying *yes*. More than he needed to learn how to play basketball, he needed a dad. And, though it was pointless to blame herself for his not having one, she did. When she'd married Jack, all she'd known was that she'd wanted his children. She'd never stopped to wonder what kind of father he'd make.

Fortunately, she thought as she wiped crumbs off the countertop, she was willing to do the only thing she could to fill the fatherly void in Toby's life. This fall, she'd enroll him in scouts. He'd get a father figure, and the only gamble she'd have to take was on ordering the right size uniform. That settled, she turned off the light in the kitchen and started back up the hall. After waiting weeks for her day in court, she'd hate to sleep through it.

Suddenly, hearing a rhythmic tapping through the muffled downpour, Zoe halted. She listened closely, and when the pattern repeated she knew it had come from the front door. Someone was definitely out there. If only she hadn't been so silly as to make her burned-out porch light the symbol of her resistance to taking up permanent residence on Magnolia Street, she could look through one of the sidelights and see who. She switched off the hall light. Then, slowly, warily, approaching the door, she prayed that lightning would reveal the identity of her night visitor.

But the lightning had gone the way of her porch light. Zoe put her ear to the door, but heard only rain nailing the wood planking and the hammering of her own heart. Perhaps whoever it was had gone. Flattening her hands against the door, she slowly leaned to her left, bringing her face before the pane of leaded glass. Seeing nothing, she pressed her nose to the glass and narrowed her gaze, trying to bore through the solid darkness.

Thunder exploded. A dagger of electricity rent the black curtain on the other side of the pane. In a gargoyle's face smooshed against it, whited-out eyes stared back at her. Too horrified to scream, Zoe jumped back.

Then, shaking her hands up and down, she turned in a circle, ordering herself to think. Think what? *Call the police.* But with her luck, she'd get Matt Ballard and a ticket for failing to fix her porch light. Besides, whoever the creep was, he'd be gone before the police got there. She needed help now. *Fetch Bruno from Toby's room.* No, he was in enough trouble already. *Wake Dad.* Might as easily wake the dead, especially when he was in love. When wasn't he? Okay. Weapon. She needed a weapon. Kitchen knife. Too bloody. She wouldn't get her security deposit back. *Poker!* Not the kind Jack played, but the kind that stood beside the fireplace in the parlor. She started for it.

"Zoe, that you?" A louder, more insistent knock came at the door. "It's me, Mitch. Open up!"

Zoe turned around, breathing hard, but not as hard as the punch she was going to deliver to Mitch Ballard's abdomen, though she'd probably break her hand. The least she could do was demand to know what the *hell* he was doing lurking outside her door at three in the morning. She tightened the belt of the soft green robe that matched her nightie, raked back her hair, then switched the hall light back on and threw open the door. "Just what do you think you're—"

At the sight of him, Zoe went speechless. His hair, even blacker when wet, hung thickly over eyes rimmed with rain-spiked lashes and smudged below with sleeplessness, perhaps many nights of it. Drops of water coursed down his face, collecting briefly on his lips, which trembled slightly, before spilling off. Below the tails of his open chambray shirt, which was soaked and tacked to his skin, his hands lay hidden inside the pockets of his wet jeans, which rode low on his glistening torso. He shifted his weight from side to side. Zoe looked down at his feet. One was bare, the other wearing an unlaced running shoe.

"I couldn't find the mate," he said.

"So you thought you'd look for it here?"

Drawing his shirt around him, Mitch sucked in a breath. "Of c-course not."

Zoe debated six feet plus of little boy shivering with cold, and lost. Taking Mitch by the hand, she led him inside and shut the door. She ordered him not to move, scurried up the stairs, then returned a moment later, towel in hand. She flung it at him. "Now, you'd better have a damn good reason for peeping through my window, because you damn near gave me a stroke."

"Yeah?" Mitch ceased toweling his hair and bent over, showing her the top of his head. "Count 'em, darlin'. I'll bet damn near fifty hairs turned gray when I saw Freddy Kreuger peeping back at me."

"Freddy—? I'm glad. You deserve every one of them." Zoe turned aside, away from the clean scent of his hair and her own sudden urge to sift its wet blackness through her fingers. When the urge passed, she turned back, her arms akimbo, and looked up at him. "What *were* you doing out there?"

"I wasn't hoping to catch you in your nightie, if that's what you're thinking." As he draped the towel around his neck, he swept his gaze over her, then quirked his lips in a smile. "Can't say I'm disappointed I did, though."

Her cheeks burning, Zoe clutched the ends of her robe over the lace top of her short gown. Why couldn't she have fallen asleep in her jeans and a T-shirt one more time? "What *were* you hoping?"

"That you all were okay. Your lights were on so long I thought something had to be wrong. Maybe one of the kids was sick. Or . . . you."

Zoe felt his gaze tenderly hold her, body and soul. "Oh. Well . . . we're fine. It was just . . . the rain . . . and the roof . . . buckets."

Mitch limped closer. "Sorry if I . . . I guess I shouldn't have . . . After all, what business do I have . . ."

As he lowered his parted lips to hers, Zoe felt him breathe her in. She parted her own lips.

Mitch pulled back. "Sorry."

"You should be." *I really wanted that kiss.*

"Well, don't make a federal case of it," Mitch snapped. He reached for the doorknob. "I won't bother you again."

Zoe stayed his arm. "Please. I didn't mean . . . You were so nice to . . ." She looked down at the sleeve she was touching. "You're soaked to the skin. You'd better get out of that shirt before you catch pneumonia."

And when he'd stripped the sopping garment away, she found herself removing the towel from around his neck and gently blotting his back dry—his beautiful broad back—and shoulders. Suddenly, she stopped, frowning over a white, jagged line about an inch long and running diagonally from his right shoulder to his shoulder blade. "How did you get this scar?"

Mitch gave a short laugh. "When Ellie didn't get what she wanted, for her birthday or our anniversary, she had a way of picking up the nearest thing and throwing it at me. As I recall, the anniversary I gave her roses instead of a diamond tennis bracelet, the nearest thing was a steak knife."

Zoe felt something stab her heart, something about the size of a steak knife. "I love roses," she said softly. "Especially redgolds."

Mitch turned, holding his shirt to the center of his chest, over his heart. "Like the color of your hair in sunlight."

Zoe leaned her head to one side. "Jack used to say things like that, at first." Giving a soft laugh, she looked away. "Later on, the only way I could get his attention was to lay odds he couldn't tell me the color of my underwear."

Crooking his fingers beneath her chin, Mitch turned her gaze back to his. "Of course, I'm only guessing, but judging from what I know about you, Zoe, I'd say the color is . . ." The fingers he curled around the towel she still held met hers. "One of a kind."

Zoe knew that if he'd wrapped her in his arms, he couldn't have held her a closer captive than he had with his slightest touch. "What *do* you know about me?"

Mitch gave her a mock frown. "Haven't you heard? You're the bestest mom in the whole world. At least, that's what Toby tells me. And Harvey says—"

"Dad? He's talked to you about me?" Zoe's eyes widened with panic. She'd sworn her entire family to secrecy about her being a banker. Of course, if Dad had taken enough time off from kissing Lou for his tongue to slip, Mitch wouldn't be here. He'd be across the street praying that lightning would strike her house. "Never mind. The only thing my father could say that would surprise me is 'Zoe, would you like me to take out the garbage?' "

Together, they chuckled softly. After a moment, Zoe asked, "What *did* he say?"

Mitch grinned. "That you were very conscientious about taking out the garbage."

"And from that you gathered I'm one of a kind? I can show you studies that prove that virtually all of the garbage in America is taken out by women."

"Or just taken by them. I see it every day."

"You really go to Booger's every day?"

Taking a deep breath, Mitch hung the towel around Zoe's neck and drew her close. "I really go for strong women with gorgeous green eyes. But there's such a thing as being too strong, Zoe." He cupped her cheek. "You've been everything to everyone but yourself for far too long."

Inhaling the man-scented mist rising off his skin, Zoe tried to tell herself she hadn't missed it. Truth was, she didn't miss Jack's scent, but she would Mitch's. "I had no choice."

"Sure you had. You could have quit at any time. But

you didn't. That's because quitting isn't in your nature."

Zoe caught the arch of his brow, challenging her not to quit on Perfection. On him. But if he knew who paid her bills, he'd be challenging her to get out of town by sunset. She pushed away. "Look, you think you know me, you think you want to know me, but trust me, you don't."

Mitch pulled her close. "You'll never convince me of that, Zoe. And maybe I'll never convince you that no matter how things are going to look to you in the morning, I really care about you. All I know is that I have to try. You understand that, don't you?"

Zoe nodded. "No. Are you sure you're not having flashbacks from that bad varnish trip?"

Letting her go, Mitch raked back his hair. "Listen, I should have told you sooner, but—"

"Mitch? I *thought* I heard your voice!" Toby tripped down the stairs and threw his arms around Mitch's knees.

Mitch ruffled Toby's mop of hair. "Sorry if I woke you, buddy."

Toby tilted his head way back. "You didn't." He yawned. "The thunder waked me up."

"Come on, honey," Zoe said, leading Toby away by the hand. "I'll tuck you back in bed."

Snatching his hand from hers, Toby ran back to Mitch. "I want you to tuck me in."

Mitch looked at Zoe, his gaze conflicted. "Is it okay?"

Stunned, hurt, and most of all worried about how Toby was going handle leaving Mitch, and whether he was going to hate her for it, she nevertheless assented.

"Hold this?"

Zoe looked at the shirt Mitch held out to her.

"I'd put it on, but I don't think Toby would like a wet piggyback ride."

Zoe took the shirt, and after he'd gone, she found

herself fingering one tip of its collar. A moment later, she brought it to her nose, absorbed its scent, and worried that Toby wasn't the only one who was going to have a hard time forgetting Mitch Ballard.

"Oh Lord," she murmured as she switched off the light. In the darkness, she wove around the unpacked cartons that stood in the parlor, finally plunking down on one, still clutching Mitch's shirt. *What have I gotten into? What have I gotten my family into?*

Later, how long she didn't know, she heard, "You've done a great job, Zoe. Toby's a terrific kid."

She looked in the direction of Mitch's voice, surprised to discover his dark, solid form at her side. She must have been in a trance not to have sensed him. "Thanks. I think so."

She felt his warm hand on her arm. "Thank *you*. For letting me be a part of his life."

Zoe stood up and faced him. "You realize the terrible position you've put me in, don't you? You knew all along I wasn't staying, yet you let Toby come to love you. And now, to do what's best for all of us, I have to hurt one of us. I have to break my son's heart."

Mitch took her in his arms, so swiftly and tightly that the breath left her body. "And mine," he murmured. Then he brought a hot, hard, plundering kiss down on her mouth, deepening it until, moaning, she went limp. He sat her back down on the carton. "Go back to Chicago, Zoe. Have a safe life. And when you remember Perfection, remember that kiss." He took his shirt from her numb fingers. "Good-bye, darlin'."

Long after he'd gone, Zoe remained seated on the crate, burying her nose in the towel, in the essences of Mitch's skin and hair.

And remembering perfection.

EIGHT

"Mom, Toby won't come. I think he's crying."

Outside Judge Angus McDowell's courtroom in the Winsome County district courthouse in the heart of Perfection, Zoe gazed over her shoulder at Bink, who was looking back at Toby. He stood a few feet away, his forehead pressed against the wall. With Bink and Harvey following, Zoe walked over to her son. "What's the matter, honey?"

Sniffling, Toby ran his finger under his nose. "You're gonna go to jail, and it's all my fault. I shoulda told Bruno to stay inside till I got back from fishing."

Squatting, Zoe turned Toby toward her. "Well, let's just say we've all learned that we need to keep an eye on him." She lifted his chin. "And I'm not going to go to jail. The worst that could happen is that I'll have to pay a fine."

With the heel of his hand, Toby wiped a tear from his cheek. "You mean *money?*"

"Now you've done it, boy. Said the secret word." Bending close to his grandson, Harvey jerked his thumb at Zoe. "You just made the slammer look good to her."

Zoe gazed up at him. "You know, Dad, I'd be touched by your concern if I didn't know how taking care of the kids would put a crimp in your porch swinging with LouAnn Ballard."

Appearing hurt, Harvey straightened. "Some habits are hard to break, Zoe."

Coming up behind her grandfather, Bink stood on her toes, reached over his shoulder, and laughingly pinched his cheek. "Yeah, like getting your face slapped every night."

"*What?*" Rising, Zoe panned her gaze from her sheepish looking dad to her daughter's Cheshire grin. "Bianca, I thought I told you, no Beastie Boys, no MTV, no spying on your grandfather."

"I didn't have to spy, Mom. You should see how red his cheeks are when he borrows my skin lotion."

Zoe gazed incredulously at her father. "And you keep going back?"

He shrugged. "It's not so bad. My left cheek gets Monday, Wednesday, and Friday, and the right Tuesday, Thursday, and Saturday. Lou rests on the Sabbath." He sighed longingly. "I do love a God-fearing woman."

Zoe turned to Bink. "Is this in *Men Are Weird?*"

Bink nodded. "Chapter Four. 'The Respect Thing.'"

Zoe gazed into the distance, wondering how much respect a handbag to the head and absolution in the back of a squad car were worth. Enough, apparently, to intrigue Mitch, to compel him to ask her to stay. To make him confess that if she left Perfection, she'd break his heart. And, as if to prove it, he'd branded her with a good-bye kiss that was so wicked her heart was still saying *hel*lo.

Saying, *Stay.*

"Mom, you okay?"

Zoe met Bink's probing gaze. "Fine. I was just thinking about—" *Staying?* "The time," she said, glancing at her watch. "Well, is everybody ready to see the Constitution at work?"

Everybody turned and walked away. Zoe stuck her pinkies in her mouth and whistled. Everybody turned back. Opening the door, she ushered her clan into the courtroom ahead of her. An instant later, she drew up, stunned to find it packed. Standing room only.

"Cool, Mom," Bink murmured. "Looks like you're hotter than Shania Twain."

"Yeah, but I have a feeling the only Twain a judge with a name like Angus P. McDowell has heard of is Mark." Nevertheless, as Zoe moved the children up the aisle, scanning the rows of seats and picking out her Magnolia Street neighbors, she took courage. They were all there, Mrs. Corbett, the Terwillikers—mother and son—and the others, smiling at her, raising clasped hands above their heads champ-style, calling out, "Good luck!" and "Don't let 'em bully you, girl!" Even LouAnn Ballard was there, standing and holding a sign above her head that read:

UnLEASH justice.
Free Zoe Laurence!

As Lou motioned Harvey to the seat she'd saved for him, Zoe wondered how Agent Mike Ballard felt, sitting directly in front of his mother while she rooted for the opposition.

More than that, she wondered where Mitch Ballard was. Working, she supposed. Construction. A man didn't get a body like his sharpening pencils. Or maybe, just maybe, he was at Booger's, pouring out his broken heart to the bartender who'd been pouring him Buds since he'd left her, a rejected man.

She could see him now, eyes red-rimmed and bleary, face stubbled and gaunt. "I'm tellin' you, Joe," he was saying. "Sheez one of a kind, an' I juzz let her walk out of my life." *Hiccup.* " 'Course I kissed her first. Kissed her—" *Hiccup.* "Good. But not good enough. If only I'da had the nerve to tell her—"

"Psst, Zoe."

Zoe started. Her dream dissolved. She looked around her.

"Over here."

Turning to her right, she saw Kathy Hardy, her coal black eyes dancing excitedly beneath the brim of the smart, pale yellow hat that complemented her rich mahogany tones. Kathy was sitting on the aisle next to Dave, and their children—adorable in suits and ties, dresses and straw hats.

"I saved you seats," Kathy said, indicating the chairs in the row in front of hers.

Zoe sent the children ahead of her. Then, taking the aisle seat, she swiveled toward Kathy. "I can't believe this turnout."

Kathy Hardy placed her hand over Zoe's. "You're one of us now. And this just isn't fair."

Zoe felt heartened, then heartsick. She withdrew her hand. "Kath, I have a confession. I haven't been totally honest and open with you and the other neighbors."

"And that's one of the things we love about you." Kathy lifted toddler Bethy, who'd crawled off Dave's lap onto her own. "Look, honey, there's little enough to do around here without you deprivin' us of the fun of suspicionin' about you the way we do about everybody else."

Zoe smiled. "I'm serious, Kath. Y'all are so good, coming out to support me. I just can't let you do it under false pretenses."

Hand in mouth, Bethy giggled, then stretched three wet fingers toward Zoe's nose.

"You tell her, Bethy," Kathy said, applying a tissue to her daughter's hand. "Zoe just said 'y'all' like a homegrown girl, and we girls don't mind a few false *pre*-tenses, do we? Fact, we kinda insist on 'em."

"But—" Glancing anxiously toward the bench, Zoe saw the court clerk take his place before it. "Kathy, please listen to me before—"

"Court is in session. The Honorable Angus P. McDowell presiding. All rise."

Feeling as heavy as she had the day she'd learned

that Jack had left her with massive debt for a mass of blonde hair on a winning streak, Zoe lugged herself to her feet. She'd never dreamed these dear people had such faith in her, or that the thought of her breaking faith with them would cause her such anguish.

Or that Angus P. McDowell would look like a much older Lyle Lovett. *Pomp and circumstantial evidence, you might say,* she thought. At any rate, he looked approachable enough, and when the clerk called her case before she could take her seat, she approached the judge fully confident of persuading him of the unfairness of the charge against her.

Until, crooking his finger, he beckoned her to the bench.

"Now then—Mrs. Laurence, is it?—this won't take long. When I ask you how you plead, you just say guilty. I'll fine you two hundred and fifty dollars, which you can pay to the clerk here, and we can all move on like everybody wants us to. Like a bunch of damn gypsies, if you ask me, but then, nobody ever does."

Zoe lurched at the bench. "But, Your Honor, I don't want to plead guilty."

The judge rolled a stick of gum and popped it in his mouth. "Was your dog on a leash?"

"No."

Chew. Chew. "Was he in your own yard?"

"No."

"Then you're guilty. That'll be two hundred and—"

"But Your Honor—"

"Now, it won't do you any good to plead ignorance of the law or some fool technicality, like you hadn't moved into your house, yet." The judge plucked the wad of gum from his mouth, wrapped it noisily in paper, and handed it to his clerk. "We need the revenue around here. That'll be two hundred and . . . what say?" He leaned toward his clerk, who repeated something in his ear. "Oh, guess we do need him. Well, where the heck is he?" The judge looked out over his courtroom. "Where's the assistant county prosecutor?"

"Here, Your Honor!"

From the back of the room, the edge of a baritone sliced through Zoe's core. She turned. As its owner approached—imposingly tall, impeccably dressed in a suit that breathtakingly framed his classic physique, a crisp white shirt that set off his rugged tawniness, and a blue tie that electrified his blue gaze—half of her thought he was the handsomest man she'd ever seen. The other half wanted to boil him in oil. No, that meant having to cook. Pour varnish down his shorts? Perfect. She knew just where to get some, too. Where he'd babied her and danced her and kissed her out of her conviction—nearly—that all men were created equal, that they were all stinkers.

So this was what Mitch had meant by "no matter how things look in the morning." From what she could see, things looked a lot less like a matter of a broken heart than broken faith. He'd lied to her. Well, maybe not lied, but he hadn't told her the whole truth, and that was wholly unforgivable. And highly prosecutable. Guilty! *She* was, that is, of not having known better.

Looking at Zoe as he approached the bench, Mitch wondered how all hell breaking loose could look so much like heaven. Of course, he wouldn't have had to wonder at all if Linda Merrill hadn't decided to go into labor last night, leaving Zoe's case to the only available prosecutor—him.

If only he'd found the words to tell her the truth earlier this morning, when he'd held her in his arms and felt she was all the woman he'd ever want to hold. When he'd tasted her sweet mouth and knew he'd never need to taste another. Right. He could have said, "Zoe, I want us to go on like this forever. Stay with me, and let me prove to you that not every man will hurt you the way Jack did. Oh, by the way, I'm the guy who's going to prosecute you today." The only difference that would have made is that all hell would have broken loose five hours sooner.

Words, words, words. What good were words, anyway? A woman wanted a man to show, not tell. For days—and nights—he'd searched his brain for a way to show her how much he wanted her to stay, not just any way, but the right way. When he'd hit on the idea of a singing telegram, he'd figured he'd hit bottom, and hit his head against the wall. But at that moment, the lights had gone on in Zoe's house, and he'd thought, *Maybe I ought to go over there and make sure she's all right. And then maybe I ought to sweep her into my arms and kiss her breathless, then just walk away. Just like in the movies.*

He saw it now the way he'd seen it then. . . . Zoe was running after him. "Mitch! Don't go! I'll stay!" He was pretending he didn't hear her, of course, but he slowed his pace so she could catch up to him. And at last she did, in the middle of Magnolia Street, in the rain. "Oh, Mitch, Mitch, Mitch. My hero." She was clinging to him, smothering him with kisses. "The minute I saw you I knew you were my destiny. Whatever the obstacles facing us, we can overcome them. Together." Music was swelling. Their children, including Sarah Jane, were gathering around them in a group hug. The dogs were back-flipping and barking, back-flipping and barking. The neighbors were pouring onto their porches and applauding. . . .

Only it wasn't applause he was hearing now. It was Zoe, slapping her hand on the bench. "Your Honor, I refuse to be prosecuted by this man after what he did to me last night."

"Last night?" Judge McDowell looked at his clerk. "This could be more interesting than we thought."

"Not to me!" Zoe snapped her gaze from the judge back to Mitch. "Oooo, when I think of last night . . ."

Judge McDowell raised his eyebrows. "Last night, again? Must have been somethin'."

"It was nothing, Your Honor," Mitch said, glancing at the judge as he took Zoe by the shoulders.

She threw off his hold. "It was not only nothing. It was irraterial and immelevant!"

Angus P. McDowell pointed his gavel at Zoe. "I'll be the judge of what is and isn't immele—Irrater—Anyway, that's what I get paid for. Now will somebody please tell this court what happened last night?"

Mitch stepped to the bench. "I believe Ms. Laurence is referring to the fact that I kissed her, Your Honor," he said softly.

The judge sat forward. "Tried to bribe you with her wiles, eh? I'd say that was *totally* relaterial to this case."

Zoe charged the bench. "I didn't even know then that he was a prosecutor. But if I had, I'd gladly have kissed him—I'd have kissed him off!" Folding her arms, she leveled a sneer at Mitch. "Thank you for making it so easy for me to leave."

And so hard for me to stay, Mitch thought. Hard having to look at that house where she'd lived, if only for a while. Hard having to wonder where she was, whether she was all right. Whether she was missing him as much as he was missing her. "Zoe, for the last time, don't go."

"You must be joking." She propped her hands on her waist. "After the way you deceived me, give me one good reason why I should stay."

"I'll give you one," the judge said. "I gotta convict you. Now, if it's not troublin' you, too much, Mr. Ballard, proceed with your case."

"Yes, Your Honor." But, after taking a deep breath and gazing from Judge McDowell to the woman who'd judged him deceptive, Mitch couldn't proceed. Not with the case, not with his life. And not just because of the angry hurt in Zoe's eyes.

Because of the hurtfulness in Sarah Jane's words before he'd left for the courthouse, when he'd told her he had to prosecute Bink's mother and she'd thrown the mother of all hissy fits. She'd said that she was going to lose her best friend all because of his stupid job, and that she would never forgive him. When he'd pointed out—desperately and foolishly—that the Laurences were probably moving, anyway, Sarah had retorted that it didn't matter because she'd probably have to move, too, in order to have any friends at all. The kids in Perfection would be afraid that he would "persecute" their mothers the way he had Bink's. Why did he have to be a "persecutor," anyway? And only an assistant one, at that. It wasn't as though he ever put anybody really nasty in jail. Just dumb ole boys who drank too much at places like Booger's and got into fights over dumb ole girls like Lila.

Why couldn't you have been what Mommy wanted, and then maybe she would have stayed and we'd all still be together?

Now, hearing for the hundredth time the recrimination in his daughter's voice before she'd run off to her room, Mitch lowered his head to his hand. Maybe he *was* to blame for the breakup of his home. Maybe, if he'd taken that job with that big law firm in Louisville . . . he'd be a partner by now. But he hadn't wanted to spend the rest of his life shuffling papers around a table at real estate closings. And he hadn't wanted to leave Perfection, where the trying of a leash law violation was enough to pack the courthouse. Folks around town still took a personal interest in seeing justice done, though when one of Booger's regulars came to trial, they came mostly to see the show. He had to admit he'd always enjoyed those cases himself. He enjoyed his work, doing his part, however small, to preserve the peace in and around Perfection. To preserve a way of life.

But that hadn't been enough to make his wife proud of him, nor now, apparently, his daughter. Maybe he'd expected too much of them. Or too little of himself. More than ever he felt like a permanent—

"Mitch?" Seeing him grow pale and sway, as that mighty tree in her front yard had under the assault of last night's lightning and wind, Zoe felt her anger give way to alarm. "Are you all right?"

At the sound of Zoe's soft voice, feeling her soft touch to his sleeve, Mitch lifted his head from his hand. Seeing her was like seeing the sun break through storm clouds. A red-gold halo surrounded her head, and her eyes had gone from murderous to ministering. Suddenly, all he wanted to do was talk to her, buy her a cup of coffee, and just talk. For weeks he'd starved himself of sleep thinking of her, of her and her family and his daughter. Of how he wanted to make them all happy, of how he worried he never could, never could be everything they needed him to be. Now, he wanted to tell her what he'd been thinking, had first thought of telling her only hours ago when she'd said she loved roses but meant that she'd love any gift a man—maybe even he—might give her, as long as it came from his heart. At least, he thought that was what she'd meant. He had to know for sure.

"Zoe?"

He not only sounded lost, disoriented, Zoe thought, he appeared that way, too. Beneath a knitted brow, his gaze was as uncertain as the haggard, haunted air about him was palpable. He was frightening her. "I'm here, Mitch," she said, stepping closer, slipping her hand into his. "What can I do?"

"Give me a straight answer to a straight question."

"If that's what you want. Shoot."

He tilted his head. "Do *you* think I'm a failure?"

Zoe's breath caught. When she'd said shoot, she hadn't meant through the heart. *"Failure?"* Letting go of his hand, she stepped back, her arms spread wide and her gaze floundering for understanding. "A rat for not telling me you were going to prosecute me, yes. But—" She raised her eyes to his. "You're an assistant county prosecutor." She turned to the crowd. "I mean, that's really important work—don't y'all think?"

A wave of assent rolled her way. In it, at the back of the room, surfaced a sweet-looking, jug-eared little man—no more than five feet two—wearing a white linen suit and a bow tie.

"Mitch Ballard's the fairest and most honest assistant county attorney we ever had, and that's for doggone sure!"

Amidst whistles and applause, Mitch joined Zoe at the railing. Turning to him, she gestured toward the crowd. "There, you see. You're a hero, and not just to—"

Realizing she was about to say, "me," she clutched her throat and swallowed, as if something had gotten stuck in it. Something had. The truth. If a hero was the kind of man who never shirked a duty to his family or to his community, who stopped to help strangers, gave his protection to women, mentored fatherless little boys, and danced like Patrick Swayze, then Mitch was a hero. Except for the part of him that was a rat for not telling her he was going to prosecute her today.

"To that little man in the back of the room," she said, completing her sentence if not revealing her thoughts.

Smiling dubiously, Mitch scratched his temple. "I'm not sure how much of an endorsement that was, coming from Booger."

Owl-eyed, Zoe took another look at the little man. *"That's* Booger? Where's the ponytail, the tattoo, the Grateful Dead T-shirt? Where's his belly button, not to mention his belly?"

"You must be thinking of his wife," Mitch replied, then raised his hands to the gallery in a signal to quiet down. "Listen folks, I'm deeply touched by your support because y'all are the ones I'm here to serve, and I mean that." He braced himself against the railing.

"I love this town, this whole county. And I love my job. But I have to tell you, it doesn't afford many extras. I'm not complaining, mind you, because since the factory closed a lot of you are having a hard enough time providin' the basics." He shoved his hands in his pockets. "But, like some of you, I've started wondering if I couldn't do better in a place like Lexington or Louisville. Or even Atlanta."

From the crowd came gasps and pleas for him not to go, and finally, the silence of disbelief. Mitch shared it, realizing it hadn't occurred to him until he'd heard his own words that if Zoe was set on leaving Perfection, he might as well, too. He might just as well follow Sarah Jane to Atlanta, much as he hated everything about the idea, and end his anguish over losing her.

Zoe, too, stood stunned. And perplexed. Her leaving Perfection was one thing. She was a transplant. Not even that. A visitor. But Mitch? Only hours ago he'd kissed her with the assurance of a man who knew who he was because he knew where he belonged. Between then and now, what emotional storm had uprooted his very identity? And threatened Perfection's? Because she suddenly had no doubt that if Mitch left Perfection, the town would never be the same. Maybe it would not even survive.

"You listen to me, Mitch Ballard," she said, yanking him around by the arm. "The judge is right. There's entirely too much moving on, and not enough staying put these days. The grass is always greener, and all of that. But what you don't realize is that some places don't even have grass. There's more to consider in life than money, you know."

Harvey stood up. "Is there a doctor in the house? Make that a priest. My daughter must be having a near-death experience!"

At all the laughter that tumbled out after her dad's remarks, Zoe charged the gallery railing. "I meant what I said! I know this sounds clichéd, but happiness really can't buy gold."

A sea of perplexed faces only encouraged her to dive in, with her new twang.

"Y'all just don't appreciate what you have here that you cain't find ever'where. Take my family and me, for example. We came to your teemin' shore a tired, poor, huddled mass yearnin' to breathe no more diesel fumes. And what did we find, we wretched refuse of the cruel city that rendered us homeless? I mean, other than a parking ticket on our windshield and where the restrooms are in the courthouse? We found a home."

Raising her finger, she began pacing.

"And I'm not talking about wood and stone, and a roof that leaks! I'm talking about a real ho-o-o-me." Here, she clapped her hand over her heart. "A place where neighbors still welcome new neighbors with bird cakes and carrot cages. Where they get to know you well enough to gossip about you, and with you. Yes, I'm talking about reciprocity! Home is where people don't wait to be asked a favor, they volunteer. Like watching each other's husbands, so some can soak in the tub and others can have candlelight dinners with their kids. Like, like coming over in a thunderstorm in the middle of the night because they saw your lights on and thought you might be awake." Her eyes wide, she shifted them between their corners. "And . . . in trouble. Naturally."

"From what I've heard, Mrs. Laurence," the judge said, drawing Zoe's gaze, "if you're awake you're naturally in trouble."

As the crowd roared, Mitch turned Zoe to himself. "I knew it. You love this place, too. It's already a part of you. You're staying!"

"You're crazy! I've heard of kiss and tell, but kiss and prosecute?"

"Errrr!" Letting her go, Mitch clamped his hands behind his back to keep them from pulling his hair out. God only knew why he wanted her to stay. Whenever he was with her, he was in danger of losing hair.

"I was merely reminding you," Zoe continued, fingering the scarf around her neck, "that there are advantages to living here you won't find in Atlanta."

Mitch released a long sigh, lowering his voice. "Try convincing Sarah Jane of that."

"Sarah? Oh, I think I see now." Zoe entwined her arms, her voice low, too. "She's behind all this talk about your being a failure and leaving town."

"She blames me for the divorce. Says if I'd just tried harder to be successful—"

Zoe gripped his upper arms, feeling the same wonder at their strength beneath the sleek fabric of his suit coat that she'd had when watching him fire basketballs with Toby. "Mitch, she's a child, and seeing how her mother lives, she confuses wealth with success. For that matter, don't most adults?" Sliding her hands down his arms, she meshed her fingers with his. "But in time, she'll realize which of her parents is the true success."

"Yeah, the one with the six-bedroom house."

"The one who gave her a home." Zoe squeezed his hands. "You've just got to stand firm and believe in yourself."

Mitch rubbed a crease in his forehead. "I'm not sure I can anymore, Zoe."

She pressed her palm to his cheek, loving the contrast that was Mitch himself, rugged yet tender. "Yes, you can," she said. "*I* do."

Suddenly, Mitch knew the reason he wanted her to stay, had wanted her to from the beginning.

The Precious Thing.

Taking her hand from his cheek, he folded her fingers in his. "Thank you."

Hearing the crack in his voice, Zoe rushed to mend it, with the truth. "Mitchell Lee Ballard, don't you know that it's just not in you to fail? Not at your job, not as a father, not as a man. I've known that ever since that night in the factory. I'll never forget the way you came charging when you heard me scream. How safe you made me feel, and when you called me 'baby', how cherished." She gazed off, a smile on her lips. "And then you just danced away all my fears." She looked back. "You still haven't told me what song we were dancing to."

As the music started inside his head, his heart, Mitch gazed down at the back of Zoe's hand in his. To the slow, sensuous rhythm he ran his thumb over it, over where it was soft and where it showed the scars of battle with that long-neglected old house on Magnolia Street. From what he'd seen of it just hours ago, Zoe had won. She hadn't unpacked her belongings, but she'd filled that house with her incredible energy, her unbeatable spirit. She'd breathed new life into it, the way she just had into him.

'Course, whether a house or a man, when Zoe set about renovating you, he thought, you'd better be prepared to be shellacked and waxed. But he could handle that, he thought as he scratched the itchy patch on his chest where new hair was growing in. If only he could make her stay. Maybe he should have sent the singing telegram, even though the only costume they had was King Kong. Or borrowed the money from Lou to hire that skywriter. Or rented that billboard out on the highway. Too late now. But she'd given him a gift, the gift of faith in himself, and the least he could do, as she'd said, was reciprocate. He could tell her the name of the song that had come into his head the first time he'd held her, and ever since, every time he'd looked into those amazing green eyes of hers— the way he was now.

"Promise you won't laugh?"

"Not unless I was right, and it really was 'La Bamba'."

Smiling and shaking his head, Mitch looked down.

He saw her lovely hand in his, and suddenly, all doubt, fear, and embarrassment left him, left him only with the truth. He raised his eyes to hers and spoke in a clear, strong voice.

" 'When a Man Loves a Woman'."

Zoe felt the ground give way beneath her, but she wasn't afraid, because she had his word, shining as brightly as the light in his eyes, to cling to. Rising on her toes, she threw her arms around his neck. "Oh, Mitch. Don't go. I'll stay. Whatever the obstacles facing us, we can overcome them. Together."

"Words, words, words." Mitch raised his hands to her waist. "Wow."

Zoe half-frowned, half-laughed. "Is that all you can say?"

"Wow, darlin'?"

Suddenly, the light in Mitch's eyes turned to fire, and Zoe knew he had oh, so much more to say. And how she loved the way the man talked. She closed her eyes. He wrapped her in his arms. And kissed her so exquisitely that she thought she would die.

And to applause, no less, which Angus P. McDowell gaveled down. Together, she and Mitch turned their faces to him.

"As I said, I get paid to judge, and in my expert opinion you two are ready to go for the gold. Only not in my court." He stuck a fresh wad of gum in his mouth. "Proceed, Mr. Ballard."

Mitch released Zoe, cleared his throat, and smoothed down his tie. "Thank you, Your Honor. The county charges that on the morning of—"

"Ex-*cuse* me?" Zoe tugged Mitch's sleeve. "Did you or did you not just tell me you loved me? Well, practically."

"Practically?" Mitch looked away, then back. "Yeah."

"And you still intend to prosecute me?"

"Darlin', that's my job. You said yourself it was important work." Mitch drew her to his side. "Now just don't say another word," he whispered, "and everything will be all right." He looked at the judge. "The defendant pleads guilty, Your Honor."

"I most certainly do—" Zoe's outrage went mute behind Mitch's hand over her mouth.

"Oh, dandy, dandy," Judge McDowell said. "That'll be one hundred dollars. I'm reducin' your fine because my godson, here, is sweet on you."

Zoe shot up, her eyes big as quarters. *'Eh-eh?'*

"How's that?"

"She said she's much obliged, Your Honor."

"Sounded to me like she said *'godson?'*—but what do I know? Tell her I'd be much obliged if she'd pay her fine to the clerk, and get the heck out of my—Huh?" Judge McDowell leaned toward his beckoning clerk, who cupped his hand around the judge's ear. "Forgot to do that, you say? Well, guess I'd better. 'Nother one of those things they pay me for." Folding his hands, he leaned toward Zoe. "For the record, the defendant will state her name, address, and occupation."

Slowly, cautiously, Mitch removed his hand from her mouth.

Silence.

"Zoe?"

She glanced anxiously at Mitch, took a step toward the bench, and rattled off, "My name-is-Zoe-Elizabeth-Laurence-I-live-at-two-twenty-two-Magnolia Street." She stepped back.

Frowning, the judge scratched his head. "Seems to me I asked for one more piece of information."

Mitch inclined his head toward Zoe's. "I'm the prosecutor, and I just got your fine reduced," he whispered. "The least you could do is tell the judge your occupation. One simple word."

"Remember when you said not to say another word? I choose that one."

"Mrs. Laurence," the judge began, drumming his

fingers, "when the only thing getting tried in my courtroom is my patience, nobody wins."

Silence.

"*Zo*-ee!"

"Okay!" She looked from Mitch to the judge. "I'm
a b-b-b—"

"A bubba-ba? Isn't that one ba too many? And anyway, shouldn't it be, maybe . . . bubbette?" Abruptly,
Angus P. McDowell shot Zoe a stern look. "Last
chance, Mrs. Laurence."

Looking down, Zoe played with her fingers.
"Imabbkrrrr."

"What's that you're mumblin'? You're a baker?"

"I'm a banker!" Hearing a world-class, giant, sucking sound, Zoe turned to the crowd. "It's true. I work
for the Progress and Pride National Bank."

"That'll still be a hundred dollars," the judge said.
"And ten days in jail!" With a rap of his gavel, he
walked off the bench.

Zoe watched her friends and neighbors walk out of
the courtroom, walk out on her. "Please try to understand! At first, I didn't see the point of telling you,
because I thought I'd be leaving. And then . . . you
all came to mean so much to me, I didn't want to lose
your . . . Kath, I tried to tell you just a little while ago,
remember?"

But Kathy Hardy didn't listen. No one listened. At
last, only Zoe and Mitch remained. She faced him. The
judge's sentence was nothing compared to the one in
Mitch's eyes.

Life without his love. No appeal.

NINE

Zoe sat in one of two cells in the jail attached to the Winsome County courthouse, alone—the most alone she'd ever felt in her life, including the time after Jack had left her. She'd had her children, then, and her mother, and a few friends that stayed around until, inevitably, their marriages and her divorce became an awkward mix. Now, her children were with her father, her mother was with the angels, and her friends were without mercy. She'd thought that by now one of them would have come to see her point of view, come around to offer forgiveness and a cake with a nail file in it. Maybe not Kathy Hardy, not just yet. After all, the Progress and Pride National Bank had put Dave out of work. But surely, after all this time, Mrs. Corbett or the Terwillikers might have softened, might have come to relieve the monotony of life on the inside. With a sigh, she checked her watch. Then, removing her lipstick from the pocket of her jacket on the cot beside her, she walked to the far wall, where she added another hash mark to the two already there. That made three hours in this hellhole.

Well, it wasn't exactly a hellhole, Zoe thought as she shielded her eyes from the blinding sun streaming through tieback chintz curtains on the window. But it wasn't 222 Magnolia Street. It wasn't home.

Of course, the house on Magnolia Street had been

home only briefly, between the time Mitch had told her he loved her—practically—and she'd said she'd stay, and the time he and an entire zip code—practically—had evicted her. From their hearts. That was why she'd never felt more alone. Jack had never really let her into his heart. When he'd left, she'd felt angry and bitter, but not displaced. Not banished from the Garden, from the Eden on Magnolia Street, from the paradise in Mitch's eyes, his arms. His word. Now retracted.

Zoe lay back in the Barcalounger beneath the window. Overlapping her hands on her abdomen, she closed her eyes and imagined the suffocating scent of carnations, the sickly sweet mournfulness of organ music, and the steady, slow shuffle of feet. She sniffled, but never quite coaxed a tear even as she realized that aside from her family, nobody would come to her funeral. The children, that was it. And maybe not even Dad, if Lou decided he finally respected her well enough.

"Zoe, honey, you okay?"

Dad, you came! But how can I be okay? I'm dead.

Abruptly, Zoe sat up and out of her daydream. "Dad?" Gazing through the bars of her cell, she saw her father smile at her as a police officer walked him by in handcuffs. She leaped out of the recliner and ran to her cell door. "What are you doing here? Where are the kids?"

"The kids are with Lou, and what does it look like I'm doing?" Harvey said as the officer opened the door to the adjacent cell and then removed the cuffs. "Gettin' thrown in stir." Hiking up his pants with his elbows, he peeled his upper lip back from his teeth. "But don't worry, doll, they haven't built the joint yet that Harvey Beck can't bust out of."

Zoe watched with horror as the officer locked her father away. After he'd gone, she scurried to the end of her cell nearest Harvey's. "What are you in for?"

"Well, it was like this, shweetheart—"

"Just give it to me straight, will you?"

There was a long silence, then, "Remember when Judge McDowell said Mitch was his godson? Well, from what Lou told me, I knew that she and her husband had made Angus Mitch's godfather as a consolation prize."

"What was first prize?"

"Lou."

"You mean he was in love with her?"

"Still is. He's been proposing to her, on and off, since nineteen fifty-seven. Yesterday, he asked her again. Lou told him she was leaning toward saying yes, but she needed more time."

"More than over four decades?"

"She said something new came up that she had to think about."

"Something by the name of Harvey Beck?"

"The man, the legend."

Zoe rolled her eyes. "Okay, so you made her think again about marrying another man. That's not against the law, is it?"

"No, but attempting to bribe a judge is. That's what he had me arrested for."

Zoe gasped. "That's ridiculous. Bribe him to do what?" Suddenly, her eyes grew wide. Grabbing two bars, she wedged her face between them. "Dad, tell me you didn't try to pay him to give up Lou."

"Zoe, you know I don't have enough money to pay Bink to take my turn cleaning the bathroom bowl. But I did suggest to him that we trade for her."

"*Trade* for her? What did you offer him, a third baseman?"

There was a long pause, then Harvey said, "I offered him Lou. I told him that if he'd let you out of jail, I'd never see her again."

As his words gripped her heart, Zoe lost her hold on the bars and on her image of her father as Mr.

Never There When You Need Him. He was not only there for her, he was in the next cell. Closing her eyes, she swallowed a lump of emotion. "You . . . really tried to give up Lou . . . for me?"

"I know what you're thinking," Harvey replied. "That all these years I haven't been much of a father to you, so why now?" He exhaled deeply. "I guess because for the first time in your life, you got into a jam you couldn't get yourself out of."

"You mean all I ever had to do to get you to love me was to get sent to the pokey?"

"I've always loved you, Zoe. You're my only child. It's just that . . . you were always so sure of yourself."

Her shoulders slumping, Zoe pressed her forehead to cold metal. "Oh, Dad, so often that was just an act."

Pause. "I wish I'd known."

Pause. "You didn't?"

"No, but I should have made it my business to know. I just figured your mother was all the parent you needed, the way you two were always together, talking and laughing. More like sisters. I felt like . . . an outsider."

Zoe looked up, then at the wall between her and her father. "Oh, I *wish* I'd known."

"You were the child, I was the grown-up. At least, that's the way it should have been, instead of the other way around." Silence settled between them and stayed awhile before Harvey breached it. "Anyway, that's why now. Because we never really knew each other the way a father and daughter should. And because—"

Zoe saw his hand, strong and open, reach toward her through his cell door.

"I was hoping it's not too late . . . Princess."

The word unearthed a long-buried memory, of a very young girl, young enough to be carried everywhere in her father's arms. He'd called her "Princess" and she'd called him—she lowered her lids over the tears welling in her eyes—"Daddy." Reaching through her own door and stretching as far as she could, she managed to grasp his fingers. "It's never too late to get to know someone you already love."

Harvey gave her fingers a squeeze. "That's what I was thinking, and not just about you and me."

"You and who else?"

"Not me and who else. You and Mitch Ballard."

Zoe drew her hand back. "That's all over, Dad. He hates me."

"He hates bankers. He loves you—well, practically. But once he gets to know you he won't hate all bankers anymore, because he'll love you *im*-practically, which happens to be the only way to really love someone."

Massaging the back of her neck, Zoe shuffled to the center of her cell and slowly turned in a circle. "You really think so?"

"You love him?"

"I *think* so."

"Then I think so, too."

"Dad? I *do* love him. Illogically, impractically, and a lot. And I want to make up for the way his ex-wife hurt him. I want him to know that he'll always be my hero, just the way he is." Zoe joined her hands as if praying and brought them to her lips. "I want to spend the rest of my life making him happy."

"One thing I've always known about you, Zoe," Harvey began, "you can do anything you set your mind to. Of course, that's only one of the reasons I'm so proud of you."

Zoe smiled softly. "Thank you." She didn't bask long in his unexpected praise, however, before a cloud of self-doubt eclipsed its warmth. "I don't know, Dad . . . Mitch loves this town, but the town hates me. So if he loves me, impractically, the town will practically hate him. I don't think that'll exactly make him happy."

"Don't you bother about this town," a female voice said.

Zoe turned toward it. "Lou?"

"Lulu!"

Dressed in a clean plaid shirt tucked into tight jeans, LouAnn Ballard propped her hands on her still small waist and called out, "If that was Harvey Beck addressin' me, he's wastin' his time, because I'm not speakin' to him!" She approached Zoe's cell and took hold of two bars. "Listen, dearie, folks around here are hardheaded, but they're not addled. They know you're the only one that good-for-nothing bank ever sent here that wanted to make a home, not just a profit so you could get sent back to whatever big city you came from. And they'll admit as much, in time. Kathy Hardy has already. She's keepin' the kids."

"She is?" Zoe beamed, then asked suddenly, "Lou, how long have you been standing there?"

"Oh, about—"

"Yoo-hoo! Remember me, Lou darlin'? Marvy Harvey?"

Lou sighed, then threw back her head and yelled at the ceiling. "The Harvey Beck I remember didn't need Miracle Ear. He'd have heard me loud and clear when I said I wasn't speakin' to him, which I'm still not!" She looked at Zoe. "As for how long I was eavesdroppin' on you and *that man I'm not speakin' to*—" Reaching through the bars, she took Zoe's hand. "Long enough to hear what a mother wants to hear from the woman her son's in love with, practically."

Zoe squeezed Lou's hand. "You're an angel," she replied. Then, lowering her voice, she added, "But um, why aren't you speaking to Dad? Not that you probably don't have a good reason."

"Why am I not speakin' to Harvey Beck? you ask."

Zoe covered her ringing eardrums.

"Well, it's like this—" The door to the cell area squealed open, and Lou looked toward it. "There you are! And about time, too."

The recipient of Lou's chiding, Zoe saw with amazement, was an officer approaching with the keys to the cells.

"Well, hurry up." Lou slapped the man's arm with the back of her hand. "Let the gal out."

As the keys clinked in the lock, Zoe hurriedly gathered her jacket and scarf. A moment later, she stood outside her cell, free and freely embracing Lou. "How did you do it?"

"I just went and told that old coot Angus that he was givin' Perfection a bad reputation as a bait and fine hick town, and I didn't much like it. Told him to wipe your conviction right off the books, too. And he did."

"Just because you told him to?" Harvey snorted. "I don't believe it. You agreed to marry him, didn't you?"

"What do you care?" Lou charged over to his still locked cell. "Isn't that what you had in mind for me to do when you tried usin' me as barter?"

"You know why I did that!"

"Well, of course I know. For your daughter, and what better reason? But if you'd come to me first, like the friends I thought we were, I'd have told you I'd already gotten Angus to order her release, and just for the asking."

"Thank God," Harvey said softly. Then, "Lou, you didn't happen to get him to release me, too, just for the asking?"

"Could be I did," she replied. "On the other hand, could be I decided you belong right where you are, you old fool!" Taking Zoe by the arm and the officer in tow, Lou headed toward the exit.

"Don't you think you're being a little hard on Dad?" Zoe whispered.

Lou tsked. "Where's your sense, girl? Can't you see I've got him where I want him?"

Zoe looked back. "In jail?"

Huffing, Lou shook her head. "You young women. So book-smart, yet so dumb when it comes to men."

"I know they're weird."

"But you don't know how to deal with 'em. Now pay attention."

"To what?"

"Wait just a darn minute!"

At Harvey's call, Lou halted. "To *that.*" Turning, she gazed past the officer. "Yes, Harv?"

"If you talked to Angus Peabrain McDowell before I did, how did you know he put me in here?"

With the touch of her hand, Lou moved the officer, who was twice her size, out of her way, and advanced on Harvey. "You sent the kids over to me, right? And you made them promise not to tell me you were going to see Angus, which that smart as a whip granddaughter of yours rightly took to mean that that was exactly what you wanted her to tell me."

Harvey looked away. "What else did she tell you I told her not to tell you?"

"To always remember two things. That you loved her and Toby, and that your favorite movie is *A Star is Born.*"

"Da-a-d," Zoe said, "I thought your favorite movie was *Beach Blanket Bingo.*"

"I get confused. They both have an ocean in them."

"You get confused," Lou echoed mockingly. "Humph. You know very well, Harvey Beck, that you wanted me to know you were going to Angus to be a big hero and give me up so Zoe could go free. What you didn't know and I *did* was that he'd be spiteful enough to call it bribery and jail you. So, naturally, I had to go and thank him for keeping you from wadin' off into the Ohio just like James Mason did into the Pacific after he gave up Judy Garland."

Zoe clutched her breast. "Dad, you didn't really plan to . . . to—?"

"To see if I'd come runnin' after him blubberin' that I loved him? That's what I figured, too. On the other hand, I couldn't be sure." Lou petted the long, thick braid cascading over her shoulder. "After all, I do have charms that drive men to distraction." She rounded on Harvey, wagging her finger in his face. "So until you swear to me that you'll never again even think of doin' anything so lamebrained, you can just keep behind bars." Folding her arms, she turned her back on him.

"Aw, Lou . . ." Harvey's voice was gentle and low as he laid his hand on her shoulder. "You *do* love me."

"Well . . ." She looked over her shoulder at him. "You have your distractin' charms, too, Harv."

Harvey found her hand, turned her toward him, then got down on one knee. Zoe watched as he looked up at Lou with a light in his eyes that spread to the reaches of her own heart. "LouAnn Ballard, will you do me the honor of marrying me?"

Between the bars, Lou cupped his cheek. "I don't know why, except you make me happy, but yes, Harvey Beck. I'll marry you." She motioned to the officer to unlock Harvey's door, then gave Zoe a wink and said, "What are you standin' there for? You'll find yours at the river, at Ballard's Point."

Zoe's heart started for the door, but her pride held her feet in place. "If you're referring to your son, the assistant county prosecutor, why would I want to find *him*? He certainly didn't object to the judge locking me up."

"And what's more, he didn't want me gettin' you out early, either."

"Oh, that man!"

"He said jail was the surest way of keepin' you here in Perfection."

"Oh, that man." Breaking into a grin, Zoe ran to hug Lou and her father. "I love you both." She dashed to the door, then paused and looked back at them. "I almost forgot. After the trouble I've caused Vi Pringle, if I don't take that transfer back to Chicago when it comes through, she'll fire me. I can't stay here without a job."

"That reminds me," Harvey said as he removed an envelope from his jacket pocket and handed it to Zoe. "This came for you today."

Seeing the Progress and Pride Bank logo and the Chicago postmark on it, Zoe tore the envelope open. She removed the letter inside and began reading.

After a moment, Harvey said, "Bad news, honey?"

"Yeah."

"You got the transfer."

"No. Constance Martin quit. I've been named the new manager of the Perfection branch of the bank."

"*That's* my girl. Since when is a promotion bad news?"

"Since it means having to foreclose on people's houses." Zoe looked from Harvey to Lou, to the ache in her heart. "Starting with Dave and Kathy Hardy's."

His tie loosened, his shirt collar open, and his jacket hanging over his shoulder from the hook of one finger, Mitch stood leaning against one of the massive bald cypresses that sheltered Ballard's Point. As the story went, the spot took its name from the first Ballard in Winsome County, MacDuff, who'd proposed to one Fionna MacTavish beneath the widespread branches of this very tree. He'd memorialized the occasion by having a portrait painted of Fionna standing in the foreground of the tree. Fionna had memorialized it by giving birth to a strapping baby boy exactly nine months later to the day, giving rise to speculation that old MacDuff had proposed more than marriage there. Ever proud of their heritage and ever since, the Ballard men had proposed marriage, and more, in the embrace of these sinuous old trees.

All except one Ballard, that is—him. He'd proposed to Ellie in the backseat of his car, and that hadn't been so much a conscious choice as collateral storm damage, though he'd been too young and stupid to know the difference, to know love from libido.

Then again, maybe he hadn't been, not entirely, he thought as he plucked a pebble from the ground and skipped it across the purling gray waters. Maybe the reason he'd broken with tradition was because he'd known, deep down, that he and Ellie hadn't shared whatever his forefathers and mothers had felt for one another that had enabled them to build lives and families, and a community. Maybe he'd known that if he'd ever stood with her on the Point, looking out at the river, he would have seen its timelessness; she would have seen only its flow. He would have wondered about the human dramas it must have witnessed, enacted on these very banks for thousands for years; she would have wondered how far away from Perfection it could take them in the little fishing boat he kept here. He wouldn't have judged her harshly for that, but then she would have asked him if he couldn't get them a bigger boat. Then she would have told him that if he couldn't, she'd just have to find somebody who could.

In a way, he was glad Ellie had found everything she'd always hoped for in a man. Charles was a bank. Hadn't he himself found everything he'd always hoped for in a woman? The problem was that Zoe was a banker. No, the problem was that Zoe was a banker and he was crazy about her, which meant that she'd have to give up banking or he'd have to give up hating bankers.

Then again, he thought as he walked down to the little boat at the river's edge, they could compromise. He'd give up hating bankers if she'd give up hating gambling, because there was talk of replacing this little dinghy with a riverboat casino. Worse, there was big talk that he was the man to get the deal done as the replacement for the current judge executive of Winsome County, who was stepping down because of ill health. As Mitch had left the courthouse after Zoe's trial, a committee of political insiders along with merchants, businessmen, and unemployed workers, including Dave Hardy, had approached him, proposing that he run in the special election to be held in six weeks for the most powerful office in the county. He was well-qualified, they'd assured him, but more importantly, he could win. Folks liked and trusted him; their outburst in support of him in the courtroom had confirmed that. But popular support alone wouldn't be enough, they'd said. He'd need money, and they could get plenty of it. All he had to do was back a referendum approving a Las Vegas casino operator's plan to build a gambling resort at Ballard's Point.

His answer had been swift and unambiguous. "Out of my way."

"Think of the jobs a casino would create."

"And the traffic, noise, pollution." He'd walked on.

They'd pursued him. "Imagine all those tourists, and the money that will follow them."

"And the crime."

"With a fortune in new tax revenues, we can afford to hire more officers."

"Great. They can make sure folks get home safely after they lose their life savings at the craps tables."

"Look at it this way, Mitch—there'll be more work for gambling addiction counselors."

Mitch had paused. "We don't have any."

They'd shrugged, laughing. "Build it, and they will come."

"And that's when I leave, for good." Mitch had looked each of them in the eye. "You're talking to the wrong man. Now, get the *hell* out of my way."

They'd parted, clearing a path for him, but at the bottom of the courthouse steps Dave had caught him by the arm. "Mitch, this casino is probably our last chance, but somebody has to convince people to vote for it. You're that somebody. You could save Perfection, man, the whole county." He'd gripped Mitch's arm imploringly. "I don't know what I'll do if I don't get work soon. I'm asking you as a friend, think about it."

What bothered him now, as he squatted beside the little boat, was that he was thinking about it. To his surprise, he found he liked the idea of running—of winning. If the committee had succeeded in anything, it was in convincing him that he could. Sarah Jane would like a father she could regard as a winner. She'd like the celebrity that would come to him, his name in the papers and his face on the news, and her share in his spotlight. She wouldn't have to worry about friends. As the daughter of the most powerful man in the county, she'd need a social secretary of her own. At last he could compete with Ellie for her. Not with money, though there would be more of that, but with something Ellie couldn't give her—distinction. In Atlanta, Sarah Jane would just be one of a number of little rich girls, but here she could be somebody. All he had to do, he thought as he rose and panned his gaze around Ballard's Point, was win.

And betray everything he believed in.

Betray a place where there were still more church steeples than jail cells, more teachers than blackjack dealers, more friends than strangers. Also, more jobless than there were jobs. For this place to survive, somebody had to shift that imbalance. Stepping on the rim of the boat, he tipped it toward him. If Dave was right, he was the only somebody.

Some somebody, he thought, stepping off the boat, setting it rocking. To save his home, he'd have to sacrifice its quiet heritage to the nonstop din of slot machines. He'd have to sacrifice his heart to it. He'd have to sacrifice Zoe, the poster girl for the innocent victims of gambling addicts. Seemed like he'd no sooner overcome one obstacle to their romance—the way his Sarah Jane felt about Zoe's Bink, he was all but certain she'd love the idea of their becoming stepsisters—than another one arose.

"Considering that my father and your mother just got engaged in the county jail, I thought we ought to talk."

Mitch looked up at the bank, where Zoe stood beneath the umbrella of MacDuff and Fionna's cypress, her hand grasping one of its branches. She was tall, beautiful, and she belonged there, where generations of women had accepted the proposals of generations of men, and the challenges of futures that had never been certain except for one thing, a love for each other and the things that make life not necessarily easy, but good. A staying kind of love.

And, if he brought the casino to Ballard's Point, the leaving kind.

Beneath the shade of a cypress, Zoe gazed from Mitch to the river. Here, at Ballard's Point, it was a body so slender and graceful that she found it hard to believe it was the same broad muddy brute that muscled past cities like Pittsburgh, Cincinnati, and Louisville hundreds of miles to the northeast, on its way to Perfection.

And it reminded her of Mitch, she thought as she gazed back at him. He was no brute, of course. Just broad-shouldered, like that other Ohio, and lithe, like this one. She recalled how he'd danced, the effortless way he'd absorbed her weight while leaving her senses to flood with his touch, his scent, his kiss, the way they were now at her memory of swaying in his embrace. Hungering for him, she prayed she wouldn't have to live with only a memory, because as she watched him begin yet another cycle of restlessly gazing from the little boat to the river—pacing the water's edge, hurling pebbles at the opposite bank, then returning to the boat and setting it rocking—she understood why he'd come to this tranquil spot. He was a man entrenched in conflict, and she had a good idea she was deep at the heart of it.

The question remained whether she was deeply enough entrenched in Mitch's heart to overcome his conflict over her being a banker. Both Dad and Lou had thought so, but that was before she'd told them she'd been instructed to foreclose on the Hardys' house. Now she'd have to tell Mitch, gamble her heart on the less than even odds she could get him to listen past that fact to an idea she had for saving the Hardys' house, and Perfection.

Drawing a breath for courage, she left the shade of the cypress and met him under a bone-baking sun, halfway down the bank. As she peered up at him, a breeze stirred his hair. She reached up to push troubled black strands back from the blue oasis of his eyes, but arrested her touch, instead. It really wouldn't be right until she'd been honest.

"You don't seem surprised at my news about the folks."

The sun was kissing Zoe's lips the way Mitch wanted to but didn't dare until he could be sure his kiss wouldn't betray her; until he'd decided whether or not to support the riverboat. Stepping back, he gave her a sideways smile. "Before Lou left to break the Laurence gang out of the joint, she told me Harvey didn't know it yet, but he was going to pop the question."

Chuckling, Zoe shook her head. "We're even, then. I'm not surprised at your news." She stared at the loosened knot in his tie, wanting to undo it completely. "Think it'll last?" She raised her eyes to his. "The marriage, I mean."

Mitch cradled his jacket in his arms, wishing that he was carrying Zoe away from all conflict, all obstacles. "Lou seems happy."

Zoe inhaled deeply, telling herself the fresh air was

good for her, knowing it was Mitch's sun-brewed cologne she wanted to take in. "Dad, too."

"You realize what this means, don't you?" Placing his fingertips on his cocked hips and looking down at the ground, Mitch saw Zoe's toes—polished with Pretty in Pink—peeking through a pair of sexy, high-heeled sandals. Of course, at the ends of legs likes Zoe's, combat boots would look sexy. Swallowing a lump of desire, he snapped his gaze up at her. "This means we'll have relations. No! I mean . . . y-yes, we will be, um, definitely related."

Zoe stared at him, wondering if he'd been standing under the sun too long. And if that Freudian slip was the result, she thought, she was going to keep him out in it on the chance that when she said "foreclosure" he'd hear "foreplay."

"I've thought about that," she replied. Then, squinting up at him, she crossed the bridge he'd unknowingly built, into dangerous territory. "So, how do you feel about having a banker for a stepsister?"

Mitch was still thinking about those sandals, and her cute toes, slim ankles, and shapely calves. And if he wanted to keep his sanity, he'd better get off that tour right now. "Believe me," he began, turning to the river and trying to picture fat, whiskered, bottom-dwelling catfish, "you don't want to know."

Zoe stared at his big, broad, rude back. "Well," she said, throwing back her shoulders and planting her hands on her waist, "I guess that tells me."

"Oh, no it doesn't," Mitch shot over his shoulder. He caught sight of her breasts, sculpted by her tightly drawn blouse and swelling on her outrage. "Not by two—no! Half. Not by half."

Zoe peeked up at the sun, then down at her blouse. She didn't know what *Men Are Weird* . . . would advise, but suddenly, something told her the way a man responded to a woman's honesty had a lot to do with her delivery of it. Something told her to unbutton the top buttons of her blouse and widen the opening. "It's so-o-o hot today," she said, strolling in front of Mitch, running her hand down her throat to the tops of her breasts then reaching inside her blouse and patting, patting. She fixed her gaze on his, which, as Lou might have said, was right where she wanted it, on the deep V neck of her blouse. "Look, I know you need to get this off your chest."

Mitch grinned eagerly. "You do? I mean, do you need help?" Closing his eyes, he breathed in sharply. "Yes, yes, I do need help getting it off my chest." He looked at her. "What was it . . . exactly . . . I needed to get off my chest?"

Zoe bellowed her blouse for air, and to give Mitch a peek of cleavage. For someone who'd never once thought of using the allure of sex to butter a man up before breaking the crock over his head, she was finding it amazingly easy, and not the least unenjoyable. "For one thing, I gave you hell for not telling me you were going to prosecute me. So naturally, you want to give me hell for not telling you I was a banker."

Mitch was quick to discover that in airing her blouse, Zoe was also airing lace and lilac. "I love natural. I'm a very . . . natural kind of guy."

"I've noticed." Smiling sweetly, she took a step closer. "Ouch!"

As Zoe stumbled, Mitch caught her, only to fall himself—into the bottomless depths of her eyes gazing up at him. "You okay?"

Zoe breathed against him, feeling her power ply his strength. "These sandals are fine for jail, I guess, but not for terrain this . . . natural. I think I'll just take them off."

"Better let me," Mitch said, righting her and holding her steady.

Zoe batted her eyes up at him. "Maybe you'd butter, er, better. I might fall."

"I won't let you fall." *Unless it's in love with me.* "Just lean on me."

"When times are bad," Zoe said dreamily. "I mean, I'd like that." *For a change.* She couldn't have leaned on Jack without yelling *Timber!*

"You ready?"

"I'm ready."

Mitch flipped his jacket over one shoulder, then did a knee-bend to her feet.

Zoe braced her hands on his other shoulder.

He slid the strap of one shoe down her heel. Then, grasping her ankle, he slowly slipped the shoe forward and off her bare foot. He dropped the shoe, but held her foot, cupping the arch in his palm, wanting to lower his lips to her instep. "I think Prince Charming had this shoe thing backward."

"I suspect he was like Jack. He wasn't going to be happy until he'd tried it on every woman in the land."

"The shoe?"

"Not in Jack's fairy tale."

Jack. Mitch pictured a man in a black suit and broad-brimmed hat, brocade vest, and string tie. He was seated at a table piled high with poker chips, puffing on a cheroot and dealing from the bottom of the deck. Behind him, Zoe, thin and haggard, was making the rounds of the tables in a patched gown, begging for milk for her children. Abruptly removing her other shoe, Mitch rose and took her by the shoulders. "Zoe, there's something I have to tell you."

"I know," she said, trailing her finger down his chest as though she were basting him. "You have to tell me how you feel about me now that you know I'm a banker."

Mitch shivered at her touch, feeling her cook his goose.

Rising on her toes, Zoe raised her lips to his. "But if that's always going to be a problem for you . . ."

Mitch swirled his mouth over hers. Oh, God, how

he wanted it, wanted her, all of her. But not like this, not with a riverboat between them. He shoved away from her. "Darlin', I can't lie to you. There *is* a real problem here."

Seeing the cold, hard set of his eyes, Zoe's heart churned. Maybe what she'd tried to butter him up with was only margarine, after all. "All right, tell me. I can take it."

"You ready?"

"I'm ready."

"No, you've gotta be *really* ready."

"I'm ready!"

Another breeze wafted, turning Zoe's hair to a shimmer of copper around the emerald of her eyes. Behind her, the cypress stood tall, and suddenly she was that portrait of Fionna that Lou, with obvious intent, had hung in his room. He flung his coat to the ground. "Well, I'm not ready, damn it!" And, scooping her into his arms, he carried her up the bank and laid her beneath the low, lush branches of the tree. Kneeling over her, he cupped her cheek. "I love you, Zoe Laurence. Not practically, because you've been nothing but a pain since the day we met, and I don't imagine you're going to stop anytime soon. But darlin', I love you with my life."

The tears that sprang to Zoe's eyes were for the words he'd sown in her heart. She reached open arms up to him. "It's such a good life."

"Only one thing could make it better. You." Not exactly a marriage proposal, Mitch thought, but there was something he had to do first. Lowering himself into her waiting embrace, he covered her body with his, her mouth with his, her heart and soul with his.

So you are a brute, after all, Zoe thought, making tracks of her nails down his back. And she was glad of it. Glad he wasn't making love to her the way he'd danced. Instead of absorbing her he was branding her, burning his lips into hers, his soul into hers.

Burning them both into the soil beneath them. He hadn't proposed, exactly, but she had no doubt they were engaged in an act of permanence. That meant commitment and trust, and truth, forever. But she'd hadn't yet told him the truth, or so much as mentioned foreclosure before they'd begun this foreplay. The way he was playing, she decided, the truth could wait a little longer.

As Zoe reciprocated his deepening kiss, swirling her glorious tongue over his, words swirled through Mitch's mind. *What do you say we tie the knot, darlin'? Jeez, Mitch! Now, there's a proposal no woman could refuse, if she was desperate enough. Zoe, will you do me the honor of*— Honor. How honorable was it of him to propose to her before he told her about the casino, and the part he might have to play in bringing it to Perfection? But how could he risk losing what he had in his arms at this very moment? The world.

She could die kissing this man, Zoe thought, twining her tongue and her hungry groans with his. But could she live with herself if she took his trust, his love, while withholding the truth?

He might be holding the world in his arms, Mitch thought, but what did a man ultimately have to give to the world but his honor?

As Zoe wedged the flats of her hands between their bodies and pushed on Mitch's chest, Mitch pulled back. Her shove, timed to his withdrawal, rolled him onto his back.

Thunk.

"Ow, damn it!"

"Oooooo." Zoe shot up and onto her knees and peered anxiously down into Mitch's dazed eyes. "What happened?"

Mitch lay motionless. "If you look closely beneath my head, I think you'll find a tree root and my brains."

"I'm so-o-o sorry," she said, trying to pull him up by his shoulders. "Does it hurt?"

Sitting up and rubbing the knot on the back of his head, he gestured to the thick, protruding root. "Why don't you ask it? You have more experience asking if it hurts than I do."

"Well, how was I supposed to know you were going to pull away from me just as I pushed on you?"

"Why *did* you push me?"

Plucking a clover blossom, Zoe sat on her hip and bent her legs behind her. "I couldn't let things go any further. I was keeping something from you."

"Oh. Me, too."

"Yeah?"

"Yeah." Gently, Mitch stroked her hair. "Whatever it is, baby, it's okay. Nothing can ever change how I feel about you. Tell me."

When he called her "baby," she'd tell him state secrets, if she had any. "I've been named the new manager of the Perfection branch of the bank. I have to foreclose on several houses, including Dave and Kathy Hardy's."

"Oh, my God!" Mitch backed away from her. "It's worse than I thought."

"I knew you'd say that!" Zoe threw her hands up. "When a man tells you you can tell him anything, he means anything that doesn't involve his best friend!"

The muscles in his jaw flinching, Mitch smacked his right fist into his left palm. "That's why I'll have to do something." The gaze he shifted at Zoe was blue ice. "Something you won't like."

Thrusting her arm out, she scooted back. "It's no use, Mitch. Bankers are like weeds. Kill one, and ten more pop up in their place."

He looked at her as though she was crazy, which he had no doubt she was. "Look, ever since we met, who's been trying to kill whom? All I meant is that the economy here is in worse shape than I thought, and I have to do something to help bring in jobs." He drew a deep breath. "I've been asked to run for the county judge executive's office."

Zoe looked at him querulously. "What's not to like about that?" She took his hand in hers. "I don't know what a county judge executive is, but I know you'd make a great one."

Mitch paused. "Even if I have to bring a riverboat casino to Perfection, right here to Ballard's Point?"

Feeling her blood chill, Zoe let go of his hand. "And you said you loved me, with your life."

Mitch grabbed her shoulders. "I do! But darlin', this place is a big part of my life, and it's dyin'. That boat's all the chance we've got."

Zoe clasped her hands around his neck. "Not . . . necessarily." After planting a kiss on his mouth, she rose and stretched her hand down to him. "Will you come with me? I want to show you something I think you can gamble your campaign on without having to bring gambling to Perfection."

Mitch looked behind him, at MacDuff and Fionna's cypress tree. *I'll bring her back. If God's kind to us, and together we can make whatever her idea is work, I'll bring her back and ask her to marry me.* Taking Zoe's hand, he sprang to his feet. "Where are we going?"

"Where else?" She shot him a sly smile. "The old furniture factory."

TEN

"Can't you just see it, Mitch?"

Among weeds and wildflowers growing in the cracks in its parking lot pavement, Mitch stood beside Zoe, looking at the big, old, two-story factory. With its windows staring like soulless eyes, its signs missing letters like teeth, and its entrance barred, it looked more like an architectural lifer than a building that could be brought back to life. Shaking his head doubtfully, he drew Zoe gently to his side. "I don't want to worry you, darlin', but doing hard time, even three hours, can cause a person to see what she wants to see."

"Hmm, maybe." Folding her arms, Zoe inclined her head toward his. "I'll admit there was a moment in that cell I thought I saw Harrison Ford taking off his shirt." Gazing up at him, seeing his scowl, she grinned. "Then I realized it was you.

"Disappointed?"

"Heartbroken. Especially when I discovered I was only dreaming." She gave him a wink. Then, wrapping her arms around his middle, she laid her head on his shoulder. "But I'm not just dreaming about putting this old place and Perfection to work again, Mitch. We can do it, all of us together."

Once again, in greater detail this time, Zoe told him her idea for turning the abandoned building into a complex of shops for local artisans and craftsmen like

Dave Hardy. Instead of one big corporation, she envisioned lots of small, specialty enterprises fueled by entrepreneurialism and providing employment for the area's abundance of currently idle talent.

"For example, have you seen the birdcages Mr. Terwilliker makes?" she asked, facing Mitch. "They're works of art. People would come from miles around to buy one."

"They'll have to wait until he gets back from his honeymoon," Mitch replied. "He stopped me on the way out of court, and he said that after seeing the way I took you in my arms and kissed you in front of God and all of Perfection, he decided to finally ask Miss Dunaway to elope with him. I believe they're on their way to Chicago as we speak."

Zoe smiled, thinking of the trip she'd planned for Mr. Terwilliker and had been so certain he'd never take. If he could not only take that trip, but take a bride, Perfection could take this old factory and manufacture hope and jobs and prosperity again.

"Look, Mitch," she said, taking his hand and directing him toward the factory. "Up there I see craft shops, and galleries filled with the work of local artists, and over there, antique shops. And below, in that corner, a restaurant featuring Kathy Hardy's fried chicken and Mrs. Corbett's carrot cake. And over there, we can build a blacksmith shop and stables, and a coach house for the horsedrawn carriages that will take tourists into town to Cousin Tilly's Ice Cream Emporium, 'Home of The World's Best Chocolate Malt,' and to more shops and restaurants, and even bed-and-breakfasts." Breathlessly, she went on describing her vision—pageants depicting local history, steamboat rides on the Ohio, fairs, flea markets, bluegrass music festivals, classic car rallies. "I don't know," she said, throwing up her hands at last. "Anything we can imagine we can do. We have the talent. All we need is the will."

The flush of excitement Mitch saw in her cheeks so

enchanted him that he hated himself for having to break its spell. "And money?" He took her warm sweet face in his hands. "I can't believe I'm about to say this, but what happened to the coldhearted, bottom-line banker I fell in love with?"

Encircling his wrists, Zoe gazed up at him through moist eyes. "She fell in love with you, and with this town. And that's when she found out that the bottom-line is really people."

At the moment, Mitch was thinking only of her bottom lip, soft and plump and delicious looking. As he watched his thumb slowly stroke it, he grew hard, and hungry for all of her. "Does that mean you'll make the necessary loans to people like the Hardys and Cousin Tilly?"

Though Zoe felt his body heat draw her to him like a backdraft, saw his mouth advertise pleasures so tantalizing her own mouth watered, she forced herself away from him. He'd asked the one question she wished she could answer differently than she had to. "A good banker knows that character can often make up for insufficient collateral, and I'll certainly bend the rules as far as I can to help anyone who's willing to work hard. But in the end, Mitch, no matter how good the people are, I can't make bad loans to them, for their sake as well as the bank's."

Mitch threw his hands up. "And if you can't lend them enough, then what?"

Zoe explained the options: a partnership with the state that would provide tax incentives, federal loans, private investors, all of the above. "It won't be easy," she said. Then, casting her eyes down at the pavement, she saw a larkspur growing in one of the cracks, the only white one in the lot. She stooped to pluck it, rose, and held it out to Mitch. "But not impossible."

He looked at the blossom, then at Zoe. "Let me get this straight. You want me to go to folks and say, 'Look, don't vote for Smedley Gasbag and those slick riverboat gamblers who'll start hiring construction workers the minute you say the word. Vote for me, because all I've got is a notion as wild as the flowers growing around the old furniture factory that we can find the money to turn that firetrap into a tourist trap?"

"Right."

"I won't be able to match the money the casino interests will pour into their candidate's coffers."

"True."

"And you still think I can win."

"Absolutely."

"Are you nuts?"

"Looney Tunes."

Hands on his waist, Mitch paused, biting his lower lip. Suddenly, he gave a laugh, then swiped the white larkspur from Zoe. "Me, too."

Throwing her arms around his neck, she pressed against him, absorbing his heat and hardness, and strength—and not only that of his body. "Speaking professionally, I'd say your character is worth a loan of, oh, about eight and one-half trillion dollars."

Mitch stroked the length of her back, bringing his hands to rest over curves so sweet that he'd never think of a banker the same way again. "And speaking personally?"

Zoe ran her tongue over her lips. "Personally, I'm done speaking."

Mitch thought he'd never seen anything so seductive as that tongue of hers. He swirled his own around the shell of her ear. "It's about time," he whispered. "I was getting ready to suggest you'd make the better politician."

Her pulse quickening, Zoe leaned away and undid the knot in his tie. "I'd rather make out with one," she said, sliding the tie from beneath his collar and dropping it to the ground. When Mitch's smile matched hers, she knew his appetites did, too. As he lowered his mouth to hers, she held her head still but let her senses loose. Oh, but he could torture her taking his time putting his flesh to hers, as though he knew that, in a breath, each peppery speck of stubble surrounding his mouth was a spark to the ether of her desire. Knowing she was about to go up in flames, she closed her eyes.

"Speaking of which, I guess I *am* a politician now."

Feeling as though he'd just smacked her in the face with something he'd just fished from the river, Zoe opened her eyes. "Excuse me?"

Mitch held her at arm's length. "This is a small town, darlin', which means that if I want to win this election, I can kiss babies in public but not babes. Especially a babe some folks are going to have a hard time forgetting is a banker."

"Thanks. I think."

As Mitch stroked her cheek with the backs of his fingers, he knew there was another, more pressing reason why he didn't want her too closely linked to him, at least not in the minds of his opposition, the casino interests. But at the moment, he didn't want to alarm her. Instead, he said, "It's better this way, Zoe. I'm afraid if I start kissing you I won't be able to stop. And I don't want to have to try."

Looking down at the larkspur in his hand, he saw the cypress tree at Ballard's Point, and himself and Zoe lying beneath it. He'd just asked her to marry him, and she'd said yes, and the tree's boughs waved, as if blessing them. But first, he had a riverboat to scuttle, an election to win, a daughter to win over, a town to save, a future to give to Zoe and Bink and Toby—to his future wife and kids. He broke off a stem of the larkspur and slipped it into his pants pocket. Then he took Zoe's hand in his. "You know there's more riding on my winning this election than stopping the riverboat, or creating jobs, or even getting Sarah Jane to stay with me—as much as I want to do all those things. Tell me you understand."

I understand, Zoe thought, *all too well.* Only moments ago, her zeal for the old factory project had pulsed in tandem with her heart-pounding desire for this man she so loved and respected. But now, both passions yielded to the bottom-line reality that whether or not their two families would become one depended on the votes that would be cast in six weeks. If Mitch were to lose the special election and a casino soon docked at Ballard's Point, Perfection would no longer be the safe harbor she wanted for her children. Beyond that undeniable fact lay massive uncertainty. She'd leave, of course, for the children's sake. Only last week, she'd read an article in a national magazine depicting chilling portraits of towns whose per capita incomes had risen while their very fabrics had been destroyed by gambling boats. They'd gone from havens to honkytonk overnight. But leaving Perfection would mean also having to leave the father she'd rediscovered only today. Surely, Lou would remain, and Dad with her.

And what would Mitch do? He hated the idea of a riverboat as much as she, but could he abandon this place, however it might change, which was in his blood? And even if he could leave with her and the children afterward, would he be the same man? Wouldn't a piece of his heart always remain here, in Perfection? The more she thought about it, the more she realized that, for all their sakes, he had to defeat whatever candidate would back the boat. And that meant she'd have to find backing for the old factory. And she had just six weeks to do it, to beat the odds. She, who'd never so much as bought a lottery ticket.

Taking Mitch's other hand, Zoe meshed her fingers with his and then raised them, so that she stood palm-to-palm with him, and heart-to-heart. "Don't worry, darlin'. I'd say we're all due for some good luck . . . you, me, Perfection." She smiled, but fleetingly.

We have to be.

That night, after they'd gathered their parents and

children around them to announce their plans for Mitch's campaign and the old factory, after they'd received the enthusiastic support of each of them, after they'd all seven held hands and prayed and then shared pizza, and even begun unpacking the cartons Zoe had kept sealed for nearly two weeks, she and Mitch stood alone on her front porch, in the dark. The kisses they shared were the kisses of two very tired people who were very much in love, impractically and completely. And so, while they were not the kind they'd shared previously—voracious, filled with barely controllable longing—they were long and filled with a quiet, steady passion for one another and for the future they were fighting for. Sex, when they could freely give that gift to one another, would undeniably enhance the union they shared—but never surpass it. For the first time in their lives, each knew a love that was fully reciprocated.

Zoe smiled to herself. She might have known that here, on Magnolia Street, she'd find reciprocity even in romance. When Mitch had said his final goodnight and started down the steps in the darkness that enclosed her porch alone of all those on the street, she said, "You know, now that I'm staying, I'm going to have to replace the burned-out bulb in my porch light."

Turning, he peered up at her, making out her lovely silhouette in the scant soft glow from the lights inside the house. He choked back the emotion that had risen from the ache of uncertainty in his heart. "Not yet, darlin'. Maybe I'm superstitious, but you and I both know that in six weeks you might have reason to put that light out, for good."

"Don't talk that way, Mitch. You're going to win."

"All right, suppose I do," he said, propping his foot on a riser and crossing his arms on his thigh. "Suppose I convince people to vote down the riverboat and open up their own shops in the old factory. They put their homes in hock, and sink every cent they have into their businesses. Then suppose the whole idea goes bust. The tourists don't come. The cash registers don't ring. Funds from investors, if we can get them, dry up. You have to call in loans. People pack up their belongings, what's left of them, and move a few counties or states away, where folks voted to let the gambling boat drop anchor and a cargo load of jobs." Mitch straightened. "Then what?"

Under the weight of his all too possible suppositions, Zoe slumped against the post at the end of the covered porch railing. "Then the town's right back where it started before the election, only worse. And everyone will hate us both. Well, everyone who's left."

"That's not the half of it, baby. We'll hate ourselves." Mitch climbed the steps. Then, pressing one hand against the post above her head, he stroked her face as he peered down at her. "Maybe we'll even come to hate each other for the hypocrites we are."

In the darkness, Zoe found his gaze and frowned into it. *"Hypocrites?* Hate each other? Look, you're tired, I'm tired, and I do *not* want to hear this." Shoving aside his arm, she headed to the door.

Mitch stopped her. "You're *going* to hear it," he said, turning her around. "Because after tonight, there's no turning back for either of us. Listen, Zoe, we say we don't want gambling to come to Perfection, but what are we doing if not asking people to gamble their futures on a plan we can't guarantee will work? Hell, we'll all of us be tossing the dice."

"Do we have a choice?"

"You do." Mitch paused to think what to say, to hope that whatever he said, she'd buy it. "You could take the kids and leave now. If things go well, you come back. If they don't, I'll join you, wherever you are."

Zoe snatched her arm from his hold. "If you really think I could do that to you and this town—quit before we even begin to fight—then you don't know me, mister. And maybe I don't know you, after all." With tears of physical and emotional exhaustion stinging her eyes, she started inside the house.

"Zoe, wait! You took me the wrong way."

"You bet I did," she snapped, rounding on him. "I thought you were as committed to this as I am. If my idea's too risky for you, go. But I'm staying and fighting that boat, and not quitting until I hear the first blast of its whistle!"

Grabbing her shoulders, Mitch pulled her close. "You don't understand. I just don't want you getting hurt!"

"Look, you can call me baby all you want, but don't you dare treat me like one." She pushed away from him. "I know what I'm up against. Besides, it's not as though I'm putting myself in any real danger."

His silence was like ice down her back.

"Mitch?" Zoe came toward him. "There is no real danger, is there?"

No longer able to conceal the concern he'd had earlier, when he'd intimated it might not be a bad idea to downplay their romance, he took a bracing breath. "We're talking about trying to stop a bunch of boys from Vegas from setting up shop outside Perfection, Zoe, and I don't know why they wouldn't play as rough here to get what they want as they do there."

"You mean—?" Zoe gulped. "They don't just help you to adopt a highway, they make you a part of it?"

"Look, they're probably legitimate businessmen, and there's nothing to worry about. But I'm a prosecutor. I think of things like that."

Zoe relaxed. She should have known that if he'd really believed his opposition could get ugly, he'd have asked her to take Sarah Jane out of town with her. But then, maybe he had. He'd said "the kids," hadn't he? And while they hadn't discussed the blending of their two families in so many words, hadn't they both come to understand that her kids and his kid would eventually be their kids? Maybe eventually had already arrived.

"Mitch, when you asked me to leave, did you mean for me to take Sarah Jane with me?"

"No."

Zoe sighed with relief. "That proves you don't think there's the possibility of violence. How did you expect to get me to leave while letting Sarah stay?"

"I'm not letting her stay. I'm going to send her and Lou to live with friends of Lou's in Paducah."

"Oh, Mitch!" Zoe flew to him, wrapping her arms around him. "You can treat me like a baby now."

Smiling gently, he rocked her in his embrace. "Good. You'll leave town, then?"

Collecting herself, Zoe gazed up at him. "I'll send Bink, Toby, and Dad to Paducah, too. Bink and Sarah won't want to be separated, and you know very well Dad won't let Lou out of his sight. As for my going, not a chance."

Taking her face in his hands, Mitch raised her gaze to his. "I knew that's what you'd say, but you understand why I had to ask, don't you?"

Over the chirps of crickets, Zoe heard the leaves of the big oak tree rustle on the sigh of a breeze that wafted the faintly sweet scent of night her way. *These are the hours, after midnight and before dawn,* she thought, *when the world seems timeless, as timeless as a man testing his courage, defending his home, protecting his family.* "I do, and I love you for it. And you understand why I have to say no?"

The air was Ohio Valley humid, not heavy but moist, and Mitch knew that even in lingering heat a sunless breeze like the one that had just passed could raise goosebumps. It must have on Zoe, because she gave a slight shiver. He turned up the collar of her sleeveless shirt, then rubbed her bare upper arms to warm her. As soft and smooth as they were, they were also well-defined if not muscular, and reminded him that what she lacked in strength she made up for in staying power—like the women who'd settled this place, and every woman who'd ever persevered against the odds in the hope of making a better life for herself and her children. And, especially precious to him, out of belief in the man she loved. Her faith was a gift so dear that he thought there was nothing he wouldn't endure to justify it. "I do understand," he said softly, enfolding her in his arms, "and I love you so much for it, I think it might take a lifetime to show you."

Zoe nibbled on his ear. "You only *think*? You're not sure?"

Mitch groaned as her tongue swirled around his ear, miraculously arousing the farther reaches of his body. "I'm sure, darlin', but I just can't ask you to share a lifetime with me until I know that that porch light of yours is going to burn all throughout it. You understand why I'm not ready?"

Gazing up at him, Zoe ran her fingers over his strong, slanting cheekbones, his straight nose, his full, fleshy lips, his stubborn chin. "Wherever I am, my love, I'll leave the porch light on for you. But I understand why you're not ready."

"You *sure*?"

"I'm sure."

Mitch turned toward the steps, then back. "You really, really sure?"

Zoe broke out laughing. "Get outta here," she cried, shoving his broad back and sending him scrambling down the steps. Once again, she started inside the house. Then, overtaken by surprise as Mitch bounded back up the steps and overpowered her in his embrace, she gave a gasp. He swallowed that, too, with a kiss so overwhelming that she went limp, so limp that when he finished he had to prop her against the jamb.

"Sorry," he whispered, "but I needed that to hold me until I win the election."

Her eyes closed, her head lolling, Zoe waved the

back of her hand at him. "Uh-huh." Moments later, after he'd gone and she'd rediscovered her bones, she walked to the edge of her porch and gazed across the street at Mitch's. She saw him there, beneath the light, open the screen door and then look back at her. Though he couldn't know she was watching him, he blew her a kiss. She blew one back. "And all I'll ever need to hold me is you," she murmured. Then she turned back to the house, smiling and hugging herself to contain the immense love inside her. She started across the threshold. Then, pausing, she looked up at the lantern. Suddenly, her smile vanished. Whether or not they'd ever hold each other again without regret for what they were about to do was a prospect as shadowy as the lantern was dark.

In the weeks that followed, Zoe had no time to worry about shadows or darkness of any kind. Time itself was what worried her—running out of it before she and Mitch could come up with a realistic proposal for the old factory mall. That meant finding out who held title to the building, what it would cost to buy it, and then renovating it.

To her surprise and delight, she discovered that the bank owned the property, had long been unable to unload it, and—according to the East Coast vice president she reported to—would be all too glad to dump it for a song. She'd smiled and asked, "How about 'When a Man Loves a Woman?' " Then, after answering the "I beg your pardon?" she'd prevaricated with something about a bad connection, she'd cleared her plan to obtain whatever appraisals were necessary to market the building. She'd stretched that okay to include consultations with architects and contractors who, unfortunately, all agreed that while the building might be had for a song, only a full-length opera could ready it for business. Nevertheless, it could be done. Assured of that but with the clock relentlessly ticking, Zoe immediately got to work on a financing package.

All the while, Mitch had been embarked on his grass roots campaign, covering the county door-to-door, speaking to church and civic groups, raising a few spare dollars here and there, but mostly raising doubts. Not that people thought the gambling boat was a good thing—just a sure one, unlike the old factory mall. Not only that, but with the boat, all they had to do was show up for work. The old factory would require some of them to borrow against their homes and risk their savings, with no guarantee of success, no ability like the boat's to provide secure jobs for others. It wasn't that they didn't trust him, it was just that they needed jobs they could count on. Now. Besides, what did they know about turning an old factory into a complex of shops and galleries and such, or putting on historical pageants and festivals, or running bed-and-breakfasts? Or attracting visitors to any of them? Of course, if an outside investor were to come in on the project, some-body with experience and know-how . . .

Mitch always assured them that Zoe was working on that, on getting commitments from private and corporate investors, and the state, to supplement the loans she was willing to make to them to open their own businesses.

But why, someone always asked, should they believe a word she said? For all they knew, she meant to strand them with a whole lot of debt just so she could take the little they had. She was a banker, wasn't she? And she hadn't even been honest with them about that.

"We didn't exactly make it easy for her to be honest, did we?" he argued. "From the moment she arrived here we made it clear that bankers weren't welcome, that we blamed them for our problems. And I was the worst of the lot. But she's proved she's not like the others, and y'all know it. She's fighting for Perfection and the rest of the county as though she's lived here all her life, which is more than I can say about some of you."

At that, Mitch invariably saw more than a few people cast their eyes downward with guilt. Then, someone would allow as maybe they'd been a little hard on Miss Zoe, but that didn't mean they would vote for the old factory instead of the riverboat—or for Mitch, instead of his opponent. It wasn't that they didn't like Mitch, even more than that other fella. It was just that they had mouths to feed, and without somebody big, like the casino operator, to do the old factory up right . . .

And how, he'd ask, did they expect Zoe to get an outsider to believe in the project if they themselves didn't?

Makes sense, someone would say. Some brave soul might even pledge his support to the project and vote for Mitch, often causing a rift within his own household. Kathy Hardy had, committed as she was to defeating the floating casino that was a destroyer to her but a lifeboat to her husband. For his marriage hitting the shoals, Dave had blamed Mitch and Zoe. Mitch had instinctively wanted to defend her, to tell Dave that Zoe had put her job on the line to save his home, inventing a number of means to stall foreclosing his loan. But knowing that Zoe would understand that sometimes all a man had left to keep him going was his pride, he'd spared Dave that humiliation. Still, he'd gained a vote only to lose a friend. And for what? With just five days until the election, the polls showed him losing by a margin as wide as the river.

"It's my fault," Zoe said that night as she sat beside him on Lou's front porch, staring at a pizza for which neither of them had an appetite. "I tried to put together a public and private partnership, but nobody wanted to be the first to make a commitment—not the state, not investors, not even Mr. Terwilliker."

Mitch laughed softly. "Give the poor man a break, darlin'. Marrying Miss Dunaway after all these years probably took just about all the commitment he had in him."

Zoe smiled, marveling that in the midst of losing an election, Mitch hadn't lost his sense of humor, or compassion. He really was a remarkable man, rich if not wealthy, strong if not powerful. Knowing him, she'd found new faith—not just in men, but in Man. Loving him, she'd found new faith in herself, too, and the God she believed had led her to him. But now, she felt that she'd let all three of them down. In her naivete, she'd underestimated the complexities of getting a project like the old factory mall off the ground; she'd failed to come up with solid backing in time to back Mitch's campaign to victory.

"Maybe," she replied. "But maybe I didn't say the right things to him and the others. Or maybe I said all the wrong things. Or maybe . . ." She walked to the railing between the porch and the lawn and, bracing herself against it, surveyed Magnolia Street at dusk. It was quiet, and she realized that the men and children no longer gathered to play basketball. The women no longer clustered to talk about their herb gardens, or the home plate umpire's bad call in last night's Little League game, or Bobbie Jo Tuttle's implants. And the reason was that even before it had been approved, the riverboat was dividing this place, pitting neighbor against neighbor, husband against wife, friend against friend. She could have prevented this strife if she'd given Mitch something more than a dream to offer as an alternative to the riverboat. But she hadn't. And now she wondered how long it would be before they, too, no longer saw eye to eye. "Maybe," she said, "it was a terrible idea to begin with. Maybe I should have encouraged you to accept the offer Dave and the others made to become their candidate. I've cost you the election and the chance to do some good, even if you couldn't stop the boat. Who knows," she began, turning to him, stretching her arms along the railing, "I might even have cost you a career in politics.

You might have been governor one day." Covering her eyes with one hand, she stifled tears with silent sobs.

"Stop it," Mitch said, taking her in his arms. "Listen, baby, I might like to be governor some day. But if I ever do get to Frankfort, it won't be because I sold out Perfection. I couldn't live with myself." Holding her away from him, he raised her eyes to his and smiled. "And turning Perfection into the kind of tourist town that's still fit for people to live in is a wonderful idea. Even our state representative and senator said it was."

"Yes, but did they have the courage to endorse it, and you?"

"Do pigs fly?" Mitch gave her a skewed smile. "Come on, Zoe. They could see the political winds were blowing toward the boat. And for that, you have to blame me. I just didn't do a good enough job convincing people otherwise."

Zoe gazed up at the dark circles under his eyes, and ran her thumb over one of them. "No man could have tried harder," she said softly.

Mitch folded her hand in his. "There is a good side to my losing, you know.

Zoe gave a snort. "To quote someone who's very intelligent, not to mention incredibly hunky, and really turns me on, 'Are you nuts?' "

Shaking his head, Mitch pinned her with a suddenly devilish glint in his deep blue eyes. "I just realized that if I'm going to lose, I don't have to worry about the boys from Vegas finding out that I'm crazy about you, because they don't have to bother getting rough with you to get to me. I can make mad, passionate love to you right here on this porch right now."

Judging from the look in his eye and the grin on his face, Zoe thought that that was exactly what he meant to do. "Now, Mitch," she began, holding out her hand and backing away. "I realize that with you campaigning and me working twelve hours a day—you know, learning a new job and getting up to speed on what's going on at the bank, and trying to find financing for the factory—we haven't seen much of each other, but—"

"I thought I really turned you on," he said, backing her toward the wicker sofa.

"You do! But—" Zoe looked around helplessly. "I can't believe I'm about to say this, but what will the neighbors think?"

Mitch gazed out at Magnolia Street. "It's dark now. There's no moon, and I haven't turned the porch light on yet. But if any of the neighbors did see us, they'd probably think it's about time." Hiking one knee onto the sofa, he pressed her down onto it, caging her even as he felt he'd kept himself caged too long. His desire for her was beyond physical—a craving in his soul. Every cell in his body was an empty vessel waiting to be filled with all things Zoe, the look of her, scent of her, taste of her, and the truth of her—which was that she was a remarkable woman whose faith had made him a new man, whose love had made him a whole one. And he worshipped her. "You ready?" he asked, his voice husky.

Zoe stretched her arms up to him. "Uh-huh. I agree with the neighbors."

Still kneeling above her, Mitch took her face in his hands. "I love you, darlin'," he whispered. Then lowering his mouth to hers, he set them both on fire.

Zoe reached up behind his back and with her palms, pressed him to her. This was so right, that they should be one, and suddenly, she knew with peaceful certainty that they would be. The threats to their future posed by Mitch's losing the election and the riverboat's coming to Perfection melted in the inferno of the love that had already been tested and had survived. And grown. Intuitively, or perhaps because of the way he was kissing her, deeply and enduringly, she knew he wouldn't wait a moment longer. He was going to ask her to marry him. Now.

His body trembling with want of her, his heart wanting to claim her once and for all for its own, and his faith telling him that no election, no riverboat, not even Perfection itself, could ever come between them, Mitch heard the words, the right ones. *For richer or poorer, in sickness and in health, in Perfection or far from it, until the day I die, I will love, honor, and cherish you, Zoe Laurence. Will you be my wife?*

Ahem. Whither-r-r the tree?

Lifting his head, Mitch looked down at Zoe. "Did you say something?"

"How could I have said something? You were kissing me. And doing a pretty good job, too." Cupping the back of his head, she lowered it, and his kiss.

Where were we? Right, Zoe Laurence, will you be my—?

The cypress tree, laddie! You must ask the lassie to wed you beneath the cypress tree, as I did Fionna. You dinna want to foul up your life agin, do you?

Great-great-great-grandfather MacDuff?

I think you forgot a great, but I willn'a hold that against you, providin' you act like a bloody Ballard this time and propose to your true love under the bloody cypress tree!

Mitch heard a sigh, then, *By the way, your great-great-great-grandmother wants you to know that this time she approves of your choice of a bride.*

I think you forgot a great, but tell her thanks. And you, sir? What do you think of my Zoe?

Whreet-whreeoo! Ow! Fionna, darlin', I dinna bring you that fancy broom all the way from Louisville for you to beat me about the head and shoulders with!

Then, in a voice growing fainter and farther away, Mitch heard, *Now don't forget, laddie, you must propose beneath the tree. Then your marriage will last as long as Fionna's and mine. On second thought . . . Ouch! I must be goin', Mitch my boy. Your great-great-great-great-grandmother's wantin' me to chase her until she lets me catch her, and I can't say as I mind. Good luck to you and your bonnie Zoe.*

"Mitch?" Pressing her hand to his cheek, Zoe turned his face back to hers. "Are you all right? You seem so far away."

"Not very. Ballard's Point." Rising, he held his hand out to help her up. "Come with me."

"To Ballard's Point? Now?"

"It'll make my great-great-great-grandfather happy."

You forgot a great, laddie!

"Sorry," Mitch said.

"Me, too. That I asked." Zoe put her hand in his. "But if it will make your great-great-great—"

"Woof!"

As Zoe got to her feet, suddenly aware of the cutting of a roaring engine and the slamming of doors, something small and wiry jumped into her arms. "Bruno? Where did you—?"

"Mom!"

"Bink!"

In a flurry of motion, Zoe pitched Bruno, Mitch turned on the porch light, Bink ran into her mother's open arms, and Toby hurled himself at Mitch, who lifted him into the air, smiling into the boy's big brown eyes and then hugging him tightly to his chest.

"We heard the latest polls," Harvey said as he and Lou mounted the porch steps holding hands. "We figured you two needed us a whole lot more than we needed to keep the kids away."

"Daddy. Lou." Her voice choked with emotion, Zoe hugged each of them in turn.

Setting Toby down, Mitch joined the reunion. Then, after trading back slaps with Harvey, he narrowed his eyes and asked, "Where's Sarah?" Gazing toward the front walk, the others guided his search to the spot where she stood holding her Cavalier, keeping her distance.

"I missed you, honey," Mitch said, starting down the porch steps, his arms reaching toward her, his heart thumping the way a puppy's tail wags when the light of its life returns home.

"Is it true you're going to lose the election because you couldn't raise the money for the old factory mall?"

Sarah Jane's tone, like the flash of a blade, stopped him cold. "Zoe and I gave it our best, but—"

"And there's going to be a riverboat at Ballard's Point?"

"Looks that way."

Stroking Chauncey's silky coat, Sarah appeared to ponder that prospect. "Will you leave Perfection?"

"Probably. But don't worry, honey." Mitch glanced back at the others. Then, lowering his voice, he said, "I'm going to ask Zoe to marry me, and I think she'll say yes. And from then on, home will be wherever the five of us are together." He moved to take her into his arms, but she evaded him.

"Well you all can just go ahead without me!" she shouted, sending a glaring look at the others.

Fear pierced Mitch like a bullet. "What are you saying, Sarah?"

"I'm *saying*," she replied with a saucy toss of her red curls, "that you'll just move to some other hick town like Perfection, and I hate Perfection! I know it's two months until my birthday, but I've decided I want to live in Atlanta with Mom. Now!"

Mitch looked down, expecting to see a hole in his chest the size of a cannonball. After a moment, breathing hard, he said, "I don't understand. You've seemed so happy since Bink moved here. You two have been like sisters. I thought . . . I thought you wanted us all to become a family."

"And have to share a room with *her*? Get real, Dad. She's a pain. She keeps me up all night, talking and laughing—"

"Stop it, Sarah."

"And she borrows my clothes, and wants us to do

everything together, and she's always telling me her stupid secrets, and—"

"That'll be enough, young lady!"

"Besides, Mom lets me do whatever I want, and Zoe's always asking what Bink and I are watching and listening to, and telling us why we can't see this movie or that one. I hate her!"

Mitch grabbed Sarah by the shoulders and gave her a shake. "I said that's enough!" He'd never shouted at her before, much less shaken her, and as stunned as she looked, as he knew the others must be, the only remorse he felt was for not having done so sooner. She'd had a wake-up call coming for a long time. Maybe they both had. Releasing her, he stood tall and slipped his hands in his pockets. "You want to go to Atlanta? That's fine with me, because I won't tolerate hate toward the people I love. I love you, Sarah, but I love Zoe and Bink and Toby, too, and I won't let you hurt them, anymore than I'd let them hurt you." He nodded toward the house. "You'd better call Charles to send the plane for you."

Hugging Chauncey tightly, the girl lifted her chin, and while Mitch saw the quiver in it, everyone else heard her tremulously defiant tone. "I already did, when we stopped at Bob Evans for dinner—if you could call it that. Charles has an eight hundred number, you know. Anyway, he said he'd send the plane as soon as he could, probably in a few days. I only hope I can stand it here that long." She ran toward the house.

"Sarah!"

Her hand on the screen door handle, she stopped and waited.

Walking toward her, Mitch said, "Apologize to Bink and Zoe."

Slowly turning to her left, Sarah faced Bink, her expression impassive. After a moment, she looked back at her father. "She should apologize to me for being such a big pain." With that, she yanked the screen door open with such force that it slammed behind her.

"Sarah Jane!" Mitch charged after her. "Come back here!"

"Wait, Mitch." With tears streaming down her cheeks, Bink stepped into his path. "She's right. I did do all those things she said I did. I'm sorry, I didn't know I was going to make her want to leave you. It's just that I've always wanted a sis—a sis—" Shuddering with sobs, she fled down the porch and across Magnolia Street toward home.

As Zoe started after her, Mitch caught her by the arm. "There are no words to tell you how ashamed I am of Sarah, and how sorry for Bink. I wouldn't have her hurt for the world. Sarah will make this up to her. I don't know how, but you have my word that she will."

"It goes deeper than that, Mitch," she replied. "How long will it be before you resent my daughter because she cost you your own? How long before you resent me? I'm afraid this is one obstacle we can't overcome." She looked down at his hand, which gripped her arm. "Please let me go. Bink needs me." When he released her, she took a few steps, then looked back at him. "I'm so sorry for you, Mitch. So very sorry for us all."

Mitch stood watching the woman he loved, the woman he'd been about to ask to become his wife, hurry away, perhaps out of his life. But, like a disaster victim, he was unable to gather the wits to stop her, so benumbed was he by the sudden destruction of his world. He didn't feel Harvey's hand clasp his shoulder comfortingly as he walked by, or hear Lou ask if there was anything she could do and then excuse herself when he didn't answer. She said she had a picture of Ellie she wanted to frame, in the center of her dartboard.

Later, after a long walk—knowing neither how long nor exactly where, only that it hadn't relieved his desolation—he found himself standing outside Sarah's door. For an instant, he thought he heard soft crying, then that he'd only imagined it. He would have given anything for a sign that the little angel who used to bring him pretend breakfast in bed and beg him not to set mousetraps still lived inside the unfeeling girl he barely recognized as his daughter.

Quietly, he opened her door, and in the wedge of light from the hall he walked to her bed. His heart wrenched as he saw that in her sleep she still looked sweet and innocent. Daddy's little girl. He lifted the top sheet over her bare legs. Then, overcome by a fresh welter of emotion, he quickly left the room, shutting the door behind him.

The walk to his room was even lonelier than the solitary one he'd just taken around Perfection as he grappled with the realization that he was a loser: he was losing the election, his daughter, and the only woman who'd ever made him feel like a real man. He was losing the family he'd always dreamed of. And the worst of it was, he couldn't think of a damn thing to do to prevent any of those things. Dejectedly, he opened the door to his room. Across his bed, in a shaft of light, he saw the portrait of Fionna standing before the cypress tree.

Despite many a storm, laddie, it still stands. Like love, if its roots go deep enough.

Though Mitch didn't say so to MacDuff, he was afraid that as far as Zoe's love for him was concerned, that could be a very big if.

ELEVEN

"Mom, I don't have any clean bras!"

Standing at the bathroom sink, pitching her comb and lipstick into her purse before leaving for the bank, Zoe paused in amazement. Last night, shattered by Sarah Jane's sudden and cruel rejection, Bink had been inconsolable. All Zoe could do was to hold her as she cried herself to sleep, something Zoe herself had gotten too little of. Aching for Bink, for Mitch, for herself—even for Sarah, who must be deeply troubled to have behaved so heartlessly—and worried about all of their futures, she'd endlessly tossed like a salad, and awakened wilted. The least Bink could do was to not bounce around at this early hour sounding so crisp and fresh, and with nothing more on her mind than clean—

"Bian-caaah!"

"Sorry, Mom." Following her collision with her mother, Bink squatted beside Zoe, helping her to gather the scattered contents of her purse from the floor. "Are you okay?"

"No, I'm not okay." Taking Bink by the shoulders, Zoe brought them both to their feet. She looked at her daughter's chest, which beneath the T-shirt she'd slept in was still as flat as the deck of an aircraft carrier. "Honey, you do not need to be wearing bras."

"You really know how to hurt a girl, Mom."

"So do you. I can appreciate that at your age, cotton undershirts aren't exactly cool. But to go to adjustable straps without telling *me*, your own mother?" Zoe returned to the mirror to put the final touches to her hair. "I mean, I would have taken you shopping, and then we'd have had lunch and talked about the meaning of life, and—"

"*Relax*, Mom. I haven't bought bras behind your back." Stepping behind Zoe, Bink brushed a few strands of chestnut hair from the shoulders of her mother's soft yellow blouse. "I just wanted to get your attention before you left for work."

"You certainly did do—" Abruptly, Zoe faced her daughter. "Oh, sweetheart. Have I been so preoccupied these last few weeks, even on the phone?"

"A little," Bink replied with a shrug. "But it wasn't like I ever thought you weren't there for me." Looking around the bathroom, she giggled. "Well, *here* for me." Suddenly, her brown eyes grew troubled beneath the straight bangs Zoe realized she hadn't asked her to trim in a long time. She probably was getting too old for them, too. "I really need to talk to you, Mom."

Zoe looked at her watch. She was going to be late for work, but that was okay. The files piled high on her desk could wait until later. *When a young girl needs to talk*, she thought, *later may be too late*. She sat on the tub, sitting Bink down beside her. "Would it have something to do with Sarah Jane?"

Hugging one knee, Bink nodded.

"I thought you sounded a little too up, considering what you went through last night."

"But that's just it, Mom. I do feel better."

"Oh?"

Bracing her arms against the ledge, Bink gazed dreamily up at her mother. "I woke up really early this morning and just lay in bed thinking. And that's when I realized that Sarah couldn't have meant the things she said last night."

Her heart aching afresh, Zoe brushed Bink's honey-tinged hair back from her eyes. "Sweetheart, are you sure your thinking wasn't just wishful?"

Bink laughed gently as she cupped Zoe's shoulder. "Mom, if I didn't do denial when my biological father left me, do you really think I'd start now?"

Zoe took a slow, deep breath. This child was really something, only she wasn't a child anymore. She was becoming a young lady, and Zoe had to fight tears of love and admiration and thanksgiving for her. "No, not really." Folding her arms, she leaned against the wall. "So, how did you come to the conclusion that Sarah didn't mean what she said?"

"Well . . ." Bink walked to the sink, then slowly turned and faced her mother. "I guess because last night, she wasn't the same person she was in Paducah. The whole time we were there, all she talked about was how she missed Perfection and how great it would be if you and Mitch got married, and then the two of us could really be sisters and always share a room and clothes and secrets. But not boyfriends."

Zoe smiled to herself. "Sounds perfectly sisterly to me." She rose and came to stand side by side with Bink. "I can see now why you think her behavior last night doesn't make sense. Unless . . ."

Bink's brown eyes looked curiously up at Zoe. "What?"

"She did say she thinks I'm too strict."

"She *said* she hated you, Mom."

"Yeah. Scary. Anyway, maybe I'm the one she really has a problem with."

"I don't understand that, either," Bink replied, tossing her hands as she stepped away. "She thinks you're so cool. Even before we left Perfection, she'd tell me I was so lucky because I had a mom I could talk to, even in the bathroom. She said her mother won't even let her into the 'mahster suite,' let alone her bathroom. And as for being too strict, she said she really liked it when you asked us where we were going, and stuff. It made her feel like you really cared about her. I thought she was crazy until she told me her own mother doesn't care what she does or where she goes or who she hangs around with, as long as she doesn't hang around the house too much." She leaned against the jamb. "That must be so awful."

"Yes, it must," Zoe murmured, one troubling thought after another parading through her mind. Too many self-involved parents talking to their kids on too many cell phones and communicating too little. Too many overlooked, underdisciplined kids who could only conclude they were unimportant and unloved. Too many irreparably damaged homes, schools, neighborhoods. Lives. But from what Bink had just told her, Sarah Jane had been on the mend. What, then, could have caused her outburst last night? She asked Bink if she had a clue.

"No, but I'm going to find out, no matter how long it takes. We were just too close for me to give up on her, Mom."

A gentle smile touched Zoe's heart and lips. "You know something, honey?" she said, gathering Bink under one arm and starting the two of them up the hall. "If every bra wearer were as good a friend as you, the world would be a better place. I just wish I could promise that after the election, Perfection will be better and Sarah Jane will decide to stay, and we'll all be together, always."

"That's okay, Mom. I know life's weird." Bink slipped her arm around her mother's waist. "But we'll deal with it."

"Yeah," Zoe said, patting Bink's hand on her waist. "We'll deal with it."

But it would help if by election day, life would deal us an ace.

* * *

Zoe didn't have to wait longer than the time it took her to drive to the bank.

"I don't know who this Arlen Samuels is, but he called twice in half an hour." Bob Peterson, Zoe's assistant, handed her a pink While You Were Out message slip.

Zoe stared querulously at the out of state phone number. "Did he say what he wanted?"

Bob shook his head. "Wouldn't leave voice mail, either. Said I was to tell you personally that if you were serious about saving Perfection, you should call him at his private number before ten o'clock. That's when he leaves for Sydney."

"Australia?"

Peterson shrugged. "All I know is that he sounded sober, in a hurry, and rich."

Puzzled, Zoe tapped her lower lip with one corner of the message.

"Thanks, Bob." As he left, she checked her watch. Nine fifty-seven. Even if Arlen Samuels wasn't a practical joker or an outright nutcase, he'd probably already left for Sydney. Australia. She crumpled the message and tossed it in her waste can, then sat down and began sifting through her mail. As she reached for a pen, she noticed a bud vase beside her nameplate, and in it, a stem of white larkspur. Bringing it to her, she rubbed a petal between her thumb and forefinger. "Oh, Mitch," she murmured, her love for him spilling over the confines of her heart. If he could still hope for a miracle, so could she. Pushing away from her desk, she delved into her waste can and retrieved the crumpled message. Then, praying that her watch was fast, she hurriedly dialed Arlen Samuels's number.

On the third ring, he answered, but in the form of a recording, and Zoe's hope evaporated. She started to replace the receiver without leaving a message, then thought, *What can it hurt?* "Mr. Samuels? This is Ms.

Laurence from the Progress and Pride Bank returning your—"

"Ms. Laurence. My Louisville office forwarded a newspaper article about the fight you and Mr. Ballard are putting up to keep gambling out of your county."

"I don't understand. Are you with Gamblers Anonymous?"

"I'm with Brown Rowan, Ms. Laurence. Commercial developers. Now about this old warehouse idea of yours—"

"Old factory."

"I don't have much time, so listen carefully."

Zoe did exactly that. Two minutes later, she hung up, feeling as though she'd been swept up by a tornado and then set down, only to discover she wasn't in Kentucky anymore. There were her notes in front of her regarding Arlen Samuels's offer for the old factory and the name of the woman who would handle the particulars of developing it into a showcase for local artisans, and Winsome County into a first-class, four state tourist attraction. Zoe had begun to rapid-fire questions at him, but he'd cut her off, assuring her that his assistant would answer them all shortly. In the meantime, he'd see to it that a letter of intent was faxed to her. "Then it's up to you and Mr. Ballard," he'd said. "You two have to get him elected, and sink that damn boat!"

Still disbelieving, Zoe dialed Bob Peterson's extension and asked him to check out a company called Brown Rowan. A few minutes later, he called back.

"Ever hear of the Fortune 500?"

Zoe's mouth fell open. "What about Arlen Samuels?"

"The CEO of Brown Rowan, *that* Arlen Samuels?"

Silence.

"You still there?"

"Uh-huh. I was just wondering if Wick's Hardware carries torpedoes."

* * *

With the polls set to open in less than twenty-four hours and not having had time alone with Mitch since the night he'd nearly proposed, Zoe frantically tracked him through unrelenting rain along the itinerary of his final campaign stops, always missing him by mere minutes—missing the chance to be with him when he needed her most, when he was about to lose not just the election but his world. At the last stop she visited, one of his young volunteers told her that Mitch had left early, saying he needed to be alone with something tall and cold. Suddenly, Zoe knew exactly where to find him. Twenty minutes later, she did, seating himself on a stool at the far end of the room.

"Make it a double," she heard him say.

Though it was the middle of the day, she couldn't blame him. Not only was it a dreaded day, but since she'd brought him Arlen Samuels's offer in writing Mitch had campaigned more like a man who was running for his life than for the county judge executive's office. In a way, he was, at least for the betterment of his life and hers and the children's, of the lives of the people he'd always known and cared about. In the last three days, he hadn't been so much a candidate as a missionary, bringing the good news of Brown Rowan's saving dollars and know-how to every square inch of Winsome County. And by all accounts, he was winning converts over from the riverboat to the old factory mall project and votes for himself. He was also hoarse and alarmingly hollow-cheeked, and—as much as she shared his cause—she'd be damned if she'd let him become a martyr to it.

After standing her umbrella against the wall and wiping mud off her shoes, she crossed the room, her steps muffled by rain pelting the roof. She eased onto the stool to his left. "Mind if I join you?"

He slid a look at her from the corner of his eye.

"As long as you don't have a baby to be kissed, or want to shake my hand." Reaching across his chest, he showed her his right hand, frozen in a permanent grip. Then he swiveled fully toward her. "So, you come here often?"

Zoe would have laughed at his bad impression of a lounge lizard if her heart hadn't been breaking for him, especially because he was bravely masking his sadness with humor. Nevertheless, she pursed her lips and played along, for his sake. "Nah. Although . . ." She ran her hand over his shoulder and down his arm, which was still well-muscled but thinner. "Now that I know that big, strong handsome guys like you hang out here, I might come more often."

"Oh, yeah?" Stretching his left arm along the back of her stool, Mitch leaned closer. "So what do you say, sweetcakes? Can I buy you a drink?"

Gazing at his lips and wanting them, Zoe brought hers as close as she dared. "I'll have whatever you're having, big boy."

Raising his finger, Mitch looked over his shoulder. "Hey, Tilly! Make that two double chocolate malts."

"Sure thing," Tilly called from behind the counter. "And now that I'm gonna have me a yogrit maker, thanks to the Progress and Pride National Bank, they're on the house." She winked at Zoe.

Mitch stared in stunned amazement at Tilly, who had never been known to utter the words "on the house" and had single-handedly turned banker bashing into a local art form. He turned back to Zoe, smiling wryly beneath an arched brow. "And can you also walk on water?"

Zoe chuckled. Then, running her fingertips across his tense forehead and down his gaunt cheek, she said, "If only I *could* work miracles."

Mitch folded her hand to his heart, taking comfort in its warmth and softness. "I know. But then I'd have to prosecute you for vote tampering."

"I wasn't thinking about the election." She pressed her cheek to his, his skin like balm, soothing her longing for him. "I was thinking about Sarah Jane." She looked into his eyes. "Any luck getting her to explain why she told Bink she couldn't wait for us all to become a family, and then decided she'd rather live with Ellie and Charles?"

He shook his head.

"Oh, Mitch, I'm so sorry." Zoe lowered her head and her voice. "Charles is still flying in to pick her up this evening, then?"

With a heavy sigh, Mitch nodded. "I'm going to drive her to the airport before going out to the high school to get ready for the debate."

As exhausted as he looked now, and as emotionally drained as he was going to be after putting Sarah on that plane, she couldn't imagine how he was going to get through the final debate with his opponent tonight. Her love for him, great as it was, was no substitute for Sarah's, but it was all she had to give him. That, and hope. She laid her hand over his. "Mitch, the other night, when you wanted to take me out to Ballard's Point . . . That's where your great-great-great-grandfather proposed to your great-great-great-grandmother, isn't it?"

"You forgot some greats, but yes. Beneath the cypress tree." The green of her eyes reminded Mitch of the soft, piney color of the leaves on Fionna's and MacDuff's tree. He grazed the backs of his fingers down her silky cheek. "Baby, you have no idea how much I want to take you back there." Lightning flashed. He smiled sadly. "When all our storms have passed."

"They will. In the meantime"—Zoe reached into her purse—"if we can't go to the tree . . ."

Mitch stared at the sprig of cypress she held out to him and was reminded of what he was fighting for, what all his ancestors, the Ballards and McTavishes and Man of the Village People, had fought for. Civilization.

And that was anywhere men and women fell in love, married, reared families, raised barns and businesses, courthouses and schools, honored beauty. And worshipped. And fought all forms of darkness, especially the human kind. And prevailed.

As would he. He took the sprig from Zoe. "I might lose the election, darlin', but I'm not done fighting for Sarah, for all of us. That's a promise."

Slipping off the stool, Zoe took his beautiful face in her hands and looked deeply into those blue eyes that had never appeared more luminescent. "So is this," she said, then laid her mouth on his, lightly at first, knowing how flammable a mix their kisses made.

But her caution went unheeded. Mitch's kiss ignited. He drew her between his knees against his body, a hot column of desire, and there in Tilly's Ice Cream Emporium, now a small business client of the Progress and Pride National Bank, Zoe began to melt like a scoop of frozen yogrit on a sizzling griddle.

"You two can come in here and act like a coupl'a soap opera characters all you like. Probably attract customers. But I'm not guaranteein' these malteds will keep."

Smiling into one another's eyes, Mitch and Zoe told Tilly to put the malteds down on the counter. "Mmmm," Zoe said, staring at the thick, creamy concoction as she slipped her straw out of its paper wrapper. "Do you know how long I've been waiting for one of these? Years." Plunging the straw into the center of the malt and seeing it stand straight up, she said, "Behold a thing of beauty," and brought the straw to her mouth. She puckered her lips around it, and then—

"There he is, fellas! Start the tape."

Zoe spun around to see a TV news crew frenziedly coming at Mitch from all directions, turning Tilly's into the streets of Pamplona. A blonde with a microphone wedged herself between Mitch and Zoe, shoving the mike in Mitch's face, forcing Zoe off the stool and causing her to knock over her malted. She narrowed her gaze on the puddling liquid, then on the reporter's back, where she mentally drew a bull's eye which she kept in focus.

She backed away to retrieve her umbrella, but she came to a dead standstill when she heard the reporter say, "Mr. Ballard, what's your response to the latest poll showing the riverboat losing support and you in a statistical dead heat with your opponent?"

Mitch's response was to send his gaze in search of Zoe. Peering through the lights and past the commotion, he saw her, her chin puckered beneath a smile, her eyes moist and filled with a love and pride he'd never known a woman could feel for him. He raised the sprig of cypress to her in a salute of gratitude, which she accepted with a nod of continuing faith. Mitch nodded back, then looked at the reporter. "I'd say that won't last."

The reporter appeared stunned. "And why is that?"

Mitch rose. "Because after tonight's debate, the polls will show that when all the votes are counted tomorrow, I'll be the next judge executive of Winsome County."

That evening, during a lull in the torrential rain that had pelted Perfection all day, Mitch placed Sarah Jane's suitcases in the trunk of his car parked at the rear of Lou's house. He couldn't have felt less like a man about to win his first election—not when he was about to lose his daughter. What saddened him most was that since the night she'd lashed out so cruelly at Bink and Zoe, he'd realized he'd lost her long before this moment. He'd lost her to Ellie, and a set of values that was as different from his as Atlanta was from Perfection.

"I just cain't understand it," Lou had said through her tears after saying good-bye to Sarah before she and

Harvey had gone ahead to the high school to save seats for the debate. "I'm tellin' you, Mitch, something's not right about that child decidin' to leave just when she was beginnin' to act like her old self again. If you could have just gotten her to talk."

But nobody had been able to, not even Bink. And now it was too late.

"I'm ready." Sarah Jane stood wearing the same yellow suit and high-heeled shoes she'd worn the day she'd returned from Atlanta.

Mitch looked at his daughter, a girl on the verge of adolescence, but saw a tot with red curls splashing gleefully as he bathed her. He heard her giggle at the suds running down his face. Then, he was tucking her into bed and hearing her plead, irresistibly, "Just one more story, Daddy." Next, he was tiptoeing into her room long after she'd fallen asleep. He leaned over to gently take her thumb from her mouth before kissing her goodnight one last time, and smelled her hair, sweetly damp amidst a halo of her favorite stuffed toys. Now, he was seeing her in a flash of lightning as she burrowed under his sheets and snuggled her little body in the curve of his—"so you won't be 'fraid, Daddy." And then, feeling her arms clinging tightly around his neck as he tried to teach her how to swim. "Never, ever let me go, Daddy. Promise."

He'd promised, but then he had let her go, when she'd been ready to solo on her first two-wheeler, and he remembered her beaming with pride when she'd realized he was no longer running beside her. But she'd ridden right back to him, jumped off, and hurled herself at him with inexpressible joy, and he'd lifted her way over his head.

"You're so tall, Daddy, I bet you can reach to the top of the world!"

"You're my world, punkin'." And he had hugged her to him, sharing her triumph, praying they'd always be that close.

But now she was a stranger, and he was letting her go again, not because he wanted to, but because *she* wanted him to. It was killing him, because this time, she wouldn't come running back, and he wouldn't lift her to the top of the world. But she'd always be his world. Always.

No! a voice inside him shouted. *It can't be too late.* Leaving the trunk open, he took her by the shoulders. "Sarah, honey, are you *sure* this is what you want?"

"I'm sure. Can we go, now? I don't want to be late."

Slowly, Mitch straightened. He'd never felt more helpless in his life, except when Sarah was born. Ellie hadn't wanted him in the delivery room—watching her with her legs in the air and "grunting like a sow"—in spite of his reassurances that she would never be anything but beautiful to him, especially when she was giving birth. But Ellie always got her way. She was getting it now. She was getting Sarah. But not his fatherhood, never that. He was about to tell Sarah they could go as soon as she went across the street and apologized to Bink and Zoe. Then he noticed something was oddly missing.

"Where's Chauncey?"

Sarah looked aside. "I gave him to Bink. I was tired of having to get up early to walk him and having to feed him."

Mitch turned her face to his. "You *love* that dog."

She shrugged. "It's a pain, loving things."

Mitch shuddered. "It's a worse pain when you don't."

Sarah rolled her eyes. "Whatever."

Disgusted, hurt, fearful, Mitch slammed the trunk lid, then opened the passenger door for Sarah. "Get in."

She did. He shut her door, and as he was about to walk to the driver's side she reached through the open window, grabbing his shirtsleeve. "When you went on that date with Lila, I put melatonin in your cocoa to make you sleepy. I . . . I just wanted you to know that."

A range of emotions from shock to outrage assaulted Mitch. But something told him Sarah's confession called more for careful thought than an immediate scolding. "We'll discuss it on the way to the airport," he said, hopeful that this one truth would lead to another, to the truth behind her abrupt change of heart and home. He started around the back of the car.

"Rreeee!" At the squeal of tires, Mitch looked up to see a midnight blue sedan speeding up the driveway toward him. It lurched to a halt, and two burly men in dark glasses jumped out. He'd never seen them before, but he knew they were enforcers and they'd come to protect their casino bosses' interests. They'd come for him. He also knew they wouldn't hesitate to snatch Sarah, too, if they spotted her in the front seat of the car. And he had just one chance of preventing that. He trotted out to greet them, smiling as if they were neighbors come to call. Then he deliberately timed a punch at one of them so that it missed, but only in the literal sense. The goons responded as he'd hoped, instantly setting on him—one holding his arms behind him while the other belted him in the gut, doubling him over. Then they hustled him into the backseat of the sedan. As they sped off, he rose up and looked out the rear window and, through a fresh torrent of rain, saw Sarah Jane running after him. *Go back, baby! Go back.* As if hearing him, she stopped. The sedan continued barreling ahead, and Mitch knew Sarah was safe. He smiled.

Then the lights went out.

TWELVE

When Sarah Jane barged into her kitchen, rain-soaked, gulping breaths and sputtering incoherently, Zoe's first thought was that the poor child was breaking down at the eleventh hour under the full import of her decision to leave her father and her home. But she soon realized that what Sarah was expressing wasn't a tangle of conflicting emotions, but a single overwhelming one—terror. The same terror that knifed through Zoe at the first two intelligible words she'd managed to soothe from Sarah—"Daddy" and "kidnapped." She knew instantly who'd grabbed Mitch and why: thugs whose casino bosses didn't like the no-better-than-even odds the latest polls had given their candidate. At best, they'd drive him around to keep him from the debate tonight, cutting his chances of taking the lead. At worst, they'd cut his throat. With no time to lose finding him, she forced herself to remain calm enough to coax a description of the hit car from Sarah Jane.

"It was blue, I *think*."

Maybe she'd seemed a little too calm, Zoe thought. Sitting down at the table, she drew Sarah to her. "Think hard, sweetheart. I'm sure you must remember something else about the car."

Sarah squeezed her eyes shut. "I think . . ."

"Yes?"

Sarah opened her eyes. "It was dark blue."

Her heart sinking as though wearing cement shoes for the occasion, Zoe nevertheless hugged Sarah and assured her everything would be all right. Then, she called the Perfection police, the county sheriff's office, the fire department, Animal Control, and Fred, the bank's security guard—everyone she could think of who owned a badge. Finally, with Kathy Hardy already gone to the high school, she phoned old Mrs. Terwilliker, asking her to come and stay with the children. Mrs. Terwilliker said she'd be delighted, considering how much time she had on her hands now that Junior had gone and gotten himself married. "Can you imagine? Married, at forty-six. What was his hurry?"

"Yes, ma'am. Um, speaking of being in a hurry, I'm really in an awful one myself."

After Mrs. Terwilliker assured her she'd be there in a jiffy, Zoe cautioned the children not to tell her about Mitch's abduction. "She's elderly and frail, and we wouldn't want to frighten her, would we?"

"*I* would." Toby giggled. Holding back a smile, Zoe ruffled his hair.

"In the first place, Mom," Bink began, "I don't see why we need a babysitter. And in the second place, if she's so frail, maybe *we* should be babysitting with *her.*"

Zoe shifted her eyes. "Good idea."

"*Mo-om!* That wasn't really an offer."

"I know," Zoe said, scrambling to find her purse and cell phone. "But humor me. I have enough on my mind without having to worry about you three here alone with the Internet. So Mrs. Terwilliker it is."

"You don't trust us," Bink said.

"I trust you, sweetheart. It's just the rest of the world I'm a bit leery of."

"But, Mom—"

"Leave Mother alone, Bink. She needs our cooperation now."

Zoe stared at Sarah, who'd melted her heart with

a single word. *Mother.* But the question remained, if Sarah felt that way about *her,* why had she decided to live with Ellie? It would have to remain a while longer. All Zoe had time to say as Mrs. Terwilliker walked in the kitchen door was, "Thank you, Sarah."

Quickly, the children gave her their promises not to mention Mitch's kidnapping to Mrs. Terwilliker. Inside of a minute, Zoe was driving off in the same direction, according to Sarah, as the car that held Mitch, who held her love. She prayed it had left a trail her heart would instinctively follow, even through the storm, which had returned with reinforcements. But after cruising every street in Perfection without glimpsing the *perhaps* dark blue car, she gave her heart a rest. It was time to use her brain.

She pulled over in front of the courthouse and turned off her screechy wiper blades, all the better to think. "Okay, Zoe. If you were the kind of big-time operator who sends horse-headgrams, and Mitch was about to sink your proposal for a floating crap game at Ballard's Point, where would you tell your goon squad to take him?"

Her mind went as blank as a check without a name after Pay To The Order Of. "For Pete's sake, Zoe," she cried, hitting the steering wheel. "You're from Chicago!" As thunder exploded over her head, a bit of gangster lore jumped from her memory. "Yeah. Wise guys *love* symbolism." Like leaving nickels in their victims' hands as a way of saying that was all their lives had been worth. Of course, these days, they probably have to leave dollar bills. Or—slot machine tokens. Zoe's chin crumpled as tears came to her eyes. Telling herself not to go there, that Mitch was all right—he had to be—she took a tissue from her purse, blew her nose, and again concentrated on figuring out where those riverboat rats had him taken. Which, if her theory was correct, was where they could make the point that they would stop at nothing to elect their candidate tomorrow.

"Omigod." Zoe turned her windshield wipers on high. "The Point!"

As she cellphoned every badge wearer she could get hold of to meet her at Ballard's Point, Zoe broke all speed limits getting there. *Nobody,* she thought, *goes to a river in a thunderstorm unless they want to dump something illegally. Like a body.* As she neared the Point, lightning revealed a sedan—dark blue, just as Sarah Jane had said. She slowly drove past it, peeking inside. Empty. She pulled in front of it and cut her engine. A hundred or so feet ahead and to her left, she saw the cypress tree that stood at the crest of the Point, midway between the road and the river. Between hope and heartbreak. "God, please don't let it be too late."

As if a sign that it wasn't, the torrent turned to a trickle and then stopped, and the clouds broke and the sky grew lighter. Zoe got out of her car and shut the door with no more than a click. Then, slowed by the muck the day's rains had made of the soil, she slogged down the embankment to the old cypress, literally sliding into it. She knew some bolt of lightning probably had her in its sights, but the tree's thick trunk and low branches provided the cover she needed to spy on Mitch's abductors. Peeking from behind it, she gazed down the steep bank to the river's edge. There, she saw Mitch's little overturned boat and, gathered around it, two baboons on steroids. But no Ballard. The baboons were looking out at the river and dusting off their hands as though they'd just completed some heavy lifting.

Zoe, too, looked at the Ohio, muddied by the storm, endlessly flowing, the ideal keeper of secrets. *Like dead heroes.* She ground her forehead against the bark of the tree, but couldn't stanch her tears.

If Mitch is indeed gone, tears willna bring him back to you, lassie, nor hold the perps until the fuzz gets here. It's bad enough they might have killed him. You do not want them to kill everything he stands for, too, do you?

Straightening, Zoe wiped her tears with the knuckles of her forefingers. "I can do it. I'll make sure they don't get away."

Spoken like a true Ballard. Ow! Go light, woman, I was gettin' to it. And a true MacTavish.

"And a true Beck," Zoe murmured, recalling her father's wacky but noble *A Star Is Born* attempt to rescue her from jail. But as she stepped from behind the tree, pasting a false smile on her face before approaching Mitch's possible killers, she prayed she wasn't about to negate Harvey's aborted self-sacrifice. Not that she didn't love the Ohio. She'd just never thought of it as her final resting place.

When Mitch came to, he knew just three things: His mouth was taped shut. His hands and feet were bound. The lights were still out. In a semi-fetal position, he lay in complete darkness beneath some kind of cover. Or lid. Of a trunk, maybe. No, whatever lay beneath his cheek was cold, wet, and earthy smelling. Maybe because it was earth—specifically, mud.

"Sure is pretty here," he heard one of his captors say. "Sort of like a chapel, right out in nature. I almost hate to see a casino take it over, myself."

"You give me a pain—you know that? The minute we get back to Vegas I'm gonna look into getting your poetic license revoked."

"I *said* almost."

"Okay, okay. Can we go now, Robert Frost? My feet are soaked."

"You sure Ballard'll keep?"

"Hell, the election'll be over before anybody thinks to look for him under his own boat."

"Buried under a boat. I *love* the symbolism."

"Will you cut it out, already?"

"What'd I do?"

Listening to the men squabble, Mitch laid plans to roll himself onto his knees and elbows and then, using his back, lift the boat and throw it off him. Then, with luck, he'd find the tackle box the goons must have dumped from the boat when they turned it over on him. Inside it was a knife he might be able to position with his feet so that he could cut his wrist bindings on it. Now, if the Blues Brothers would just get the hell out of here . . .

"Why do you always gotta pick on me?"

"Why? Because—hold it. Who's the broad standin' up there by that tree?"

Mitch's heart lurched. Zoe might be Looney Tunes, but she wouldn't be crazy enough to come after him by herself. *Would she?*

"I don't know, but she's got great legs."

She would.

"Yeah, and I just figured out where I seen her before. On the news today, havin' a malted with Ballard. Maybe she'd like to join him underneath that boat."

Along with his fists, Mitch's whole body clenched for a fight he couldn't wage. *For God's sake, Zoe, go back!*

"Excuse me, gentlemen! I'm looking for Perfection, and I must have taken a wrong turn somewhere."

You got that right, darlin'. Now will you please turn back?

"How do I get—?" Zoe cautioned herself that if ever there was a time to ask the right way, this was it. "Would you lovely gentlemen be so kind as to tell me how to get there?"

"It would be easier if we drew you a map, ma'am. Why don't you come on down?"

Don't you do it, Zoe!

"And they say chivalry is dead. I'll be right— aaaaaaa!"

Hearing Zoe's scream, Mitch threw off the boat in

time to see her sliding down the bank on her butt, her gorgeous legs in the air, a human mudslide heading right for the two stunned apes. "Hm Hmhm!" he moaned, which was duct tape for, "Go, baby!"

As if in response to his cheer, she picked up speed, and the goons, suddenly putting it in gear, tried to get out of her way. But, unable to get a foothold on the soggy bank, they slipped and slid until, arms windmilling, they plunged backward into the roiling Ohio. The bad news was that Zoe was still barreling after them, headed straight for the swollen river.

"Hmmmm!"

"Don't you think I'm trying to stop?" Zoe shouted back at Mitch. Finally, digging the sharp heels of her pumps into the mud, she did stop, so close to the water that one of her arms plunged into it. Seeing her lying there motionless, Mitch got onto his haunches and began scooting toward her.

Recovering her senses, Zoe pulled her arm out of the river, rose on all fours, and shook like a wet dog, sending mud flying in every direction. Wiping the muck from her eyes, she looked out at the river and saw the two apes flailing against the current, which carried them downstream. "Damn! They're getting away." Somehow, she had to get back up the bank to her cell phone and alert her search crew, but first, of course, she had to cut Mitch loose of that duct tape.

"Mitch?" Still on all fours, Zoe turned and looked up the bank. "Oh, no!" He was coming at her like a skeeball, and unless she stopped him they'd both end up in the water. Actually, they could both do with a bath, only he couldn't swim because his hands and feet were bound, and she couldn't swim because she'd never learned. Plunking onto her rump, she braced her hands at her sides, drew her knees back, and closed her eyes. Then, as an afterthought, she crossed her fingers for luck. That must have done the trick, because a split second later something slammed into the soles of her shoes, hard. She shoved against it, holding it in place, then opened her eyes.

"Mitch!"

Mitch wanted to ask her how she could recognize him, but his mouth was still taped, which was why he hadn't been able to yell when her heels skewered his backside.

Getting on all fours again, Zoe groped through the mud from his stern to his bow. Taking his face in her hands, she stamped it with ecstatic kisses. "Oh, darling, you're alive!" She went to kiss his mouth. Then, seeing the duct tape, she smiled. "Well, this won't do."

Mitch's eyes widened with fresh terror. "Hmmm!"

Rip!

Zoe's own eyes popped at the grimace on his face "Oooo. I'm so sorry. Are you all right?"

Pursing his mouth, Mitch twitched it from side to side. "Fine. I didn't really need my lips, anyway. They just get in the way when I shave."

"But *I* need them," Zoe murmured. Hooking her arms around his neck and tilting her head, she pressed her lips to his, lightly at first. Then she deepened her kiss with such force that she rocked him onto his back, forcing his taped wrists and feet in the air. "Oh, Mitch. I want your arms around me so much I could die."

His eyes filling with panic, he rolled onto his side, removing his wrists from her reach. "That's what I'm afraid of. Only you won't be the one doing the dying."

Zoe tsked. "You know you're really getting paranoid."

"And just because I've been kidnapped, rabbit-punched, hit over the head, bound, buried beneath a boat, and de-lipped, all in little over an hour. What can I be thinking?"

"Exactly. Do you realize that if we don't hurry, you'll forfeit the debate?"

Mitch directed Zoe to his tackle box, which he'd

spotted several yards behind him. She retrieved a knife from it and hurriedly cut away his bindings. Then, holding onto one another, they started up the slippery bank toward the cypress tree. When they reached the crest, they abruptly drew up at the sound of sirens. Looking toward it, they saw two county patrol cars, a Perfection police squad car, a hook and ladder truck, the Animal Control wagon, an ambulance, three school buses, and Father O'Reilly on his bicycle leading a convoy of pickups, minivans, and assorted cars to a stop. Out poured Harvey, Lou, Tilly, Mike Ballard, Mr. and Mrs. Junior Terwilliker, the mayor, Mrs. Corbett carrying a carrot cake, Booger and his wife, and Dave and Kathy Hardy holding hands—the whole county, it seemed. They all gathered around Mitch and Zoe beneath the cypress tree.

"You two okay?" Lou asked.

Seeing the fright in his mother's eyes, Mitch planted a reassuring kiss on her cheek. "It was a hell of a fight, Ma, but—"

"The mud won," Lou said. She started to rub the visible sign of sentiment Mitch had left on her cheek, then stopped, took his face in her hands, and kissed him squarely on the mouth. Then she hugged Zoe with the strength of a mother bear before passing her into her father's waiting arms.

"You've got one brave daughter there, Harv," Mitch said. "Nuts, but brave."

Harvey smiled into Zoe's eyes. "That's no surprise to me."

With Kathy's arm in his, Dave Hardy stepped forward. "You're quite a hero, yourself, Mitch. When we got word at the high school that you'd been kidnapped by five guys with AK-47s and stuffed into the trunk of a dark blue, bulletproof stretch Mercedes with tinted windows, we knew you were right about the boat bringing worse trouble than we've got now. We should have listened to you from the beginning, before you had to risk your life for us." He extended his hand to Mitch. "I'm so sorry, man."

Clasping Dave's hand, Mitch joined him in renewing their friendship. "Forget it, man."

"Not until after we vote tomorrow." Dave looked around at the crowd. "Right, y'all?"

A thunderous assent went up. Meshing her fingers squishily with his, Zoe smiled up at Mitch. "Congratulations, Mr. County Judge Executive." They kissed, knowing that this particular kiss was nearly complete because their lives were now nearly complete. All they needed was to complete their family. All they needed was—

"Daddy!" With Bink, Toby, Bruno, and Chauncey tramping behind her, Sarah Jane pushed through the crowd. She hurled herself into Mitch's arms and clung to his neck.

"It's all right now, baby," he said, lifting her off the ground, hugging her to him, stroking her hair. "It's all right now."

"Oh, Daddy," she cried. "If I'd known the money was going to make them hurt you, I'd never have—"

"What?" Mitch set Sarah on her feet. "What money, sweetheart?"

Quivering, Sarah stole a glance back at Bink.

"Go on," Bink said. "Tell him what you told me on the way here."

Sarah turned back to Mitch. "When I found out you were going to lose the election because you and Zoe couldn't find the money for the old factory mall, I called Charles and asked him to fix it so you could have as much as you needed."

Mitch and Zoe exchanged looks. "Five will get you ten the conglomerate Charles runs owns Brown Rowan," Zoe said.

Mitch nodded agreement. Then, bending over, he looked Sarah in the eye—or tried to. She wouldn't look back. "That was quite a gesture, honey. But

Charles is a pretty shrewd businessman. You must have offered him something in exchange for his investment, something he wanted very much." He lifted her chin and her gaze. "What did you promise him, Sarah?"

Sarah Jane stared at him for a moment. Then, all of a sudden, she broke like a dam. "Oh, Daddy, I never ever wanted to leave you and the rest of the family, but I just couldn't stand to see you lose the election because it was so important to you, and you'd be such a great judge, and besides I just couldn't let that nasty riverboat come here and ruin Perfection and the whole county, because I love this place so much, and I love *you*, Daddy." Her shoulders shaking with her sobs, she wrapped her arms around her father's waist and pressed her cheek to his heart. "Please, *please* say you don't hate me."

Mitch stood holding her, looking down at the top of her precious red head through the tears that welled in his eyes before spilling freely down his face. She was back. His little girl was back, only she wasn't a little girl anymore. She was a budding young woman, plain to see—not because of the designer suit and high heels and sheer stockings she wore—the extent of Ellie's understanding of womanhood—but because of her sheer courage. And heart. "I could never hate you, sweetheart. You're my flesh and blood. And I've never been more proud of you than I am at this moment." He held her away from him. "But now that I know the truth, I can't let you go to Atlanta. You're staying right here with me and"—looking up at Zoe and Bink and Toby, at Harvey and Lou, he smiled—"the rest of the family."

Visibly overjoyed, Sarah half-laughed, half-cried. Then she asked, "But what about the money for the old factory mall?"

"Don't worry, baby," Zoe said, smoothing back the lovely red hair of the girl she'd come to think of as her own daughter. "We'll just keep looking until we find it."

The others offered to pitch in. Mrs. Corbett, for one, started selling slices of her carrot cake on the spot. Accepting payment for the last slice, she looked at the money in her hand and shrieked. "A thousand dollars!"

"I'm sorry," said the man who'd given her the bill. "Since I don't have anything smaller, I guess you'll just have to keep the change."

Moving Sarah behind him, Mitch walked up to the meticulously and expensively dressed man who was in his mid-fifties and looked it. "The deal's off, Charles. Sarah's staying with my family and me."

"Which is where she belongs. I know that now."

"You tell him the whole story, dear," Mrs. Terwilliker said.

"Be glad to." Handing his carrot cake to the beaming old lady, Charles began. When Mitch and Sarah didn't meet him at the airport or answer the phone, he had become concerned, rented a car, and driven to the house. Finding no one at home, he knocked on several neighboring doors, meeting Mrs. Terwilliker, who was minding Sarah, Bink, and Toby. The children told him what had happened, and then they heard sirens. Mrs. Terwilliker demanded to know where the fire was. He told her, and before he knew it she was behind the wheel of his rented car, ordering him and the children to hurry up and get in so they could join the search party.

"Just like I kept tellin' Junior, if you don't hurry up and marry that darlin' Miss Dunaway, she's gonna get away from you."

Smiling, Junior Terwilliker and his bride each put an arm around his mother.

"Anyway," Charles continued, "on the way here I realized that Sarah Jane belongs where her heart is, and that she's lucky to grow up in a place like this,

where people still look out for one another. Ellie won't
like it when I tell her Sarah's staying in Perfection, but
for once in her life Ellie's going to do what's best for
someone other than herself."

Mitch grasped Charles's hand. "Thank you."

Charles smiled, then turned to leave. "Oh, I almost
forgot. Brown Rowan's offer still stands. The old factory mall is a great idea, and I intend to make a profit
on it."

Mitch and Zoe stood with their arms about each
other and the children, watching Charles depart to
cheers and back slaps.

"Hey, y'all! Look what I got!" Perfection police officer Matt Ballard came over the crest of the bank,
holding his revolver on the two sodden, handcuffed
thugs as he shoved them forward.

Drawing his own revolver, the chief of police of Perfection's three man force met Matt. "Good work, Ballard. You'll get a citation for this," he said. Calling
over his two other officers, he took the kidnappers
away.

"Congratulations, Matt," Zoe said.

"Well, I was just doing my duty," Matt replied, replacing his revolver in its holster. "The credit should
go to the chief. He understands that you let two guys
swim where no swimming signs are posted, and the
next thing you know, you've got a crime wave on your
hands." Touching the brim of his cap, he walked away,
leaving Mitch and Zoe's cheeks puffy with suppressed
laughter.

Shortly afterward, they stood alone on Ballard's
Point, beneath MacDuff's and Fionna's tree.

Well, go on, lad. Do I have to ask for you?

Taking her hand in his, Mitch gazed at Zoe. Tears
had streaked her dirt-stained cheeks, her hair had
dried and was sticking up like quills, and her clothes
looked like the BEFORE in a detergent commercial. But
with those green eyes of hers no longer storming, just

shining brightly, steadily, and eternally with Zoe spirit and Zoe love, she was the most beautiful creature he'd ever seen.

"Darlin'—"

"I can't stand it anymore, Mitch. The waiting, I mean." Zoe dug her fingers into his upper arms. "I almost lost you once, and I'm not going to take that chance again. Just marry me, okay?"

Squeezing his eyes shut, thrusting his hands over his head, Mitch threw his head back. "Nonono! *I've* got to do the asking. It's tradition."

Don't you believe it, laddie. Your great-great-great-great-grandfather will never admit it, but I'm the one who did the proposin'!

Great-great-great-grandmother Fionna?

You forgot a great, but I willna hold it agin you, providin' you answer your lassie's question the way MacDuff answered mine.

Abruptly, Mitch fixed Zoe with the glint in his eye. His grin defined roguish. "Are you ready for my answer?"

Zoe's laugh defined rogue loving. "I'm ready."

"You sure?"

"I'm—"

Mitch pulled her into his arms and answered her with a kiss so complete that she felt it ream her very bones. He didn't stop until her arms hung limply at her sides. "And to think," she said, letting her head loll and gazing up at the cypress green umbrella over their heads. "I didn't even ask right."

Three weeks later, with the riverboat defeated and Mitch sworn in as the new county judge executive, they were married. On their wedding night, Sarah, Bink, Toby, Bruno, and Chauncey stayed in the house that now belonged to Lou and Harvey, who had been married the week before. Hand in hand in the dark, Zoe and Mitch climbed the porch steps to the front door of 222 Magnolia Street, which they'd bought, and where they would rear their family. As Mitch bent to carry his bride over the threshold, Zoe shied away.

"Open your wedding present first," she said.

"You're my wedding present," Mitch replied, reaching for her. But she eluded him again, disappearing inside the house and returning a moment later carrying a small package wrapped in silver paper and tied with a white ribbon. Excitedly, she watched him unwrap it.

"Oh . . . wow. A lightbulb."

Zoe looked forlorn. "Don't you get it? It's for the—"

"I know what it's for, darlin'," Mitch said. He stroked her cheek. Then, stepping past her to the lantern beside the door, he replaced the burned-out bulb with the one Zoe had given him. The one that meant they would be together always, right there in Perfection.

Maybe.

"How do you turn it on?" Mitch asked, staring at the still dark lantern.

"I thought I had," Zoe replied, referring to the switch beside the door, which she'd always assumed controlled the porch light. "I don't understand why . . . wait." Abruptly, she ran into the house, skidded into the dining room, and flipped on the mysterious switch in the middle of the wall. Then she dashed out to the porch, which was now aglow with light.

It was no match for the light in their eyes as the newlyweds smiled at one another. Without having to ask if she was ready, Mitch swept his bride into his arms and, while they kissed, carried her over the threshold of their new home. "I have a present for you, too, you know. You want it now?"

"You just bet I do."

"Ah, ah, ah. No betting allowed in Perfection."

Sighing, Zoe propped her left hand, bearing the plain gold band she wouldn't trade for all of Tiffany's, on her waist. "I can see there's going to be no living with you, Judge Ballard. Just tell me where it is, okay?"

"Not fair, baby. You know I can't resist when you don't ask right." Setting her down, Mitch took her by the hand and led her into the kitchen. He opened the freezer door. "Go ahead and look."

"In the freezer?"

"Of course, if you don't want it . . ." Mitch started to close the door.

"No, that's fine," Zoe said, grabbing the door. "A side of beef is a perfectly thoughtful gift." She peered inside the freezer and instantly saw a tall wrapped cylinder topped with a bow. She tore open the wrappings. "One of Tilly's double chocolate malteds! Oh, Mitch!" Holding the container behind his neck, she hugged and kissed him.

"Go ahead. Have it now," he said. "I know how long you've been waiting."

Zoe looked at the malt, then at the man she'd searched for all her adult life, even when she hadn't known she was looking. "I can wait a little longer," she replied, putting the container back into the freezer. Then, taking his hand in her two, she tugged him up the hall toward the stairs leading to their bedroom. "After all, it's not every day a woman finds perfection."

He cocked a smile, along with a quizzical look. "The town or the man?"

Zoe looked back at him from atop the first step. "Both, my love. Both."

AFTERWORD

As of this writing, in the spring of 1999, the Commonwealth of Kentucky does not license riverboat or land-based casino gambling, both of which would require the statewide ratification of a Constitutional amendment. Despite recent studies indicating that wherever gambling has been legalized it has cost communities more revenue than it generates—principally in unpaid debts, bankruptcies, check fraud, thefts, embezzlement, and other crimes—the governor has proposed an amendment to allow fourteen land-based casinos. Debate is currently underway. It is the fervent hope of the author—who, after looking for many years, found near perfection in beautiful Kentucky—that such legislation will never come to pass.

BOOK YOUR PLACE ON OUR WEBSITE AND MAKE THE READING CONNECTION!

We've created a customized website just for our very special readers, where you can get the inside scoop on everything that's going on with Zebra, Pinnacle and Kensington books.

When you come online, you'll have the exciting opportunity to:

- View covers of upcoming books
- Read sample chapters
- Learn about our future publishing schedule (listed by publication month *and author*)
- Find out when your favorite authors will be visiting a city near you
- Search for and order backlist books from our online catalog
- Check out author bios and background information
- Send e-mail to your favorite authors
- Meet the Kensington staff online
- Join us in weekly chats with authors, readers and other guests
- Get writing guidelines
- AND MUCH MORE!

Visit our website at
http://www.zebrabooks.com

Put a Little Romance in Your Life With
Janelle Taylor